1998

**More praise for the
Cal & Plato Marley mysteries
by Bill Pomidor**

"INTERESTING PLOT . . . THE SUSPECTS
ARE WELL DRAWN."
—*Cleveland Plain Dealer*

"NO ONE GETS AWAY WITH IT WHEN
FORENSIC PATHOLOGIST CAL AND
HER GERIATRICIAN/FAMILY PRACTITIONER
HUSBAND, PLATO, ARE ON THE CASE."
—*Akron Beacon Journal*

Mind over Murder

"Plato?" she cried. *"Plato?"*

Cal glanced up and down the aisle, but saw no
sign of her husband. Instead, she caught a flash of
orange in the next row over—Jimmy Dubrowski's
hunting jacket. . . .

Cal frantically wormed into the narrow gap between two trees, feeling the spiky branches prick
and tear at her coat. . . .

"Cal?" Like a specter, or maybe an officer
beamed down from the starship *Enterprise*, Plato
materialized at her elbow. He was breathing hard
too, and his boots and pants were spattered with
mud. "What's ~~wrong? I~~ ... d you yelling—"

...~~~~... " she cried, reaching
...ere—he's *after* me!"

"It's Jimmy Dubrowski," someone yelled,
out to clutch his arm. "He's here

MIND
OVER
MURDER

A Cal & Plato Marley Mystery

Bill Pomidor

A SIGNET BOOK

SIGNET
Published by the Penguin Group
Penguin Putnam Inc., 375 Hudson Street
New York, New York 10014, U.S.A.
Penguin Books Ltd, 27 Wrights Lane,
London W8 5TZ, England
Penguin Books Australia Ltd, Ringwood,
Victoria, Australia
Penguin Books Canada Ltd, 10 Alcorn Avenue,
Toronto, Ontario, Canada M4V 3B2
Penguin Books (N.Z.) Ltd, 182–190 Wairau Road,
Auckland 10, New Zealand

Penguin Books Ltd, Registered Offices:
Harmondsworth, Middlesex, England

First published by Signet, an imprint of Dutton NAL,
a member of Penguin Putnam Inc.

First Printing, November, 1998

10 9 8 7 6 5 4 3 2 1

Copyright © William J. Pomidor, 1998
All rights reserved

 REGISTERED TRADEMARK—MARCA REGISTRADA

Printed in the United States of America

Without limiting the rights under copyright reserved above, no part of this
publication may be reproduced, stored in or introduced into a retrieval system, or
transmitted, in any form, or by any means (electronic, mechanical, photocopying,
recording, or otherwise), without the prior written permission of both the copyright
owner and the above publisher of this book.

PUBLISHER'S NOTE
This is a work of fiction. Names, characters, places, and incidents either are the
product of the author's imagination or are used fictitiously, and any resemblance to
actual persons, living or dead, events, or locales is entirely coincidental.

BOOKS ARE AVAILABLE AT QUANTITY DISCOUNTS WHEN USED TO PROMOTE PRODUCTS OR
SERVICES. FOR INFORMATION PLEASE WRITE TO PREMIUM MARKETING DIVISION, PENGUIN
PUTNAM INC., 375 HUDSON STREET, NEW YORK, NEW YORK 10014.

If you purchased this book without a cover you should be aware that this book is
stolen property. It was reported as "unsold and destroyed" to the publisher and
neither the author nor the publisher has received any payment for this "stripped
book."

For Dan Holtan, M.D.,
and the rest of the Healthcare for the Homeless Project

ACKNOWLEDGMENTS

Being a doctor rather than a lawyer, my under-standing of the criminal justice system and espe-cially the issues of competency to stand trial and the insanity plea are limited. John Pomidor—yes, my brother is a *lawyer*!—helped clarify the issues for me. Sam Hibbs, of the Ohio Department of Mental Health, offered specific details about the in-sanity and competency laws currently in effect in Ohio. I appreciate their help and insights, which helped me assemble a reasonable scenario for the saga of Jimmy Dubrowski, schizophrenic univer-sity student and convicted serial killer.

I beheld the wretch—the miserable monster
whom I had created.

—MARY SHELLEY,
Frankenstein

CHAPTER 1

"Dr. Marley," said the cadaver in a soft, oily voice. "It's so *good* to see you again."

Cal Marley, deputy coroner and anatomy professor, had seen a lot during her career. She had dug bodies from the frozen wastes of Lake Erie and the muddy banks of the Cuyahoga, carved up hundreds of corpses in the County Morgue, and embalmed dozens of cadavers here in the basement laboratory of Siegel Medical College.

Cal Marley knew cadavers. And one thing her vast experience had taught her was that cadavers never talked. Sometimes an occasional specimen would make an odd noise, shifting in its stainless steel sarcophagus over in the anatomy lab, settling into its winding sheets or burbling as the oily embalming fluid trickled through its flaccid blood vessels.

But the cadavers never, ever talked.

Which was why Cal spilled her coffee all over the embalming room floor. Just minutes ago, she had undressed the lab's latest donation, flushed his arteries with saline fluid and then "juiced" the body, pumping its blood vessels full of preservative embalming fluid. And while the pump did its work, she had stepped next door for a cup of coffee. She returned just a few minutes later, planning to tie off the cadaver's arteries, tuck him into a cozy shroud and a man-sized plastic baggie, and slip him into place beside his comrades on the wall rack.

It had been a busy day; the first week of December and the height of flu season had brought a wave of fresh donations. Three bodies today—two already embalmed and snoozing in the wall rack, and the third sprawled on the table, waiting for his shroud.

And a fourth cadaver, lying in the lowest wall rack. A new donation?

If so, the doctors had been a bit hasty in pronouncing this one dead. He sat up on the rack, smacking his head on the stainless steel bunk overhead, and smiling ruefully.

"These beds are *awfully* hard."

To her relief, Cal saw that this new "cadaver" was fully dressed—overdressed, actually. For instead of the *de rigueur* shroud and baggy, or perhaps a hospital gown, this fellow was wearing a three-piece suit. The very suit Cal had just removed from the body on the table.

Stiffly, the visitor rolled over and climbed down from the rack. He shrugged his massive shoulders and shook his pantlegs down, but it didn't help. Although the body on the table was enormous, the borrowed suit was still far too small for the visitor. The sleeves of the dapper pin-striped jacket stopped halfway down his forearms, and the neatly pressed pantleg cuffs dangled a good four inches above his ankles. The buttons of the borrowed vest strained with the pressure of each breath, and the shirt collar squeezed the man's neck like a well-tailored noose.

The visitor looked like the Incredible Hulk just before he pops his clothes.

"I hope you don't mind me taking these clothes, Doc." He shrugged tightly at the cadaver on the metal table and smiled a vacant smile—a grin that was oddly reminiscent of the cadaver's rictus, as though they were sharing in the same joke. But his voice was the dull, pressured monotone of a tired auctioneer. "I figured *this* guy didn't need them any more."

To Cal, the whole situation held the surreal menace of a developing nightmare. Her mind spun in place, like a car trapped in the snow. The harder she tried to make sense of it all, the more incomprehensible it seemed.

"Cold beds, cold beds, flower beds, flatbeds . . ." The man's voice fell to a garbled mutter—something about the cadaver racks and the cut of the dead man's suit. As he talked, the man was in constant subtle motion, his huge body writhing and twitching like a cobra with poison ivy.

"But then, I guess it doesn't really matter how cold these beds are, does it? I mean, dead bodies can't *feel* anything, right?" He cocked his head at Cal and smiled again. One side of his mouth twitched down and then up, down again, up again. An involuntary motion, like his constant writhing. "That's something I always wondered, I used to ask Mom about it but she couldn't tell me *then*. Now she's dead and she could, but she *can't*, you know what I mean? Jelly bean?"

"I—"

"Still, it's awfully nice of you to play Christmas music for them. Even if they can't hear. Can they? Hear, near and dear?"

From the CD player in the corner, Nat King Cole was wondering if reindeer really knew how to fly. The embalming pump was still pushing fluid into the cadaver's neck. Two dead men on wall racks watched the drama unfold from inside their cellophane wrappers.

"*And so, I'm offering this simple phrase,*" the man crooned off-key. "*To kids from one to ninety-two . . .*"

Cal's mind spun helplessly, tires spinning on the glare

ice of insanity. She reached out to switch off the pump, then glanced up at the man again.

He stopped singing suddenly, lifting his head as though a familiar voice had just called his name. He nodded, and turned to the cadaver on the table. "How about you, huh? I mean, you can't feel anything anymore, can you?" He cocked his head in that odd listening posture again, then glared at Cal. "Fenton says he's cold. He says you better give this poor guy some clothes."

Cal took a cautious step toward the door. "Fenton?"

"Sure." The man frowned. "Don't you *see* him?" He turned and pointed. "He's right over there, next to that rack. Say hi, Fenton."

"Nice to meet you," Cal muttered to the empty air.

"That's better. You betcher."

He turned back to the cadaver, and she darted for the door. But not quickly enough—the man was incredibly fast. In an eye blink, he had scrambled over to block her path. Shaking his head, he glared at Cal. "*No!* I've gotta talk to you!"

He shifted his gaze to the empty air, then sighed. To Cal's relief, the frown slowly faded, replaced by an apologetic smile. "Mrs. Abernathy's right—sorry."

"It's okay." Trapped in the embalming room, Cal murmured a silent thank you to Mrs. Abernathy.

She took a step back, and the man-mountain relaxed even more. But Cal's heart was still pounding; she wanted to yell for help, to turn and run, to call Security—*anything*. But she was trapped, and nobody would hear her scream. It was late Saturday afternoon; the college was all but deserted.

Even if he hadn't dressed himself in a dead man's clothes and talked with invisible friends, this guy was obviously ten watts short of a bulb. The mood swings, the glazed look in his eyes, the pressured, flighty speech—he was either psychotic or flying high on drugs. Cal forced herself to remain calm, take a few deep breaths, and smile up at the intruder.

"Can I help you?" she asked calmly, as though talking cadavers routinely showed up in her anatomy lab.

"My name is Jimmy," the man finally responded. He took a step closer, towering over her. "But I bet you know that already. Yup, you got it. You betcher."

Keep calm, she told herself again, taking another quiet step back and swallowing a scream. Cal was just five feet two inches tall and barely topped a hundred pounds dripping wet. The intruder was huge—even taller than her husband Plato, and twice as wide. His hairy forearms jutted from the ill-fitting suit like the paws of a grizzly bear. His head was a huge boulder perched atop the mesa of his shoulders. His rubbery lips constantly puckered and twisted and smacked.

Tardive dyskinesia—a side effect of long-term antipsychotic drug treatment.

"Don't you remember me?" Jimmy asked with a frown.

"Sorry, no," Cal replied. But as the man stepped closer again, she frowned. His face *did* look vaguely familiar somehow. A face from the past, from a few years ago, maybe—except he looked *younger* than the person she recalled, which didn't make a bit of sense. Somebody's brother? Somebody's son? She took another step back and shrugged. "Should I remember you?"

"You better, you better, you bet," Jimmy replied. Quick as a flash, he lashed out and grabbed her wrists, locking them both in a steely grip. He smiled down at her in triumph. "You're the lady that sent me to prison. Yup."

Cal screamed.

*   *   *

"Where the hell is Cal?" Homer asked impatiently.

"Embalming cadavers," Plato Marley replied. He shrugged at his cousin. "Take it easy—she should be home any minute."

Homer Marley was circling the kitchen like an aquarium shark at feeding time. The burley assistant prosecutor opened the oven and peered lovingly at the simmering tray of burritos, then took a sniff.

"Maybe we should start without her," he suggested hopefully.

"No way," Jeremy Ames replied. The county homicide detective shook his grizzled gray head; he was a stickler for procedure. "We all eat *together*—that's the rule."

Nina Ames, the detective's fourth and final wife, nodded firmly. "It's *tradition* that we should wait."

Homer Marley harrumphed but sat down. Nina Ames was right. It was poker night at Plato and Cal's, a Saturday evening tradition for the past three years or more. Once a month, the five of them assembled for a long evening of dinner and beer and penny-ante poker. When it was her turn, Nina Ames usually cooked meals from her homeland—saltimbocca alla romana, vitello ala parmagiana, and her own lasagna con pollo. Plato prepared more traditional fare—grilled steak and baked potatoes, homemade chili, and Homer's favorite—triple cheese and chicken burritos.

Homer, the perennial bachelor, typically treated his guests to take-out pizza.

"How about some more chips and salsa?" Plato suggested.

"I'm chipped out," Homer complained. He signed mournfully. "But I'll take some anyway."

"I'll get it," Nina insisted. She headed over to the pantry for a fresh bag.

Jeremy Ames followed his wife like a fond puppy trailing its master, then turned his schnauzer nose back to Plato. "Maybe you should try paging Cally, huh?"

"I *tried*," Plato replied. He waited for Nina to refill the bowl, then shoveled a chipful of salsa in his mouth. "I paged her three times in the last hour. Her beeper's on the fritz."

"How about calling the school?" Homer suggested.

"Maybe I should," he agreed. It wasn't like Cal to be this late without calling—especially on poker night. Besides, she liked Plato's burritos almost as much as Homer did. "Cal got a last-minute donation at the lab, but she *still* promised to be home an hour ago."

Just as Plato reached for the telephone, a pager went off. Plato, Homer, and Jeremy all glanced at their belts. Jeremy unclipped his pager and grinned.

"I win." He stood and dialed the phone. "Homicide office downtown—they probably forgot I've been on vacation this week."

"I didn't know you ever *took* vacation," Homer muttered.

"He doesn't," Nina replied. The statuesque blonde sighed tolerantly and turned her wide brown eyes to the ceiling. "On our cruise last month, I thought Jeremy would *kill* somebody just so he could solve the case." She smiled fondly at the detective. "My husband is a very restless man."

Restless was an understatement. Detective-Lieutenant Jeremy Ames had the bulging eyes and jittery manner of a Rottweiler on speed. The human bloodhound took as much overtime, night, and weekend duty as the sheriff's department could dish out. During his few off-hours, he taught police procedure and Tai Chi at a local community college.

And since he had given up smoking, Jeremy was even jumpier than usual. He had worn out his first three wives like a savage mustang tossing novice riders, but Nina was somehow able to handle him. The gorgeous, sloe-eyed Mediterranean beauty was as calm and unflappable as her husband was hyper, and she could tame him with a simple look or gesture.

But nothing could tame Jeremy Ames now. He hung up the phone and whirled, eyeing first Homer and then Plato. His eyes bulged even more than usual, and his long snout twitched the air anxiously. All the color drained from his face, and he swallowed heavily.

"That was a friend of mine from the Homicide Division," he explained, pulling a tab of Nicorette gum from his shirt pocket. "Something awful happened. Jimmy Dubrowski's escaped."

"Oh, my God!" Plato breathed.

Homer glanced at his cousin blankly. "Jimmy Dubrowski?"

"Don't you remember him?" Plato asked. "The West Side Strangler?"

"Killed three people before they finally caught him," Jeremy said. He popped the gum into his mouth and eyed Homer skeptically. "Guy was a total nutcase—tried to cop an insanity plea, but the jury didn't buy it. He ended up in maximum security at Mansfield. God only knows how he broke out."

The story brought back a tide of wonderful and awful memories; the whole thing had happened right around the time Plato met Cal. Their relationship had blossomed in the shadow of the Strangler case; Cal was the deputy coroner who handled the evidence. She was stalked for weeks even as the city spread a dragnet to bring Jimmy Dubrowski in. Four years ago now, though it seemed like a lifetime.

And now, the Strangler was free again. Plato closed his eyes, feeling his heart pounding in his chest. *Cal!*

"He's out—but that's not the worst of it," Jeremy continued. He was chewing the Nicorette furiously and drumming his fingers on the countertop. "They searched Jimmy's room after he broke out, and found a scrapbook."

"A scrapbook?" Homer asked.

"Full of news clippings." The detective glanced up at Plato. "Clippings about your wife. Every single case she's handled for the past four years." He grunted. "The prison shrink wouldn't say much in the interest of 'confidentiality.' But he claimed Jimmy Dubrowski is 'obsessed' with your wife. And that he should be considered extremely dangerous." Ames rolled his eyes. "Like we didn't already know that."

"*Madre di Dio*," Nina Ames breathed.

Plato glanced at the clock on the wall. Cal was almost ninety minutes overdue now, yet she hadn't called. It wasn't like her, not at all.

"Oh, God," he murmured in a shaky voice. He couldn't move, couldn't think.

"I already sent the cops over to the medical school," Jeremy continued. "They should be there any minute."

"We should start praying, I think," Nina suggested.

"*You* pray," Jeremy told his wife. "Stay here and pray—and answer the phone."

She nodded slowly, pulling her trusty rosary from her purse. "And you?"

"We're going to the medical school," the detective

replied simply. He spun on his heel and headed for the front hall.

Homer grabbed Plato's arm and followed the detective, seeming to understand his cousin's helplessness.

"Don't worry, pal," he said in a soft voice as they pulled on their coats. "Cal's a tough girl—she'll be all right."

"You got it," Jeremy agreed with a sickly, unconvincing grin. He scrambled into his car and waited for Homer and Plato to pile in from the other side. "I bet she's just fine."

"But what if she isn't?" Plato asked quietly. "What if she *isn't*?"

Jeremy Ames spun the wheel as they pulled into the street, tires screeching. He leaned across Plato to open his glovebox and pull out a heavy black police-issue revolver. The detective glanced at the cylinder to make sure it was loaded, then set it down on the seat beside him.

"In that case, Jimmy Dubrowski will be dead." His voice was as cold as the gun barrel.

Plato stared dully out the window as the bare trees and barren fields flashed by. He knew Cal was in trouble; he could *sense* it somehow. And there wasn't a damn thing they could do about it. By the time they got there, it would all be over.

If it wasn't already.

Behind him, Homer reached up to pat his shoulder. "Don't worry, pal," he repeated. "She'll be just fine."

Plato wished he could believe him.

CHAPTER 2

"Fenton says you're the smartest coroner around." Jimmy Dubrowski's mouth widened with an awkward smile; the twisted grin of a dragon trying to charm its virgin maiden. "I've read *all* about you—every single case in the papers for four years, now. You're good. Good-good-Robin-Hood. Yup, you betcher."

Still imprisoned in the killer's vicelike grip, Cal managed a weak shrug. But Dubrowski didn't seem to notice.

"Those Chippewa Creek murders—remember them, huh?" he asked. When Cal nodded, he continued. "And those bones they found—nobody knew who they were, but *you* did. You figured it out and caught the killer. Killer-diller-Phyllis-Diller. Yup. Even the lady that ended up down here in the cadaver lab. *Nothing* gets past you, nope, no way." His huge bowling ball of a head nodded firmly. "I'm a big fan of yours, see."

"Thank you." Cal looked away, trying to think, to adjust to Jimmy Dubrowski's quickly changing moods, his shifting manner. A moment ago, he had been angry, menacing. His voice had been a low growl, and his manner had slowly grown more threatening—and less coherent. Now, he had reverted to an almost agreeable, affable mood, and Cal could follow his thoughts reasonably well.

He had acted much the same way four years ago, she

remembered—once rising from the witness stand to launch a long, rambling tirade against the police who had trapped him, then slumping back into his seat and delivering a whispered apology for his outburst.

"I've got all your pictures, too, every single one, yup, yup." He smacked his lips again and leaned close, like a man admiring a rose in a vase. "You're one pretty lady."

"Thank you," Cal repeated, smiling tightly. She twisted her hands against their bonds, a futile gesture. The serial killer hadn't relaxed his hold on her in the ten minutes since she screamed; his huge hands clenched her wrists gently but firmly, like a pair of steel handcuffs. And as he held her, Dubrowski had continued his rambling, pointless speech. Cal still wasn't sure why he had come here, to her anatomy lab, but she had a pretty good guess.

And that guess scared the hell out of her.

"Smart, and pretty, pretty smart, Pop-Tart." Dubrowski cocked his head at her, squinting down at his next victim. Remembering all the others, maybe. "But not perfect. No way, nope, negatory allegory. You know that, don't you?"

"Nobody's perfect," Cal replied softly. Least of all Jimmy Dubrowski. He'd bungled his first murder, leaving behind a trail of blood and DNA evidence that a first-year medical student could have traced, then followed it up with two more grisly stranglings on the west side of Cleveland before a frustrated police force finally ran him to ground.

The crimes seemed largely motiveless—insane—a trio of almost random killings, an aimless Angel of Death stalking the streets of Cleveland. But it didn't matter; Dubrowski himself was insane—a paranoid schizophrenic who had stopped taking his Haldol and apparently suffered a psychotic break.

The county prosecutor had called it the easiest case he'd ever tried. But Cal's testimony had been pivotal: her DNA tests had linked the suspect with blood found at the scenes of two of the killings. But Dubrowski had hammered the last nails in the coffin himself—he insisted on pleading not guilty and participating in his own defense, then broke down on the witness stand and apologized to the families of the victims.

After just three days of testimony, his lawyer persuaded him to shift his plea to not guilty by reason of insanity. But it didn't help—the insanity plea is notoriously hard to prove in Ohio, and the judge and jury weren't convinced. Jimmy was convicted and given three consecutive life sentences. The West Side Strangler had finally been caught, the jury had done its work, and Clevelanders had rested easier.

Until today.

Jimmy Dubrowski's face was going through another slow contortion: a march of worms beneath the skin of his cheeks and forehead. The grimace had returned, and his voice dropped to a low rasp.

"Fenton says you screwed up big-time," the killer said sadly. His grip was no longer gentle; Cal's wrists and hands were swallowed up in his huge paws. He leaned closer, his fetid breath moist against Cal's forehead, his wild blue eyes boring down into his victim's. A trail of spittle cut a glistening path through the grime on his chin. "And now, we're going to do something about it. Somebody's got to pay."

Cal's breaths came in quick gasps, and her heart thudded in her throat. Smiling a ghastly smile, she shook her head and tried to wriggle away, tried to scream, but nothing came out. It was still like a nightmare—one where you open your mouth and the best you can manage is a thin, sheeplike bleat.

"No," Cal finally gasped. "*No.*"

"You got me all wrong, Dr. Marley." Dubrowski smiled again. A predatory grimace, like a dragon apologizing for its table manners. "Wrong, wrong, sing along with a Christmas song. You see that now, don't you, huh, huh, huh?"

"We could *help* you," she stammered. Cal's pulse hammered futilely at the pinched arteries in her wrists. Her hands were gone now, pale numb ghosts of their former selves; all sensation terminated at the stumps above her wrists. "Maybe an *appeal*, another trial. New evidence—"

She was blubbering now, terrified beyond coherent thought, certainly beyond dignity. Cal would promise the killer anything, fool him any way she could, if he would just let her go.

And to her complete amazement, that's exactly what he did. The vices unclamped, letting Cal's hands fall limp to her sides. She tottered, stumbling into the cadaver on the table, bracing her dead hands against its naked chest. Dubrowski's sad smile had brightened to a broad grin.

"You *understand*, then. You know why I have to—" He cocked his head, listening, then paced over to the door.

Behind him, Cal staggered to the pump beside the autopsy table. Willing her numb hands to function again, she yanked the flexible plastic catheter from the cadaver's neck and flipped the pump on to full blast. The force of the flow almost jerked the tubing from her clumsy grip, but Cal pressed it between both of her hands.

Dubrowski whirled just as the pump started up. He

lumbered back into the room, back toward Cal, opening his flabby lips to speak.

And got a mouthful of embalming solution. The killer gasped in shock, only making things worse. For good measure, Cal pointed the hose up at Dubrowski's eyes, blinding him. He staggered back, groaning in horror and pain like a buckshot grizzly bear. Hands swiping at his eyes, he stumbled past the desk and barely caught himself against the door.

Hot needles of pain shot up Cal's wrists and arms, but she kept up her barrage. The trouble was that Dubrowski was still blocking the door—an outraged cyclops barring the mouth of his cave. Embalming fluid—full of formalin and acids and oils and all sorts of other nasty things—was caustic even in low doses. The medical students always double-gloved during their dissections; even then, the toxic fumes always seeped through the latex and into their hands.

A *direct* dose was something else entirely; Dubrowski howled in anger and pain as he squeezed his eyes shut and reached for Cal in a deadly game of blind man's bluff. He moved just a few inches sideways, just far enough to leave a tiny Cal-sized hole near the door. But just as she poised to lunge through, the pump made a sickly, gasping sound.

Sucking air—the reservoir had finally run out of embalming fluid.

Still, Cal lunged into the tiny gap, squirming through Dubrowski's oily grip. She was almost free when he caught the tail of her white lab coat, wrenched, and reeled her back in. Cal struggled and clawed, but the half-blind killer batted her hands away effortlessly. He finally clenched both of her wrists in one hand and found a box of Kleenex to dab at his eyes. Through a bloodshot haze of formalin and tears, he shook his head at Cal. The sad smile had burned away. His voice was a scratchy rasp again.

"That was *mean*, Jelly Bean. You've been a bad girl."

Jeremy Ames hung up his cellular phone and set it on the dashboard. Turning to Plato, he shook his head. "Maybe we shouldn't bother going to the medical school after all."

Plato gasped. *"Why?* What *happened?"*

"Hey, take it easy." The detective reached out to pat his arm. "It's just that Cal wasn't there."

"She wasn't?"

"Nope—the security guard says she signed out two hours ago." He frowned worriedly. "So the cops didn't even bother going inside."

"That's right around when she called me," Plato said. "Then where the hell *is* she?"

He turned to look grimly out the window. They were headed north on Route 77, Cleveland's southern artery, passing under the Harvard-Denison bridge. The sun had long since set and the city skyline was flickering to life. Up ahead, the chisel tip of One Cleveland Center carved a hole in the black snow clouds, while the lights of Jacobs Field kindled memories of hot summer days and brisk October nights. Closer at hand, the foundries and forges of Cleveland's half-dead industrial past spewed steamy lava into the stratosphere. A gloomy yellow-brown pall hung over the freeway here; Plato shivered.

"I think Cal's still there," he finally decided. "She probably signed herself out just before the donation came."

"Donation?" Jeremy frowned.

"The cadaver. The body she was embalming." He

shook his head. "The lab director's got the flu, so Cal is helping with the bodies."

"Oh." Jeremy didn't ask about it, obviously didn't want to hear about it. The tough detective had seen hundreds of grisly killings in his days, but he had a notoriously weak stomach for autopsy suites and especially the anatomy lab. As Jeremy put it, he didn't mind *fresh* bodies, he just couldn't stomach the pickled ones.

"I *still* don't see why that means Cal's at the school," Homer broke in from the back seat. "She could have left by now."

"That's right," Jeremy agreed. "I bet she's back home eating burritos with Nina and laughing her head off."

"She's probably just fine." Homer patted Plato's shoulder. "Anyway, if Dubrowski *was* looking for her, he sure as hell wouldn't check the medical school."

"Yeah." Jeremy nodded. "He'd try the morgue, first."

"Or her house." Homer gasped as he realized the implication of his words, then turned to Jeremy. "Forget I said that, pal."

But Jeremy was already picking up the phone again, and dialing the Marleys' number. He broke into a smile as the phone was answered, nodding his head quickly.

"Yeah, honey—lock all the doors and windows, just in case. No sign of her yet, no calls or anything? Right, you just go on praying." He hung up the phone and turned to Plato. "Nina's fine; she wants you to know she's got the rosary humming on all cylinders."

"Thanks."

"But Homer's right," he continued. "How the hell would Dubrowski ever find her at the medical school, for Christ's sake?"

Plato shrugged gloomily. "If he's as well-read as that doctor says, he'd know she works there."

"That's right," Homer chimed in. "And there was that profile of her in last month's *Cleveland Magazine*. They talked about how she spends Saturdays helping out at the school, didn't they?"

Jeremy whipped his head around. "You're just a *fountain* of good news, aren't you? A regular Jehovah's Witness."

Homer gave a guilty sigh and slumped back into the seat.

"Don't listen to him," Jeremy advised Plato. "I doubt if Jimmy Dubrowski reads *Cleveland Magazine*—too highbrow for his type."

But Plato wasn't listening. He was leaning forward as they crossed the Veterans' Memorial Bridge over the Cuyahoga. Straining to peer upriver at the western bank, at the crumbling granite pile that was Siegel Medical College. Straining to see if he could spot the fiery red Acura in the dimly lit patch of asphalt that was the college's parking lot.

He turned back to Jeremy. "This is the turn."

"I know."

They pulled into the parking lot just a minute or two later, and Plato's heart gave a sick lurch. Sure enough, Cal's car was parked near the main entrance.

"Son of a bitch," Homer muttered.

"God-damned worthless security guard," Jeremy snapped as he slammed on the brakes. He hammered the steering wheel for good measure. "Stupid shit couldn't even check the parking lot."

Plato barely heard them. He staggered out of the car and stumbled up the icy sidewalk to the main entrance with Homer and Jeremy trailing behind. Plato yanked open the door and paused in the vestibule, then tugged on the inner door handles. Both were locked.

A tinny voice crackled through a metal speaker grille in the door frame. "Can I help you, sir?"

Plato turned, spotting an unfamiliar face behind the heavy window of the guard's station. Great—a new recruit who wouldn't recognize him. And Plato hadn't brought his ID badge.

"I'm Dr. Marley," he began. "I'm on faculty here. My wife—"

"Let us in," Jeremy snapped, muscling his way up to the window. "Police business."

"Can I see your badge, sir?" the guard asked, leaning forward skeptically. He was tall and slender, with clean-cut good looks and perfect hair. His uniform was neatly pressed and his gunbelt gleamed. He didn't look like a real security guard; he looked like an actor *playing* a security guard.

"Here." Jeremy wrestled the badge from his wallet and pressed it to the window.

"Badge 342." The guard nodded, jotting the number on a note pad. "If you'll just wait a minute while I dial the sheriff's office—"

He pulled a thick telephone directory from his desk and leafed through the pages.

"But this is *urgent*," Plato sputtered.

"Cuyahoga County, right?" the guard asked politely. "It should be listed in the blue pages."

"I can't *believe* this," Homer groaned.

"Lemme handle it." The homicide detective reached into his belt and pulled out his revolver. He pressed it against the window, training it on the shiny badge over the left breast pocket of the guard's immaculate shirt. "Let us in, *now*."

The security guard looked up, eyes widening with shock and dismay.

Jeremy smiled grimly. "Or do you want to find out if this is *really* bullet-proof glass?"

The guard reached down and pressed a button. The door buzzed open.

Plato's footfalls echoed down the dusty first-floor corridor. Behind him, Homer was puffing and panting to keep up, and Jeremy was still arguing with the irate security guard. The hallway seemed endlessly long, a marble-floored treadmill leading nowhere.

But it *did* lead somewhere—to the stairwell down to the anatomy lab. Plato rushed to the heavy steel door and yanked it open; the crash echoed back up the corridor. Behind him, Homer huffed and panted and waved him ahead. Jeremy Ames was running a distant third but closing fast. And the security guard was still standing by his desk, apparently unsure whether to call the police or give chase.

Plato dove through the doorway and bounded down the steep granite staircase, taking the steps two at a time. He had started the second flight when he heard the scream—a bloodcurdling yell made all the more horrifying because it was *Cal's!*

Halfway down the second flight now, Plato hurdled the last six steps, slipping on the slick linoleum floor below and crashing into a row of battered steel lockers on the far wall. He scrambled to his feet just in time to glimpse a huge man in an incredibly ill-fitting suit dashing away in a wave of formalin fumes.

It didn't matter. Nothing mattered but getting to Cal in time. Crashes and clatters echoed from the embalming suite at the end of the corridor. Plato sped up the hallway and skidded right past Cal's door in a tangle of arms and legs and oily embalming fluid; someone had apparently coated the floor with the stuff. He slammed through the swing doors leading to the anatomy lab proper, slipping and sliding and finally tumbling into an empty stainless-steel cadaver box.

Sprawled there on the floor, Plato tried to gather his dazed thoughts, to figure out what the hell had happened, to remember what the hell he was *doing* here, when a familiar figure rushed to his side.

"Plato!" Cal crouched beside him, frowning with concern. Her white coat was torn and rumpled, and her long blond hair was scraggly and wet. She looked like she had just taken a dip in the Cuyahoga River on foundry-cleaning day, but she was the most wonderful thing Plato had ever seen. "Are you all right?"

"I'm supposed to be asking *you* that." Gingerly, he felt a lump on his forehead and peered up at the side of the cadaver box. Sure enough, he had left a dent.

"I'm fine, but *you've* got a nasty bump on your head. Poor clumsy dear." Cal clucked over the lump, then eyed him curiously. "What are you doing here, anyway?"

"Rescuing *you*," Plato answered peevishly. He struggled to his feet and reached out for Cal, to make sure she was really there. "And I'd have done it, too—if somebody hadn't planted an oil slick on the floor."

"It's not an oil slick." She raised a hand to touch the growing bulge on his head. "It's embalming fluid."

"I figured that out." He wrinkled his nose. "No wonder he ran away."

"*Cally!* Thank God you're all right!" Homer Marley skidded through the door, lumbered across the lab, and sniffed. He peered at her skeptically. "*Are* you all right?"

She laughed, far too loudly. The sound echoed from the tile walls and steel coffins. It was a laugh Plato recognized—fear and relief tinged with hysteria. He'd heard

Cal laugh that way once before, in an ambulance speeding to Riverside General.

Plato reached out to take her in his arms. Seconds later, she started sobbing into his shirt. Homer shot him a worried glance; he had never seen Cal upset before. For that matter, even *Plato* had hardly ever seen her cry. Cal always seemed too tough, too strong for that. She always met her worries and disappointments with anger instead of tears.

Plato knew *that* from experience.

"Maybe I'd better see how Jeremy's doing," Homer suggested quietly. Staring at the floor, he scuffed his feet in a puddle of embalming fluid. "He took off after Dubrowski and sent me over here."

Plato nodded, and Cal turned to touch Homer's arm. "Thanks—for coming down here. I don't know if I—"

Her voice broke off, and Homer reached up to squeeze her fingers. It looked like a child's hand in his grip. "Don't worry, Cally. You're safe now."

Watching him turn and drift out through the doors, Plato nodded firmly. "He's right, you know. You'll be just fine."

"I'm sorry." She pulled away, shaking her head.

"What for?"

"For crying like this." She dabbed at her face with a dry end of her lab coat. "But I was *so* scared."

"It's okay—I'd probably be crying too." He reached out to pull her close again. "But everything's going to be just fine."

She pulled her head back to look up at him. Her copper-brown eyes were filled with fear and dread. "No, it isn't."

"What do you mean?" Plato stroked her hair and smiled confidently. "Jimmy's gone, now. You're safe."

"I'm not safe at all." She shook her head and shivered. Pressing herself against him once more, she murmured into his shirt. "Before he ran out, Jimmy said he wasn't giving up." Her voice dropped to a barely audible whisper. "He said he would find me again . . . no matter what it takes."

CHAPTER 3

"Monday Night Football," Jeremy Ames announced as he shuffled the cards. "Downcards for pregame, postgame and half-time, ups for the quarters. Threes and sevens wild, show a suicide king and you match the pot."

"The guy with the ax?" Nina asked Cal.

"Right," Cal replied with a smile. Nina was a great card player, but she still had trouble with American poker. She had been raised in Italy on pinochle and bridge and euchre; she couldn't get used to the absence of a trump suit. And the endless variations confused her; she was accustomed to a rigid set of rules.

On the other hand, with her stolid, placid temperament and her utter immunity to being shaken by anything short of an earthquake, Nina was a fantastic bluffer.

"Ante's two bits," Jeremy continued, dealing a round facedown for the pregame and another faceup: the first quarter. "Homer starts the bidding."

Beside him, Homer Marley tossed a red chip into the pot. He had a seven of clubs showing, but he was too preoccupied to concentrate on the game. His fork was ploughing through a chicken-cheese burrito like a bulldozer demolishing an abandoned house.

The earthmover paused for just a moment while Homer mopped his forehead; as usual, Plato had made the sauce hot enough to sear their lips, draw tears to their eyes and sweat to their brows. And as usual, Homer had pitched into his third burrito before anyone else had finished their first.

They were gathered around the kitchen table, polishing off the huge tray of burritos, Plato's infamous Tijuana rice, the chips and salsa, and a cooler full of Great Lakes Brewery beer. More Christmas music was playing on the boombox: Harry Connick Jr.'s rollicking *It Must've Been Old Santa Claus*. A chill wind whistled through the eaves, but Marley Manor was snug and warm with a toasty fire in the fireplace and a thousand dollars' worth of new insulation in the attic.

It might have been a typical poker night except for the long silences at the table, the strained heartiness as they played cards and ate dinner, and the sidelong glances Cal kept getting from the others. It seemed like they still weren't quite sure she was really there, as though they all expected Jimmy Dubrowski to pop out of the refrigerator and drag her screaming from the house.

They had been quiet and pensive ever since she came home. Jeremy and Nina even offered to leave and cancel tonight's poker game, but Cal had insisted that they stay. For one thing, she didn't want to think about what had happened just yet. For another, she simply didn't want them to go—she wanted as many people around her as possible.

The memory of Jimmy Dubrowski's wild eyes, his hot breath on her cheek as he whispered his threats, hadn't faded from Cal's mind. She was far more frightened, far less confident than she had ever felt before. It was more than just the fear of physical harm; Cal had been through closer scrapes in the past. Instead, it was the absolute powerlessness she had felt there in the lab, the total loss of control.

The attack, down there in the quiet sanctuary of the embalming suite, had violated Cal's self-confidence, her nerve, her *soul*. She wondered if she would ever feel safe, ever feel whole again.

"Ten cents to you, Cally." Beside her, Plato frowned with concern.

"I'm in." She tossed a red chip into the pot without looking at her cards.

"You okay?" he asked softly. "You haven't touched your burrito."

"I'm sorry." She forked a bite into her mouth, then shrugged apologetically. "I guess I can't stop thinking about it."

The others heaved a collective sigh, as though Cal had finally uncorked the topic for discussion.

"I don't blame you, not one bit." Nina patted her arm and frowned. "It must have been *awful*."

"It was just such a shock."

"If only I could have caught the bastard," Jeremy muttered. He dealt another round of faceup cards and grimaced. "He's awful damned quick, for such a big guy."

Jeremy had spotted Dubrowski running out of the lab's fire exit. The detective had chased him across the parking lot and into the street, but the killer had darted down an alley and disappeared into the darkness.

"They'll catch him," Homer pronounced confidently. He shoveled the last bite of burrito number three into his mouth and offloaded a fourth from the pan. "Where the hell can he hide?"

"It took three weeks to find him last time," Cal sighed. "Didn't it, Jeremy?"

"Yeah." The detective nodded, then smiled confidently. "But he wasn't wearing a cadaver suit that was three sizes too small. We'll get him—the whole *city's* looking for him."

He dealt the rest of the hand and Nina calmly scooped up the pot.

"They caught him in the city library last time, didn't they?" she asked.

"In the basement, using the computers," Jeremy agreed. "That's how they tracked him down."

Nina nodded quickly, and touched her husband's arm. "Thank goodness."

They exchanged fond glances, remembering. Jeremy had been the senior detective on the Dubrowski case, and Nina had been a witness for the prosecution. Jeremy had met with her several times to discuss her testimony, eventually putting her under police protection while the West Side Strangler was still at large. And then, a few months after the case was closed, the thrice-divorced detective had taken one more shot at the dating game. The rest was history.

Fourth time's the charm, Jeremy had told his friends. And to Cal's eye, he seemed to be right.

"I remember hearing about it," Homer mused, looking up from the wreckage of his burrito. He hadn't moved back to Cleveland until after the trial. "Didn't Jeremy think he was innocent?"

"Not *innocent*," Jeremy told them. "I just had some doubts—but I was wrong. It's happened, once or twice."

Cal remembered now. On the last day of testimony, the defense had indeed called the chief detective on the case back to the witness stand. Jeremy's uncertainty about Dubrowski's guilt had been obvious. Dubrowski's lawyer—an earnest young public defender—had unraveled an impressive string of doubts and inconsistencies from Detective-Lieutenant Ames. Luckily, the prosecutor's cross-examination had tied Jeremy up in knots, further muddied the waters, and caused the jury to forget the detective's doubts.

Cal's own testimony later that day had sealed the verdict, placing Jimmy Dubrowski at the scene of two of the crimes by matching blood stains on and near the victims with Dubrowski's own DNA.

"They caught him using the *computers*?" Homer asked. "I thought the guy was crazy."

"Crazy like a fox," Jeremy replied. "One of these screwy genius types. He was getting a degree in computer programming before he went off the deep end."

"But what was he trying to accomplish?" Nina asked.

"He was trying to tap into the hospital," Cal replied. "His doctor's office—where that first lady was killed."

"That's how we tracked him down," Jeremy concluded. "Somebody picked up the after-hours activity at the library, and they caught him."

"Pretty impressive, for a schizophrenic," Plato mused. "Outrunning the police for three weeks, then tapping into the computer at Riverside."

"Jimmy was pretty sharp, as long as he took his medicine. That was the problem, according to the doctors. They figured he hadn't taken his pills for a couple of weeks."

"He was on Haldol, but his blood level was zip." Cal turned to Jeremy. "Maybe you guys should check the library."

"They're looking into it," the detective replied, eyeing the hand Homer had dealt. His schnauzer nose twitched disdainfully, as though he had just found bargain-brand dog food in his bowl.

Plato touched her arm and smiled. "Don't worry, kiddo. They'll find him."

She nodded, faking an assurance she wished was real. And doing a little reminiscing of her own.

Like Nina and Jeremy, she and Plato had also met four years ago—just before Jimmy Dubrowski's murder trial. Maybe that was why the case was imprinted so firmly in her mind. That whole unreal winter: her first case out of fellowship, the deluge of work at Riverside General where she was a part-time staff pathologist, the tall, handsome young doctor who had come down to her lab to witness an autopsy on one of his patients. Luella Huckleby—an eighty-year-old woman who had fallen down her basement stairs and died. She'd been on half a dozen heart medications; the fall had seemed like a simple accident.

Dr. Marley had been brisk, professional, and remarkably quiet—almost *cold* during the entire procedure. Cal wrote him off as just another one-dimensional workaholic doctor—the kind who couldn't admit failure, maybe, so he had to come to the lab and see for himself what went wrong, assure himself that Luella's fall wasn't his fault. The autopsy only confirmed Cal's impression of Plato: he had watched over her shoulder, badgering her every step of the way, focusing on every detail, subtly forcing her to perform a far more thorough autopsy than the poor old woman's death warranted.

But after almost two hours, during which Cal's courtesy had worn thin, all that thoroughness finally paid off. Dissecting the neck, Cal had found a cracked hyoid bone—a sign that she might have been strangled.

Later, investigators discovered a connection between Luella Huckleby and Jimmy Dubrowski: Luella had taken the strange young man from the apartment next door under her wing, seeing him almost every day and cooking him dinner once a week.

Oddly enough, Cal's autopsy showing that Luella's doctor wasn't at fault hadn't seemed to relieve Plato Marley. The coldly clinical physician remained just as aloof, just as unhappy as before. After thanking Cal for allowing him to observe the procedure, he helped wheel Luella's body into the cooler, lingering behind as Cal went off to write up her summary.

Ten minutes later, she glimpsed him still standing in the cooler, still bent over the old woman's body. Holding Luella's dead hand and murmuring something, then brushing his face on the sleeve of his white paper coverall. She ducked away quickly, feeling like she had just overheard someone's confession. Collecting her thoughts then, thinking back to the autopsy, Cal suddenly realized that she had mistaken genuine grief for cold professionalism. All her annoyance and exasperation were swept away in a sudden tide of empathy; Plato Marley's irritating questions and annoying persistence now made perfect sense, like a jumbled reflection on a rippled pond suddenly calming to become mirror-clear. And Cal knew she wanted to see more of this man.

A few days later, he sent her a thank you note and a small basket of flowers for "putting up with him" during the autopsy. He had followed the Dubrowski case closely after that, through the newspapers and through his contact with Cal. Eventually, she learned that Luella Huckleby had been one of Plato's first patients, and one of his favorites.

"Your bet, Cal," Homer reminded her.

"Sorry." She smiled and tossed a blue chip into the pot. The others were still talking about Dubrowski.

"How did he get into the lab today, anyway?" Plato asked.

"That emergency exit, probably," Jeremy replied. "It was propped open when he ran out."

Cal nodded. "The medical students sometimes leave it open."

"Why? Doesn't it get cold down there?"

"It's *always* cold in the anatomy lab," Plato griped.

"They like the fresh air," Cal answered. "It gets kind of stale down there, and the embalming fluid doesn't help."

"No kidding," Homer grunted. He leaned toward Plato and sniffed critically. "You *still* smell like the frog I dissected in fourth grade."

"The one you put in Sister Gertrude's lunch box?"

"Not the *whole* frog," Homer replied. "Just the legs. They're supposed to be a delicacy."

"Homer Marley!" Even the stoic Nina Ames was scandalized—her eyebrows rose a full eighth of an inch, and a frown flickered at the corners of her mouth. She had put her rosary away only a few minutes before. "You did that to a sister? A woman of the habit?"

"Shame on you," Cal said.

Jeremy shrugged. "What else would you expect from a *lawyer*?"

"She was the principal—and she took away my lunch," Homer protested. He pushed his empty plate away and gave a satisfied burp. "She said I was gollupping my food."

Cal eyed the wreckage and shook her head. "I wonder whatever gave her that idea."

"Dead Man's Curve," Plato announced as he dealt the cards. "Seven-card stud; twos and nines wild, king high, ace low."

Cal nodded; Dead Man's Curve was one of Plato's fa-

vorites—a game based on the deadly intersection between Routes 2 and 90 in the heart of Cleveland. Speeding in Dead Man's Curve could be lethal in real life as
well as the game: not only were aces the low cards, but a
face-up ace meant you had to match the pot.

Jeremy Ames hadn't dealt *his* favorite game tonight,
though, and he probably wouldn't. It was a perfectly
mundane game of five-card draw, played with standard
ante and rules until all the bets were in. Then, just before
the cards were shown, the dealer "killed" each player's
hand by randomly drawing one of their cards and replac-
ing it with another from the deck; of course, he had another player murder *his* hand as well.

A fun game, except for one thing: it was called Psy-
chopathic Killer. Cal doubted their group would play it
again any time soon.

"Sister Gertrude," Plato mused. "She was a pretty
good principal."

"The best," Homer agreed. "I still send her a card
every Christmas."

The telephone rang before Plato dealt the face-up
cards. He scrambled to answer it before Cal.

"Hello? Hello?" He frowned at the receiver. "Who *is*
this?"

Suddenly tense, Cal started to stand, but he waved her
back to her chair. Finally, he shook his head and grimaced.

"No, thanks. We're not interested." He reached over to
hang up the phone, then turned and rolled his eyes at the
others. "Somebody trying to sell aluminum siding. On a
Saturday night—can you believe it?"

Cal *didn't* believe it. For one thing, she couldn't imagine anyone selling aluminum siding in the dead of winter.
For another, Plato was a horrible liar; the side of his

mouth always got a funny little twist whenever he wasn't telling the truth.

"Telephone solicitors." Jeremy shook his head. "I always tell them we just built our house. That way, they don't call back."

Plato avoided Cal's gaze as he dealt the cards. Homer and Jeremy both had aces in the first round of face-up cards. It was a huge pot by the end of the hand, and Nina Ames scooped it all in.

Just like she did for the rest of the evening. Usually a mediocre player, Nina was the runaway favorite tonight; by the time they quit, her pile of chips was taller than all the other players' combined.

"Hard to believe I started with fifteen bucks," Homer groused as he cashed in his meager pile. "There goes tomorrow's lunch money."

"Poor Homer." Nina Ames patted his hand and smiled. "I appreciate your contribution—Jeremy and I are going to need this money."

"What for? You already went on your cruise."

"For what happened *during* the cruise," Jeremy replied. He eyed his wife hopefully, like a puppy waiting for a treat. If he'd had a tail, it would have been wagging. "Should we tell them?"

Nina nodded, beaming radiantly: it was the most emotion Cal had ever seen her display.

"Tell us what?" Cal asked.

"We're expecting," the detective announced proudly.

"Expecting *what?*" Homer asked.

"A baby, of course." Nina patted her stomach, then measured her piles of poker chips. "This may be enough money for that crib blanket I saw at Penney's."

"You're *pregnant?*" Cal gasped.

"The baby should come in August," Nina replied. "So the doctor tells us."

"That's *fantastic!*" Plato gushed. Cal thought she heard just a trace of envy in his voice. They had been trying to get pregnant for the past few months; Plato was already getting impatient. He glanced over at Nina and chuckled. "No wonder you made Jeremy take a cruise."

"He couldn't get away from me," she replied.

Beside her, Jeremy's ears were a bright neon red. "Nina—"

"And now, I'll have someone to keep him home at night," she continued.

"No kidding," Homer agreed. He glanced down at the paltry remains of his fifteen dollars. "At least my money's going to a good cause."

"I think this calls for another beer." Plato opened the cooler and passed them around.

"Beer—and *cigars.*" Jeremy pulled a handful from his pocket and winked at Cal. "I brought enough for *all* of us."

"The baby can't smoke," Nina scolded. "And neither can I."

"And I don't *want* to." Cal wrinkled her nose. "Take those awful things out on the porch. Last time Jeremy brought cigars, this place smelled for a whole *week.*"

Much later, after the others had left and the dirty dishes were stacked in the sink, Plato slipped his arm around Cal and smiled.

"Great news about Jeremy and Nina."

"I know." Cal nodded. "She's *so* excited—and worried."

"Worried?"

"*You* know. About her epilepsy."

Plato nodded. They both knew about Nina's problem.

She'd been in a car accident as a child, and a head injury had left her prone to seizures.

"I told her the baby would be fine, as long as she followed her doctor's orders." Cal shrugged. "She seemed relieved."

"She'll be all right," he replied.

"I know." Cal grinned. "You should have heard her—talking about cribs and comforters and baby bottles. She sounded so *domestic*."

"Don't laugh—it could happen to you." He led her upstairs to their room and slumped onto the bed.

"I'm looking forward to it." She climbed into bed beside him and unbuttoned his shirt, moving close and nuzzling his neck. "Really soon."

He tilted her chin up and met her gaze with those green eyes of his—clear and guileless, the eyes she had seen above that surgical mask on the day they had met. Cal remembered seeing those eyes of his that first time and wishing all the good-looking guys weren't pinheads; at least she had found *one* exception to the rule. He kissed her, long and sweet, and she remembered their first embrace, their first date, the other time Jimmy Dubrowski was on the run.

Thinking about that date, Cal couldn't help thinking about the Strangler. Those threatening phone calls in the middle of the night, the face she once spotted in her apartment window. Being stalked even as the police struggled to track the killer down. Cal couldn't help shivering.

"What's wrong?" Plato asked, drawing away.

"I'm just remembering our first date," she said absently.

"That bad, huh?" He grinned. "I hope I've gotten a *little* better since then."

"It's not *you*," she protested, then explained. She told

him about her terror in the lab, the utter certainty that her life was over, the helplessness she had felt. And the fear that still chilled her now, that she worried might never go away. The words tumbled out—a stammered confession of weakness, of terror. Sharing it with Plato made her feel just a little bit better. "Just hold me. Please. Okay?"

He held her close, stroking her back, murmuring soft reassurances, keeping her safe and warm. Soothing her fears away. Their lovemaking was different this time—comforting, like the sanctuary of home during a loud thunderstorm, making her relax and forget, if only for a while.

She fell asleep then, safe and secure in his arms. Until the pealing of the telephone split the quiet night. Plato went on snoring, comatose with sleep; Cal wondered how he ever managed to hear his pager—even if he *did* tuck it inside his pillowcase every night.

She rolled over and grabbed the phone from the nightstand.

"Hello?"

"Hi, Dr. Marley," said a familiar voice. "It's me, Jimmy. We've got a lot to talk about, you betcher."

Cal swallowed a scream, then slowly reached over and hung up the phone, disconnecting it for good measure. The logical thing to do would be to call the police, to get a tap placed on her line, to keep Dubrowski talking next time until they could track him down.

But Cal wasn't feeling very logical. And somehow, she knew it wouldn't do any good. Jimmy Dubrowski was psychotic, but Jeremy Ames was right. He was crazy like a fox—he'd never let them catch him that easily.

She scrambled into her bathrobe and scurried downstairs, checking that all the doors and windows were locked, patting their Australian shepherd's head and feeling just a little safer for his presence. Ghost looked up at her and then at the windows, seeming to understand.

Finally, she climbed upstairs and got dressed, then pulled her trusty baseball bat out from under the bed. Cal lay there alone in the darkness, staring up at the bedroom ceiling. Straining her ears for a telltale creak, the crash of a broken window, Ghost's frantic barking. Wondering if she would ever feel safe again.

And falling asleep, fully dressed atop the covers, snuggled up to a 26-inch Easton aluminum T-ball bat.

CHAPTER 4

The cold winter sun seeped through the bedroom curtains, oozed through the blanket covering Cal's face, and leaked through her tightly closed eyelids, nagging her from a fitful slumber. She hadn't slept very well—partly because of the sharp pain in her chest, the hard lump of Plato's arm under her ribs.

She rolled over, reached down to push his arm away, and gasped. Plato's arm was gone, replaced by a changeling: a rock-hard aluminum T-ball bat. *What the hell?*

And then it all came rushing back—the cadaver stirring to life in the embalming suite, the wild look in Jimmy Dubrowski's eyes, the sheer terror of being trapped alone in the medical school's anatomy lab. Her wrists were still swollen and sore, as though Cal had worn a pair of tight handcuffs all night. She held her hands up to the light and gasped, shocked at the strange pattern of livid purple bruises circling both wrists. Four thick lines on the back of her left wrist, and a single oblique smudge on her right.

The forensic pathologist in Cal understood immediately, even as she herself was appalled. Four fingers and a thumb: Jimmy Dubrowski had left his mark on her. Cal felt naked, violated, and somehow humiliated—as though the attack was somehow her fault. As though the Strangler had taken something from her: stolen a piece of her soul, of her very private self.

She sat up in bed, still studying her wrists, wishing Plato were here in bed and wondering where he could possibly be. Plato *never* got up early on Sundays: sleeping in was a sacramental rite for him, a strictly and zealously observed ritual. But she could hear him up and stirring, bumbling around in the living room downstairs. A strange noise filtered up from the first floor—an eerie metallic screech, punctuated by a steady drumming rattle and Ghost's frantic barks. And Plato's muttered curses as something clattered loudly to the floor.

Curious now, Cal changed and headed downstairs. As she approached the living room, the odd screeching resumed, now accompanied by the acrid whiff of ozone and a sad, plaintive whistling—like the call of a mourning dove whose mate had just succumbed to a long and painful illness.

Cal rushed into the living room, but she could never have been prepared for the awful sight that met her eyes: Plato sprawled on the floor in front of the sofa, imprisoned by a jumbled mass of wires, twisted metal, rusted machinery, and mildewed cardboard boxes.

And dust. Lots and lots of dust.

The immaculate living room Cal had so carefully tidied and vacuumed yesterday morning, in preparation for last night's poker game, looked like the site of some tragic accident—a cornfield littered with debris from an airplane crash, or a beach strewn with wreckage from a sunken ship.

Plato was oblivious to his surroundings and to Cal. Clad in a pair of oil-smeared sweats and a tattered AN-TIGUA, W.I. T-shirt, he was gently massaging a strip of metal with a ball of steel wool. His tongue was clenched tightly between his teeth and his eyes were hooded with concentration; he might have been sculpting a master-piece—or defusing a bomb.

Gently, carefully, he laid the metal strip on the floor beside him and looked up. He gestured at the mess, smil-ing with the rapture of the prodigal son's father, with the joy of a shepherd who has found a lost sheep.

Cal would have preferred a sheep.

Arms folded, she frowned around the room and winced. "What, may I ask, are you *doing*?"

"Just getting this cleaned up," Plato replied airily. But he glanced at his surroundings and frowned, stroking his beard thoughtfully. Plato seemed just as surprised as Cal by the wreckage, the total demolition of the living room. From his innocent expression, he might have seen the mess as the work of demonic elves, or maybe a slovenly poltergeist.

"What *is* all this stuff?" she challenged, coming closer and prodding a lump of wire with a cautious slipper. "Alexander Graham Bell's first telephone? Some kind of exotic torture device?"

"Hardly." He shook his head quickly, then dove into a moldering cardboard box tucked behind the coffee table. He emerged with a wide smile, another smudge on his shirt, and a piece of heavy black metal in his hand. Some-thing with wheels, and a little smoke stack.

A toy locomotive. A choo-choo.

"Watch this." With obvious pride, Plato set his prize on a short length of rusted track he had assembled on the floor, then reached over to a dangerous-looking box on the coffee table. The box featured a long red handle, a dial, and a pair of indicator lights. Its frayed and dusty cord was plugged into a wall socket. Plato pushed the handle down and turned; the dim lights changed from red to green and the device droned like a buzzer on a game show. Sparks flew from the locomotive's wheels as it quivered and clattered to life, shuddering down the track like an injured thoroughbred stumbling across a finish line. Plato pushed a button, and the black box made its widowed-dove noise. Apparently, it was supposed to be a whistle.

The whole scene was very painful to watch.

"You're playing with a toy train?" Cal asked when the demonstration was finally over.

"Not just *any* train," he replied earnestly. "This is an *American Flyer*."

He paused, presumably to let the significance set in. Cal raised one eyebrow very slowly and deliberately. But Plato didn't notice. He was fondling the locomotive, massaging its tired wheels with a happy smile.

"I've had this set ever since I was a kid." He glanced up at Cal. "It was my *father's* set."

"You guys didn't take very good care of it, did you?"

Plato frowned over the wreckage. "It just needs a little cleaning, that's all."

"It needs to be *sandblasted*." She picked up a length of track and studied it critically. The twin rails were coated with a thick patina of rust, and the metal crosspieces were bent and twisted, as though an itsy-bitsy tornado had struck the Marley & Marley Railroad many years ago. "On second thought, don't bother. There's probably not any metal under here." She set the track back on the coffee table—gingerly, so it wouldn't shatter into dust. "Why don't you just buy a new set?"

Plato gasped at the suggestion. "They don't make *real* American Flyers any more. This is an *antique*."

"I'll say." She shrugged. "So why not just get a Lionel?"

"Very funny." He set the locomotive back on its track. The controller box had stopped smoking. Mercifully, he unplugged the fire hazard from the wall. "Besides, even generic S-gauge sets are expensive."

"So is burning down the house." Cal shifted a few tattered boxes and slumped into the easy chair, watching her husband with bewildered dismay. She felt like one of those wives you see on the cover of the *National Enquirer*—the poor gals whose husbands turn out to be space aliens or Elvis Presley's illegitimate sons. During almost four years of marriage, Plato had carefully hidden this train-fanatic side of his personality, this Lionel-scoffing elitism.

Maybe it was an early midlife crisis, Cal mused. What the hell *was* an American Flyer, anyway? Plato even pronounced the name with reverence, like a modern art collector discussing Picasso.

What other awful secrets might Plato be hiding?

"I'll get it fixed up," he promised as he stroked the steel wool along another length of track. "You'll see— we'll have a train running around our Christmas tree this year. Just like when we were kids."

"You're *still* a kid," Cal muttered. "Hey—speaking of trees—"

"I thought maybe we'd go to Storyland this year." Plato handed her a newspaper, folded in half. It was the *Beacon Journal*'s annual Christmas-tree shopping guide, listing most of the farms in Northeastern Ohio. Storyland was circled with yellow highlighter. "Just like old times. We could get another ten-footer."

Plato was into big trees. Last year, they had to settle for a measly eight-footer.

Cal glanced up at the date—yesterday. "Didn't the Sunday paper come yet?"

"Probably not." Plato shrugged. "Tommy's *always* late on Sundays. Especially in the wintertime."

She drifted across the living room to the front door. Sure enough, little Tommy Jorgensen—all of fourteen now, but still wispy and frail—was just making the turn into their drive. He was bent double under the heavy load of the Sunday *Plain Dealer*s, and his bike skidded and slid along the icy asphalt. But he trotted up to the front door and rang their bell to make his delivery personally.

"Hi, Dr. Marley!" Tommy handed over the newspaper and shot her an admiring grin. With his orange hair and freckles, he looked like a reverent jack-o-lantern. "You made the front page again. You and Jimmy Dubrowski. God—that must have been *radical!*"

Cal turned the paper over and studied the headline. Sure enough, yesterday's saga was splashed across the top of the page in big, bold letters: DUBROWSKI ESCAPES PRISON, TERRORIZES DEPUTY CORONER.

"Is Dubrowski as crazy as they say?" Tommy asked. "I mean, I heard he was, like, as bad as Jeffrey Dahmer. Maybe even worse, except he didn't *eat* anyone. Nobody they *know* about, anyway. . . ."

Reading the story, Cal reeled beneath a fresh wave of fear. It had really happened—it wasn't just a dream, or something she could laugh away or forget about.

"Thanks, Tommy." Gently, Cal reached out to close the door.

"Do you think he might come down *here*?" the paperboy asked hopefully. "I mean—"

"Thanks, Tommy." Still studying the paper, she slowly closed the door. In a trance, she turned back to the living room. The shivers were coming again. "Plato?"

"I'm right here."

And he was—just behind her. He folded Cal into his arms and held her close, banishing the trembling and the fear once again.

Two hours later, they pulled into the gravel-covered driveway of Storyland Forest. A plump old Santa Claus handed Plato and Cal a pair of Dum-Dum suckers and directed them to an empty parking space. Plato pulled into the spot, switched off the Corsica and turned to Cal with a frown.

"You sure you're up to this?" he asked. "We could do this some other time, if you want to stay home." He swallowed heavily. "Or we could even get a *cut* tree."

"Poor Plato." She grinned, patting his cheek with her mittened hand. "Such sacrifices you're willing to make for me."

"What?" He frowned curiously. "What?"

"I know you—a cut tree is just one step above *artificial*." She grabbed the bow saw from the floor and scrambled outside, beaming at him. "This year, *I'm* going to cut it down. Just lead me to it."

Cal had grown up in the heart of Chicago's near northside: Lincoln Park, where the best Christmas trees came from a seedy little lot under the L-station a couple of blocks from her and Mom's apartment. The trees there were cheap and reasonably fresh, but the annual shopping trip was always rather frightening—following Mom through back streets and deserted alleys, darting into the dimly lit enclosure and hoping the leering owner wouldn't notice the two unescorted females, slinking down the shadowy rows of trees to pick a spruce that would fit into the tiny corner of their living room, and finally hurrying home with their prize slung over their shoulders.

It felt less like a Christmas outing than a commando raid into an enemy P.O.W. camp.

Before meeting Plato, Cal had never seen a Christmas tree farm before, never imagined a place where ordinary saw-carrying civilians might cheerfully harvest their own trees in broad daylight.

It had been their very first date: over lunch not long after Luella's autopsy, Cal had confessed that she wasn't going to bother with a Christmas tree this year—she was new to the area, living alone, and didn't think finding one was worth the hassle.

"*Hassle?*" Plato had replied, astounded.

Hunting for a tree was half the fun, he had told her. Tracking the wild spruce through the snowy fields of Ohio, stalking the ideal prey and pouncing before someone else got it, then finally bringing it down with a sharply aimed band saw. Laughing, she had asked to join him on his next hunt.

So he had taken her to Storyland Forest—a vast Christmas tree ranch near the Pennsylvania border—a huge spread covering hundreds of acres with every kind of tree imaginable: Scotch pine and blue spruce, Frazier fir and Norway spruce, and a dozen other varieties. The fields were too far-flung for walking, so half a dozen tractor-drawn wagons shuttled shoppers into the fields.

Scrambling onto the cart and onto a hay bale beside Plato, Cal couldn't help remembering that first Christmas tree shopping excursion together. It had been a viciously cold December day, with a bitter north wind whipping across the rows of trees. Between the frigid weather and the lateness of the season, they were the only two passengers on their wagon. After picking out a blue spruce for his apartment and a small Scotch pine for Cal's, Plato had finally noticed that his date was shivering and turning blue. On the return trip in the wagon, embarrassed and apologetic for having dragged his date out on a day when the wind chill was in the double-digits *below* zero, Plato had gallantly offered her his coat. Instead, she had snuggled close against his leeward side, worming her way into his awkward and shy embrace.

The tractor driver, through some form of intuition or clairvoyance, had gotten "lost" on his way back to the parking lot. After two more trips around the farm, he had finally found the proper trail. By that time, Plato had recovered his confidence and found a new way to keep his date warm, and Cal had discovered that he was a very good kisser.

It wasn't nearly as cold today, and they were sharing their wagon with a family of five: three little girls with obvious head colds, a mom with an overstuffed diaper bag and a huge box of Kleenex, and a gloomy-looking dad in a suit and tie who sat sullenly on his hay bale, studying his bow saw like a Neanderthal eyeing the latest model of spear and finding it lacking.

The tractor came to life with a roar and a cloud of smoke, jerking the wagon into motion and setting off down a rutted lane. As the endless rows of evergreens swung into view the two older girls sat up excitedly, gesturing at one tree after another and begging their father to stop the tractor.

. "We'll wait," he finally replied, lifting his head mournfully. "We're getting a Scotch pine. They don't shed as much."

The youngest girl eyed Plato with a shy smile. Finally, she bounced out of her mother's grip and skipped nimbly across the floor of the cart, colliding with Plato's knee and grabbing his hand for support.

"You've got a beard," she announced.

He eyed her curiously. "No, I *don't*."

"You *do*." She tucked a hank of blond hair under her pink knitted ski hat and pointed. "There. On your chin."

Plato reached up, fingering the whiskers thoughtfully, then smiled. "Oh, *that*."

The girl nodded.

"That's not a *beard*," he continued. "That's *Harold*. He's an otter that lives on my face."

"*Plato!*" Cal scolded. She glanced over at the mother, but the poor woman was too busy plying her Kleenex on her other two girls to hear Plato's crazy ramblings.

"An otter?" the little girl asked. For a three-year-old, she spoke very clearly, with just the faintest of lisps. She leaned to the side, apparently searching for Harold's eyes and teeth. "How come he lives on your face?"

"It keeps him warm." Plato shrugged. "And sometimes, when I don't like my supper, I let Harold have it."

The girl nodded—she had found a kindred spirit. "I do that too—with Scamp. She's my dog."

Then, without the slightest hesitation, she grabbed Plato's sleeve and wiped her nose on it, then danced back to her mother. She leaned close to whisper into Mom's ear, and the woman glanced up at Plato, frowning suspiciously.

"Did you see that?" he asked Cal, pulling out a tissue and wiping his sleeve. "She wiped her nose on my coat."

"Serves you right." Cal shrugged, then leaned close to whisper. "Still want to have kids?"

"Seven of them," he replied with a nod. "They can wipe each others' noses."

Cal glanced across the wagon and shook her head. "Heaven only knows what that poor girl told her mother."

They would never find out—the Mucus family disembarked at the next field, and another couple climbed aboard with a stately Douglas fir.

"Another blue spruce this year?" Plato asked.

She nodded, and he signaled the driver to continue. The tractor clattered along to the northeast corner of the farm, picking up another Douglas fir and two Scotch pines along the way. Finally, they reached the blue spruce zone—several dozen acres of widely-spaced evergreens, planted in neat rows and neatly pruned by an army of seasonal workers last summer.

The blue spruces were expensive, but Cal liked their shape. And the short needles didn't clog up their vacuum cleaner. On the downside, the trees tended to be far heftier for their height than the wispier pines in the other fields.

Of course, those subtleties were lost on Plato. He had a Charlie Brown attitude toward Christmas trees, invariably gravitating toward the most awkwardly shaped trees in sight—the hopeless rejects most likely to end up as next spring's mulch. He claimed it was pity, but Cal had another theory: Plato seemed to identify with the gawky trees—the wallflowers and outcasts of the tree farm.

"Look at *that* one," he gasped excitedly.

Sure enough, he had led her straight to the most crooked, misshapen tree in the area: a ten-foot blue spruce with a perfectly S-curved trunk—an arboreal Hunchback of Notre Dame. The tree had at least three top leaders, and its windward side was almost devoid of branches. The side that *had* branches looked diseased; the needles were a pale greenish-brown, as though rust had somehow set in.

He danced over to look at it, and Cal smiled grimly.

"Maybe they'll give us a special price on it," she said.

"Why?" he asked cluelessly. "I think it looks great."

"Aside from the fact that it's shaped like a corkscrew and it's missing half of its branches."

"Only on *one* side," he argued, stepping over to the left. "If you look from here, it's almost straight."

Cal wasn't listening. From the corner of her eye, she had noticed a tall, solitary man studying them from a distant row of trees. He was broad-shouldered and powerful-looking, wearing an orange hunter's jacket and an Indians baseball cap tipped low over his face. She paced over for a closer look, but the man quickly turned away to frown at the spruce beside him.

Probably nothing—she was just being paranoid. But what was he doing out here *alone?*

"You can hardly see the bare spot at all," Plato was saying.

"It's pitiful," Cal replied. "I'm not spending six dollars a foot for—"

"Seven," he amended. "Blue spruces are seven. Good Christmas trees are getting expensive."

"This isn't a Christmas tree." She frowned at the charity case. "It's a prop from a Dr. Seuss show."

"Okay, okay. Maybe next year, buddy." Sadly, Plato reached out to pat one of the branches. A shower of needles floated down to the muddy ground. "If you're still alive."

They finally settled on a choice of two trees—another Charlie Brown special of Plato's with a spiral trunk but a reasonably full shape, and a ruler-straight spruce with a perfectly conical shape and a regal bearing: the sap of a hundred White House Christmas trees seemed to course through its veins. But even Cal had to agree that it seemed a little *too* perfect—almost artificial. On such an ostentatious tree, their collection of ornaments would seem plain and tawdry.

"Stay here and guard this tree with your life," she finally told Plato. "I want to take one more look at *your* choice."

Leaving him behind, she darted down the next row to find his Charlie Brown special. They had tied Cal's scarf to one of its lower branches, both to help it stand out from its lookalike cousins and to ward off other prospective buyers. Not that anyone else was likely to want the thing.

But the tree—and Cal's scarf—weren't there. She checked down the next row, and the next. Plato's tree was nowhere to be found. Surely nobody had cut it down already—except for that weird guy in the hunting jacket, they had spotted just one other family in this corner of the farm. And Cal was pretty sure those people had already left—*without* Plato's tree; they looked far too sensible for that.

She hurried down the next row, searching for Plato's lost tree. And over the next five minutes, Cal somehow got turned around in the evergreen maze. Plato had a much easier time finding his way around—he could see over the shoulders of most of the trees, while Cal's five-feet-two-inches of height left her surrounded by solid walls of green. She frowned, wondering if she could even find her way back to Plato, wondering whether she might actually be *lost*.

It wouldn't be the first time—Plato often teased that she didn't have enough direction-sense to find her way out of a cul-de-sac. Cal could simply shout his name to find her way back, but she wouldn't give Plato the pleasure of another chuckle at her expense. Instead, she would find him by herself.

Cal stopped at the end of a row and looked around. A few hundred yards to the left, she recognized a huge weeping willow—the very tree that stood at the end of the row where she had left Plato standing. Relieved, she threaded her way back through the rows, always keeping the willow tree in sight. And just a minute or two later, she stumbled on Plato's top selection with its spiral trunk and Cal's scarf tied to one of the lower branches.

She bent over to retrieve her scarf, then stood back to study the tree. Maybe Plato was right after all. It wasn't a *bad* tree, really. It just needed a little love.

She smiled, starting to walk back to tell Plato the news. But a voice behind Cal froze her in her tracks.

"Dr. Marley. It's so *good* to see you again."

CHAPTER 5

Like a startled jackrabbit, Cal sprang into action, bounding across the aisle and vaulting over a four-foot Scotch pine. She sprinted down the next row, made a left turn and then a right, and dove through a solid wall of blue spruces to the spot where Plato was waiting.

Except he wasn't there. The perfect tree was standing just where they'd left it, with Plato's scarf dangling from one of the limbs. The muddy ground surrounding the tree was trampled and cratered with his size-thirteen boot prints. But Plato himself was nowhere to be seen.

"Plato?" she cried. "*Plato?*"

Cal glanced up and down the aisle, but saw no sign of her husband. Instead, she caught a flash of orange in the next row over—Jimmy Dubrowski's hunting jacket.

She lurched into motion again, haring down the path as fast as her clumsy hiking boots would permit, churning through the soft mud and tearing into another wall of trees. The main wagon trail was just on the other side, and a tractor was rounding a bend and heading this way. Cal frantically wormed into the narrow gap between two trees, feeling the spiky branches prick and tear at her coat and slacks like the grasping claws of a dozen demented witches. The trees here were older and tougher; their limbs were locked together like the wires of a chain link fence. Needles scratched and scraped her face and hands, her hat was snatched away, and a dead branch slashed through the fabric of her ski jacket with a sickening *r-r-rip!*

But she was *through*—staggering up the wagon trail toward the oncoming tractor, flagging it down, and smiling with crazy relief as the driver approached. The tractor with its empty wagon ground to a halt, and the driver frowned down at her in puzzlement.

"Where's your tree, lady?"

Cal simply shook her head, waiting to catch her breath. Finally, she replied, "I don't have one. I need help—my husband is—"

"Cal?" Like a specter, or maybe an officer beamed down from the starship *Enterprise*, Plato materialized at her elbow. He was breathing hard too, and his boots and pants were spattered with mud. "What's wrong? I heard you yelling—"

"It's Jimmy Dubrowski," she cried, reaching out to clutch his arm. "He's here—he's *after* me!"

Plato tensed. He stared over Cal's shoulder, then gallantly pushed her behind him. She peered around him, spotting the now-familiar orange hunter's jacket and Indians' cap.

But the huge man wasn't Jimmy Dubrowski after all. He was a ruggedly handsome older man, with iron-gray hair and a wide and perfectly sane smile. He strolled closer, waving to the man on the tractor and nodding at Plato.

"Get back," Plato growled. He wiggled his hand in his pocket menacingly. "I've got a gun."

The man's jaw dropped, and he backed up a step or two. With his leathery face, blue jeans and tall snakeskin boots, he might have been the Marlboro Man's grandfather. He was vaguely familiar to Cal; she was sure she had met him sometime in the past few months.

"Easy, fella." The leathery smile had hardened to a rigid mask of fear. "No need for any of that."

"Plato," she muttered. "It's not Dubrowski."

He whirled on her. "What?"

"You thought I was Jimmy Dubrowski?" the man exclaimed. "*Shit*! No *wonder* you took off like that." He shook his head, chuckling now. "Course, what with Jimmy being about thirty years younger than me, I wouldn't think there was much chance of you mixing us up."

"Is everything all right?" the man on the tractor asked. He was holding a small CB radio in one gloved hand, and eyeing the group with a puzzled frown. "You still need help, lady?"

"No," Cal replied with a reassuring smile. "It was just a mix-up. I'm fine, now."

The tractor started up and rumbled off, and the man in the orange jacket extended his hand to Plato. "Otto Browning. I assume you're Dr. Marley's husband?"

Plato didn't shake his hand. Instead, he glanced down at Cal. "What's this about?"

Before she could answer, Browning replied. "I'm a freelance reporter—I do a lot of work for the *Cleveland Post*." He edged past Plato and took Cal's hand. "We met at the courthouse last summer, Doc."

She shook his hand numbly. "I remember."

"But what are you doing *here*?" Plato asked.

"I just wanted to ask you a few questions," he told Cal, ignoring Plato altogether. "About Jimmy Dubrowski. Is there any chance that the coroner's office will reopen the case?"

"No." Cal shook her head, caught off-balance by

Browning's rapid delivery. "We have no reason to. No new findings have appeared, and the jury seemed quite satisfied with the evidence."

He nodded, then flashed a curious smile. "But are *you* satisfied with the evidence?"

Cal paused, and Plato broke the silence. His voice was gruff, impatient.

"Hold on a minute." He edged between the reporter and Cal again. "Do you mean to tell me you came all the way out here just to question her?"

"I don't mind," Browning replied modestly. "I might even pick out a tree while I'm here. *After* the interview, of course."

"How did you know we were here?" Plato asked sharply.

"He followed us," Cal murmured.

"All the way from Sagamore Hills?" He shook his head in disbelief. "That's over an hour away."

"It's a very important story," Browning replied. He turned to Cal again. "A story that I think will evolve with time. What exactly did Jimmy Dubrowski *say* yesterday, Dr. Marley?"

"I don't believe this," Plato growled. "You *followed* us all this way? What'd you do—camp outside our house last night?"

"There's no law against following people," the reporter answered quickly.

"There are laws against *stalking*, against *harassing* people." Plato's voice shook, a sure sign that he was angry. He clenched and unclenched his fists, and took a step closer to the reporter.

Despite his size, Plato was half a head shorter than Browning. The reporter smiled down at him confidently. "I would hardly call this *harassment*, Mr. Marley."

"That's *Doctor* Marley, and I *would* call it harassment." He pointed an angry finger at the man. "You scare my wife out of her mind, chase her around this farm, and then you have the *nerve* to try to badger her into an interview. Why didn't you just call for an appointment?"

Browning shrugged. "She wouldn't have given me one." He turned to Cal. "Right?"

She nodded reluctantly.

"I'm sorry if I startled you, ma'am." The reporter's voice dropped to a half whisper, and he smiled ingratiatingly. "But I don't see any reason why we can't have a little chat." He shot a pointed glance at Plato. "That is, if your *husband* will allow it."

Cal felt a surge of anger at the implication—that she needed Plato's permission to talk with a reporter. But almost instantly, she understood Browning's strategy. The reporter was just pressing buttons, manipulating her into answering his questions.

"It's not a question of what Plato will allow," she replied. "I make my own decisions, but I happen to agree with him." Her voice rose as she found her own anger, directing it at the annoying reporter. How *dare* he follow them here, frightening her half to death and ruining their day in the process? "I resent being followed by *anyone*—whether it's Jimmy Dubrowski, or you, or the mayor himself. Outside of the coroner's office, my life is my own." She took a step forward, glaring up at Browning. "You've spied on us—violating our privacy and purposely waiting until I was alone before approaching me. At least Jimmy Dubrowski has a *reason* for acting crazy."

Browning simply nodded. "Then you agree that he has a case for appeal?"

"*No!*" Cal shook her head, frustrated. The man hadn't heard a word, hadn't understood a thing she said.

"Go away," Plato snarled. He took another step toward the reporter and stuck his chin out angrily; they were standing toe-to-toe, and Plato's fists were clenched into stones. Not for the first time, Cal noticed how broad her husband's shoulders were, how powerful he was. Browning had three or four inches and a few dozen pounds on Plato, but most of the reporter's weight was centered in his gut: a round bowling ball slung just above his belt.

Cal remembered Steven Prescott—the only person she had ever seen Plato fight with. His roundhouse blow had knocked Prescott off his feet and laid him out cold. She shivered, worrying that Plato might actually *hurt* the reporter, secretly wishing he would, but fretting over the consequences.

Luckily, Browning blinked first. His cocky smile melted to a lame grin, and he backed another step or two, raising his hands apologetically. "Hey, I'm sorry. I didn't mean to intrude."

"Sure," Plato said.

"Listen—if you ever *do* want to talk, just give me a call." He pulled a business card from his pocket and handed it to Cal, then smiled over at Plato. "No hard feelings?"

"We'll see." Plato folded his arms. "Just leave us alone. Okay?"

"Fine." The reporter turned on his heel and headed up the trail toward the parking lot. Another tractor was rumbling down the trail; it halted and he climbed aboard. As it clattered past, Browning smiled down at them, his confidence restored.

"Thanks," she said once the tractor had disappeared. "I was afraid you were going to *kill* that guy."

"*Me?*" Plato asked in a tone of wounded innocence. "I was just trying to protect him from *you.*"

"Come on." Cal took the bow saw in one hand and grabbed his arm with the other. "I want to go chop something down."

The midwinter darkness had fallen by the time they made it home. Plato's crooked spruce was bound up tight in a net of plastic mesh, strapped to the roof of the Corsica, and glazed with a thick coat of sleet and melted snow that had accumulated on the hour-long drive home. They wrestled the tree off the car and into the garage, where Plato stood it in a corner while Cal watched dubiously.

"It's pretty wet," she observed.

Already, a pile of melting slush had formed beneath the tall spruce. Plato lifted the massive tree trunk and slammed it down onto the floor two or three times; a half-gallon of grimy water rained onto the concrete. Still, the branches were glazed with a thick layer of ice and dirty snow. It hadn't been snowing that hard, but the poor tree seemed to have collected every bit of slush and road grime from the interstate between Youngstown and Cleveland. Blue salt crystals clung to the needles, and the branches were spattered with clumps of ash and asphalt.

"I think it needs a bath," Plato told her.

"*You* give it a bath," she replied irritably. "I'm getting something to eat. I'm *hungry*."

Plato nodded. A hungry Cal was a dangerous thing; without regular feeding and watering, his sweet, diminutive wife morphed into a ravenous and bad-tempered lioness. The confrontation with Otto Browning was making her even more irritable, Plato knew; the barbaric satisfaction of felling their Christmas tree had only sated part of Cal's anger at the reporter. During the drive home, she had grumbled and growled and snarled at the nosy reporter's impudence in following them around. And groused about how she hadn't *really* had the time to give him a piece of her mind.

On the bright side, the incident seemed to have deflected Cal's attention from her original worries: she seemed to have completely forgotten Jimmy Dubrowski's attack yesterday. Cal was still angry about Browning; beyond the door to the kitchen, Plato could hear her muttering imprecations and slamming pots and pans around. If Browning ever *did* show up again, Cal would probably beat him to a pulp.

Dubrowski too, for that matter.

Plato heaved a sigh of relief, thankful to have an excuse to stay outside, to stay clear of Cal. He undid the net and studied the poor tree in its corner, wondering how he would ever get it clean. Even to Plato's sympathetic eye, the spruce looked pretty horrible. It had a nasty case of scoliosis, patches of pattern baldness in the middle, and a tangled knot of upper branches that looked like the antenna network of a communications satellite.

The filthy coating of road grime just put it over the top.

Maybe a bath wasn't such a bad idea. Or not a bath, exactly, but a *shower*.

Plato nodded and set to work, wrestling the tree outside, standing it up against the back of the garage and dragging a garden hose to the spot. Cal had lopped the trunk off two feet up from the ground, but the tree was still a full ten feet tall. Plato grabbed the stepladder and a flashlight from the garage, stood the ladder beside the tree, and opened it up.

And that was when he spotted the footprints. Huge, muddy boot marks covering the ladder's wooden steps. Reasonably fresh, which meant they weren't his; Plato hadn't used the stepladder in weeks.

Cold fingers clutched at Plato's heart. He dropped the hose and sprinted into the garage, then burst through the door to the kitchen. Standing by the stove, Cal glanced up at him with alarm.

"What's wrong?"

"Huh?"

"You look like you've just seen a ghost."

"Oh—er—nothing." Plato kicked off his boots and sauntered into the room. "Just checking to see what's cooking."

"Hamburgers." She relaxed, smiling. "So you're hungry too, huh?"

"Yeah." He chuckled. "But I want to hose down the tree first. You haven't seen my other boots lately, have you? The waterproof ones?"

Cal shook her head and turned back to the stove. Relieved, Plato hurried through the kitchen and switched on the lights in the courtyard; it was empty. He moved back through the house, checking every hallway and room and closet on the pretense of looking for his boots. He even sifted through the piles of junk in the basement and shone his light around the crawl space under the west wing. Upstairs, he grabbed Cal's T-ball bat and climbed into the attic, but found no sign of an intruder.

All the while, Ghost followed along behind him, cocking his head and squinting with puzzlement at his master's odd behavior.

"It's okay, boy," Plato finally told him. "There's nobody here."

Ghost nodded his head in seeming agreement, and Plato hurried back down to the garage. He decided he was just being over-cautious after Dubrowski's attack yesterday and the odd phone call last night—from a man who had asked for Cal and then hung up.

That was it: Plato was just being paranoid. Most likely, he had used the ladder himself in the past few days and just forgotten about it. He turned on the water tap and climbed the ladder, carefully hosing down the tree until all the road salt and grime and even the dead needles were washed away. He coiled the hose and packed the stepladder away while the tree drip-dried, then finally hoisted the spruce onto his shoulder and lugged it onto the front porch.

Propping the tree up against one of the posts, Plato realized that his suspicions weren't so crazy after all. Under the dim glow of the front lights, he spotted four neatly spaced dents in the ground beside the porch. A perfect square: the prints of a step ladder.

The front door slammed open, and Plato nearly jumped out of his skin. But it was only Cal.

"The burgers are done," she announced. "Are you coming in?"

"Umm—yeah." He dragged his gaze away from the ladder marks beside the house. "Sure. In a second."

"Is something wrong?" she asked, frowning suspiciously. "You seem awfully jumpy."

"Huh? No—nothing." He shook his head and forced a smile. "Just standing this tree up to dry. How's it look?"

"Better." She shrugged. "At least it's clean."

Once Cal was back inside, Plato hurried over to the garage and retrieved the stepladder. He stood it beside the porch, matching its legs with the four imprints in the ground; a perfect fit. The ladder didn't quite reach up to any of the windows, but by scaling it, an intruder could climb to the top of the porch. Standing near the top of the ladder, Plato spotted the familiar muddy boot prints crisscrossing the flat tin roof of the porch. The intruder had apparently tried all three windows before giving up. Plato scrambled up onto the roof and checked, just to make sure.

All three windows were locked. Dubrowski had apparently given up, for now. Or perhaps Plato and Cal had surprised him when they returned home.

Standing on the roof, Plato peered away into the deep, dark forest surrounding Marley Manor and shivered. Jimmy Dubrowski—the West Side Strangler—might still be out there, lurking in the woods, waiting for his chance.

A chance Plato was determined he would never have.

Late that night, after Cal had finally drifted off to sleep, Plato quietly picked up the bedside phone and dialed a familiar number. Jeremy Ames answered on the first ring. As usual, the detective was wide awake.

"What's up, Plato?"

"I've got a favor to ask," he replied in a hoarse whisper. Quickly, he filled Jeremy in on the latest developments: last night's anonymous phone call, the reporter who followed them to the tree farm, the marks of the stepladder and the footprints on the roof of the porch.

"I think he's gone," Plato concluded. "Maybe we got here before he could break in. Or maybe Ghost scared him off."

"Or maybe you just got lucky." Jeremy grunted. "You guys just go to sleep. I'm coming out to take a look around."

"Jeremy, you don't need to come right now—"

"Listen, Plato. I want to *find* this guy, before he kills anyone else." He paused. "Especially you folks."

Plato nodded soberly, then frowned at the inert lump snoozing beside him. "Cal doesn't know I called you."

"And she won't know I came," Jeremy promised.

"Neither will you. No need to come downstairs—I'll just check around outside."

"I'll help."

"No, you won't," the detective barked. "Just get some sleep."

"Yeah, sure." Plato paused. "Thanks, Jeremy."

After his friend hung up, Plato lay wide awake, staring at the ceiling. He would wait until he heard the detective's car, then steal downstairs and take him a cup of coffee. It was the least he could do.

Actually, he could do even less. For just a few minutes later, a tide of drowsiness seeped through his defenses, washed away his awareness, and drowned him in a gentle wave of sleep.

But beside him, Cal was still wide awake. She had dozed only briefly, waking up when she heard Plato dial the telephone. Cal had overheard the entire conversation—Plato's side of it, at least—and sleep was the very last thing on her mind. She waited until Plato's breathing steadied and slowed, until she knew that nothing short of a bomb would jar him awake, before grabbing her T-ball bat and sneaking out of bed.

After waking Ghost and putting him on the leash, she grabbed the cordless telephone and stealthily crept around the old mansion, double-checking that all the windows and doors were locked. She paused at each window, peering out into the night with her finger on the speed-dial button, making sure that Jimmy Dubrowski wasn't on his way inside. She paused at the three windows of the guest bedroom—the windows looking out over the front porch—and studied the ominous pattern of boot prints on the roof. They crossed and crisscrossed each other, approaching each window two or three times, as though the killer had tested the windows over and over again. Like an animal pacing its cage, constantly searching for a way to reach the spectators just beyond the bars.

Cal shivered, and turned away from the window.

Just then, a pair of headlights split the darkness in front of the house. Stifling a scream, Cal raised the telephone, ready to press the speed dial button that would connect with the Sagamore Hills police station.

But the police were already here. She recognized the car—it was Jeremy's silver Honda. The detective climbed out of the car and flicked on a flashlight. He was holding a heavy black object in his other hand; Cal shuddered when she realized it was a gun.

Jeremy hurried to the side of the porch, shone his flashlight on the spot where Plato had seen the ladder prints, and flicked the beam up to her windows. Cal edged back against the wall until the light had passed. Then, with a sort of horrified fascination, she watched as one of her best friends methodically searched the grounds and forest surrounding her house, hoping to find a deranged killer bent on murdering her.

For almost an hour, the flashlight beam sniffed back and forth, to and fro as Jeremy conducted his search. Finally, the detective returned to his car and Cal sighed with relief. She *almost* felt safe enough to go upstairs to bed. Not that she was likely to sleep, though.

Cal waited for Jeremy to pull away, but he didn't. The detective merely backed his car halfway down the driveway, switched off the lights, and waited.

And waited.

And waited.

Finally, Cal realized what he was doing for them. Jeremy Ames's lack of a need for sleep was legendary; rumor had it that he got by on just an hour or two a night. In the days before he made detective, Jeremy had moonlighted as a night security guard for one of the downtown office buildings. The only reason he had stopped moonlighting was that Nina wanted to have him home at night.

But still, Jeremy Ames almost never slept.

And so, he was watching, and waiting. Hoping Jimmy Dubrowski might show up. And making sure of that, if he did, Cal and Plato would be safe.

She considered heading outside with a cup of coffee or a sandwich, but rejected the idea instantly. Jeremy would be embarrassed—and maybe offended—by the attention. It was something he wanted to do; letting him know that *she* knew would disappoint him.

So she let Ghost head back downstairs while she returned to bed with her T-ball bat. Picturing Detective-Lieutenant Ames on guard in the driveway, Cal finally relaxed, let the bat slip to the floor, and drifted off to sleep.

CHAPTER 6

Monday morning, Plato Marley took Riverside General's main elevator up to the eighth floor, walked to the heavy steel door halfway down the corridor, and rang the nurses' station. On the other side of the shoulder-high window, a pretty nurse recognized Plato's face behind the wire-reinforced glass, smiled, and pressed a button. The door buzzed, unlocked, and Plato passed inside.

"You're here early today," the nurse noted curiously.

Janice Hathaway was a knockout, both literally and figuratively. The psych ward's head nurse had long brown hair, glittering brown eyes, and more curves than a Rorschach print: she might have been Vanessa Williams's younger sister. Janice also had a black belt in karate and a brown in jiujitsu—she was quite handy to have around on the psych ward. Many an uncontrolled schizophrenic had underestimated the dazzling nurse's physical abilities, only to find themselves on the wrong end of a syringeful of Thorazine.

"I couldn't sleep," Plato explained, "so I figured I'd come in."

Janice nodded soberly; like most of Riverside's staff, she seemed to know the whole story. Thankfully, she didn't ask for details—a welcome switch from everyone else Plato had encountered so far this morning. It was only six a.m.; most of the early arrivals in the physicians' lounge were surgeons rolling in for their first case. And surgeons were notoriously direct; three of them had cornered Plato and badgered him into recounting the attack, and one had advanced the opinion that Cal wouldn't last the week unless Dubrowski was caught.

The pessimist was probably down there right now, launching a betting pool.

"Poor Cal," the nurse said simply. "I hope she's all right."

Plato grimaced. "She'll be a lot better once they catch him again."

"I bet." Janice glanced down the hall. "Dr. Cummings is here—maybe he'll have some ideas."

Plato frowned curiously.

"He was Jimmy Dubrowski's psychiatrist."

"Wow." Plato was surprised. Tyler Cummings was one of Cleveland's top psychiatrists—and he came at a very high price. Tyler had privileges both here and at the Cleveland Clinic, ministering to the city's wealthiest neurotics. He hardly seemed like the type of therapist to have treated a serial killer.

Then again, Plato knew very little about Jimmy Dubrowski—just what he had gleaned from the papers and picked up from Cal during their first weeks of dating. And at the time, Plato had been far more preoccupied with Cal than with the meager details she shared about the case.

"You're here to see Francine?" the nurse asked.

He nodded, and she handed over a blue three-ring binder—Francine Pryce's chart. Several of Plato's patients had psychiatric problems, but luckily, few of them required hospitalization. Francine was an exception; the wealthy computer magnate admitted herself to Riverside's locked ward at least twice a year, when the stress got to be too much.

She had called Tyler Cummings over the weekend and asked to be admitted; Plato was visiting her simply as a courtesy call. He hardly felt qualified to treat her complex amalgam of symptoms and diagnoses.

Francine Pryce could have occupied several pages of the *Diagnostic and Statistical Manual of Mental Disorders*, the psychiatrists' bible. She had the classic symptoms of at least three major disorders, yet the combination of Tyler Cummings's treatment and some cutting-edge psychiatric medication kept her generally functional.

Most of the time, anyway.

"Is she up yet?" Plato asked the nurse, though he already knew the answer.

"Up, showered, dressed, exercised, showered, and eaten breakfast." She smiled sadly. "If you hurry, you might catch her before she hits the shower again."

"That bad, huh?"

Janice nodded. "She's getting chemical burns from the soap."

Plato winced. Poor Francine's primary diagnosis was obsessive-compulsive disorder—most of her other psychiatric problems were related to that. She had an irrational obsession with cleanliness: during periods of stress she might wash her hands a hundred or more times a day. Her office featured a full bath and shower, so that she could "tidy up" before important meetings. She changed her clothes up to a dozen times a day. And Francine generally avoided dining in restaurants, or anywhere else she couldn't be sure the dishes and utensils had been thoroughly sanitized.

Luckily, she trusted the hospital's kitchen—more than Plato did, anyway. Breakfast in her lap, Francine was sitting by the oversized window in the activity center, staring down at the parking lot below. The large common room was almost deserted; most of the patients were still in bed, asleep. Thankfully, much of yesterday's cigarette smoke had dissipated, and the few patients scattered in the corners of the room hadn't lit up yet.

The psych ward was the only place at Riverside where smoking was permitted. If it weren't, the patients would rebel en masse. Cigarette smoking was so common among psychiatric patients that nonsmokers were actually the exception. The practice seemed to calm many patients down; ironically, the latest research seemed to show that nicotine actually improved the symptoms of schizophrenia. Certainly, patients' psychoses seemed to worsen when smoking was prohibited. Psychiatrists were learning to view the noxious habit as a form of self-medication.

And the patients did a *lot* of self-medication. The ceiling tiles of the common room were stained brown with smoke residue, and the stale odor of yesterday's tobacco bonfire still hung in the air. Dozens of ash trays were scattered around the room. By mid-morning, the halls and common room would be choked with cigarette smoke; patients and staff would fumble through the corridors like strangers on a fogbound London street. But this early in the morning, the air was almost fresh.

Still counting cars, Francine Pryce heard Plato approach and gestured to the chair beside her.

"Have a seat—I'll be done in just a minute."

"No hurry," he replied.

She turned and smiled, recognizing his voice. "At least the parking lot isn't too crowded yet."

Plato chuckled. That was the irony of obsessive-compulsive disorder: patients knew that their obsessions were perfectly irrational, that their compulsion to wash hands or count cars or step over cracks in the sidewalk were nonsensical, but they couldn't help themselves. Francine Pryce was a highly intelligent woman, a successful entrepreneur, and a wonderful mother, but she was still a slave to her compulsions.

Especially when she was under stress. Waiting for her to finish the hourly ritual, Plato noticed the scaly skin on the backs of her hands, the bloodied cracks between her fingers that highlighted the severity of this attack.

With medication and weekly visits to Tyler Cummings, the obsessions and compulsions hardly affected Francine's ability to function. She could get through a day with just a shower or two, could fend off the need to wash her hands more than once every hour, and wasted little of her precious time in meaningless counting rituals. But during a flare-up, all bets were off.

Plato had flipped through her chart on the way down the hall. As always, this attack had started with the little things: pre-holiday stress, the loss of a critical account in her software consulting business, and her husband's hospitalization for heart tests. Everything had come out all right—the client had changed his mind, and her husband's heart was healthy. But Francine's precious balance had been thrown off-kilter; she had already fled to the comforting shelter of rituals to relieve her stress . . . until the rituals themselves had become the stressor, a burdensome habit just as addictive and destructive as drug abuse.

By the time she called Tyler for help, Francine had missed a full week of work: when she wasn't showering, she was washing her hands, or alphabetically sorting the cans in her pantry, or scrubbing her floors until they were mirror-bright.

Or counting cars on the busy street outside her Lynd-hurst home.

"It's good to see you again," Francine finally said. She turned away from the window, momentarily satisfied, and smiled.

In her early forties, Francine Pryce was quite attractive: blond hair, classic features, and a bright smile. And blue eyes that sparkled whenever she laughed—which was pretty often. She had a way of focusing on Plato, of listening, of hanging on his words as though he had just said the most profound, insightful, and entertaining thing she had ever heard.

It was a magical quality—an inborn talent that few people had to any great degree. The other psychiatric patients loved her, especially the depressives. Tyler Cummings joked that Francine delivered more therapy than she received during her hospitalizations, and he was probably right.

Coupled with her doctorate in computer science and a keen business sense, Francine's charm and talent for listening had taken her a long way in an often male-dominated field. Dr. Pryce ran one of the most successful computer-consulting businesses in the midwest.

Few if any of her clients had any hint of the psychiatric problems she suffered.

"I'd rather have seen you in my office," Plato confessed. "Feel like talking about it?"

"It's the same old story," she replied with an airy wave of her hand. "Too much happened too fast. No control over *anything* . . ."

And now, it was Plato's turn to listen as Francine unburdened herself—describing the fear and dread of her husband's possible heart problem, the worries over her company's loss of a major client, and some problems with her son at school. This was Aaron's second year at Princeton, and something had gone wrong this fall.

"He's *changed*, Plato. He's just not himself." She shook her head worriedly. "His grades have fallen off, and he's kind of withdrawn. Like he's tucked himself inside a shell, and I just can't break through."

"He's almost grown up now, Francine." Plato smiled reassuringly. "Maybe he's just learning to stand on his own."

"Maybe." She took a deep breath and sighed. "Maybe."

She stared out at the parking lot again, counting, counting. Watching her, Plato realized that her worries about Aaron were probably the last straw, the catalyst that had brought her whole world tumbling down. Aaron was the Pryces' only child, a son who carried more than his fair share of his parents' hopes and dreams.

Across the room, a tall elderly man in a three-piece suit and bow tie stood in the doorway. He cocked his head at the occupants, nodded three times, and paced over to a small stereo tucked in the corner. Kneeling before the machine, he chose a cassette tape from the pile nearby and slipped it into the deck.

As Bing Crosby quietly crooned "Christmas in Kilarney," the man slid into an orange vinyl chair and dug in the canvas sack he was carrying. Two blunt-tipped plastic crochet needles appeared, along with a bundle of yarn. And a little baby bootie, complete with a tiny locomotive and itsy-bitsy puffs of smoke.

The man's hands shook from long-term antipsychotic medications, and the crochet needles were as big and clumsy as a pair of railroad spikes. He rocked back and forth in his chair as he knit: a classic schizophrenic motion. Plato marveled at the man's ability to knit such an intricate pattern with his constant rocking and his quivering hands.

Francine turned away from the parking lot again. "I just don't know."

Plato frowned curiously.

"Aaron is so *young*." She shivered. "And nineteen is such an *important* age."

In a flash of insight, Plato finally understood. Francine's own problems had started during college—in her sophomore year, according to her chart. She had dropped out of Case Western's nursing school after missing several important clinical sessions. That was when the hand-washing and showering habits had begun, the obsessions and compulsions that had eventually ruled her life.

Francine had even attempted suicide before her family finally took her to see a psychiatrist. Tyler Cummings had been fresh out of residency then, but he was still quite good. Not only did Francine have obsessive-compulsive disorder, but she suffered from chronic anxiety and depression. All those psychiatric problems had formed a tangled and confusing web, one which might never have been unraveled. But after several hospitalizations, a year of intense therapy, and quite a bit of determination, Francine was ready to return to school.

Rather than resuming her nursing career, she had chosen a totally different path—one that focused on a fledgling technology: computer software. She always told Plato that she had never looked back.

Until now.

Plato had seen many of his patients worry themselves into fits as they approached the age their parents had died: a son whose father had died of a coronary at age fifty was likely to worry as his own fiftieth birthday approached. At the very least, he might start exercising and cut back on red meats. And in some cases, Plato had seen people worry themselves into full-blown panic attacks.

Francine Pryce was just the opposite: she was worried that her *son* would suffer the same fate she had.

"Aaron seems like a pretty well-adjusted kid," Plato said. He patted her hand. "Are you afraid he'll have the same problems you did?"

"No—that's silly," she began. "I mean—"

Francine tilted her head thoughtfully, closed her eyes, and nodded slowly. Finally, she took a deep breath. "You know what? I think maybe you're right." She beamed at Plato, then shook her head. "But it's *crazy*."

"Not at all." He explained the "anniversary syndrome," and told Francine how her worries were very similar, only reversed. "It's normal to worry about something like that. Lots of parents worry about passing problems on to their children."

She sucked in her breath. "My problems . . . Are they—are they—*genetic?*"

"Not really," he assured her. "There might be a weak link, but obsessive-compulsiveness is generally pretty random. Most psychiatric problems are."

"I see." Francine still didn't seem quite satisfied. She cast a hopeful glance at Plato. "Do you think, maybe, you might—?"

"See Aaron?"

She nodded gratefully. "Just to *talk* to him, to see how he's doing. He's seen you before, Plato—he trusts you. I know you mostly see just geriatrics patients—"

"You're hardly *geriatric*, Francine," he told her. "I've got several other ordinary family practice patients, too. I even have a few *babies* in my practice now."

She chuckled. "Then you don't mind?"

"Hardly."

"I can't send Aaron to see Tyler Cummings; he would suspect in an instant—and then he'd clam up even more." Francine grinned slyly. "But maybe he could stop by your office for a check-up."

"You know, I was just wondering about Aaron," Plato agreed, playing along. "I haven't seen him in a while—it might be a good idea if he dropped by for a physical."

She laughed again, more relaxed now. "I'll tell him you said so."

"Good." Plato started to stand. "Just tell him to call my office. I'm not *too* busy now—we can set something up during his vacation."

"Thanks." Her smile faded abruptly. "I just wish I could do something to help *you*."

"What do you mean?" He sat down again, puzzled.

"I knew Jimmy Dubrowski. Not very well, but I knew him." She glanced at the parking lot but fought the urge, instead turning her attention back to Plato. "He worked part-time at my company. To help pay for school."

"Oh." Plato swallowed heavily—the last thing he wanted was for Francine to get involved in his problems. Her own life gave her quite enough to worry about.

Luckily, another figure appeared in the doorway of the common room. Tyler Cummings had stopped by to see Francine. He crossed the room, smiled a greeting at Francine, and shook Plato's hand.

"Nice to see you again," he said. "How's our patient?"

"Much better, thank you," Francine replied. "I just had a *very* illuminating conversation with Dr. Marley."

"I'd love to hear all about it," Cummings replied, in a tone of utter sincerity.

That was an important part of the psychiatrist's talent—unlike many in his field, Cummings conveyed the impression that he genuinely cared. And that feeling came through regardless of whether his patient was a well-adjusted business executive or a schizophrenic veteran on disability.

Cummings glanced at Plato and passed a hand through his curly gray mane. "But I'd like to have a word with you first, Plato. As long as Francine doesn't mind." He turned to her. "All right?"

"No problem." She chuckled, waving a hand at the parking lot outside the window. "I'm sure I'll find something to do."

"Do you have a minute, Plato?"

"Sure." He shrugged, and followed Cummings out of the common room. The hall was getting crowded now, but the psychiatrist ploughed easily through the crush, tossing bluff good mornings and hellos left and right. Patients spotted him and smiled, nurses beamed happily, and even the angry young paranoids softened their suspicious frowns.

Cummings was one of the most popular psychiatrists at Riverside General—perhaps because he hardly seemed like a psychiatrist at all. His manner this morning was more like a jolly innkeeper checking on the welfare of his patrons. The man's portly build, ready grin, and heavy gray beard only reinforced the impression: he looked like a Santa Claus in training.

The patients followed his passage through the hallway with fond smiles and chuckles, like a crowd watching the bobbing progress of a cartoon balloon in the Macy's parade.

Cummings led Plato to the locked entrance and pulled an impressive set of keys from his pocket. He unlocked the heavy steel door and they passed through; a buzzer sounded at the nursing station behind them but was quickly silenced by the slamming of the door.

Just past the elevators, the psychiatrist turned down another corridor housing therapy suites, offices for the attendings and residents, and the ECT room, where depressed patients were treated with electroconvulsive therapy. Walking past the open door, Plato caught a glimpse of the padded table with its extremity restraints, the ventilator and anesthesia cart, and the wires and electrodes bundled beside the Big Black Box that delivered electrical shocks to the brain.

He couldn't suppress a shudder.

Cummings spotted his expression and chuckled. "We've come a long way since you were a resident, you know."

"I know." Plato nodded. He had read all the research about the breakthroughs, the surging popularity of a technique once shunned by reputable psychiatrists and dreaded by the public. "It seems to have done Francine a world of good."

Aside from her obsessive-compulsive disorder, Francine suffered from anxiety and depression. The depression had been debilitating and dangerous; she had attempted suicide several times. But electroconvulsive treatment had helped; so had the latest generation of antidepressant drugs.

"Unilateral treatment, low voltages, and careful patient selection," Cummings mused as they approached his office. "We see very few cognitive side effects, and even *those* fade with time."

Plato nodded again. He understood all the arguments. But he couldn't help remembering his own experiences during medical school and residency—watching his patients' anxious, hopeful eyes as they were strapped to the table and went under the ether, seeing the psychiatrist fiddling with the dials and electrodes like a mad scientist bringing Frankenstein to life, hearing the momentary hum of the machine as the shock was delivered.

Plato remembered how the patient's left hand would tremble and twitch as though it had a life of its own. To prevent injuries, patients were anesthetized and paralyzed before the procedure began. But in order to monitor the seizure's progress and duration, a tourniquet was tied around one arm while the paralyzing medication was injected.

That single twitching hand had seemed almost obscene: the quivers and tremors barely hinted at the electrical hurricane spreading across the surface of the brain.

Yes, electroconvulsive therapy was more helpful and safer than ever before. But Plato still couldn't overcome his prejudices, his memories of how the treatment used to work. One of Plato's first patients as a medical student on the psych floor had been a hopelessly confused depressive. Her suicidal impulses had been cured by the treatment, but many of her most precious memories had been destroyed.

Looking back, Plato realized that the woman's case had been one factor in his decision to study geriatrics, where so many more people were robbed of their pasts. But those cases resulted from a *disease*, not a treatment.

"Nurse Ratched is gone," Cummings continued, seeming to read his thoughts. Like most people, Plato's first impressions of ECT were shaped by the scenes in *One Flew Over the Cuckoo's Nest*. "No more Fog Machines, no more Chief Bromdens."

"I know," Plato replied, then shrugged sadly. "Some prejudices are just hard to shake."

"You're not kidding." The psychiatrist ushered him through a waiting room with a plump and genial hand. At the other end of the room, a receptionist poked her head through the open window.

"Oh, Ty—Dr. Cummings." She disappeared and hurried around to swing the inner door open with a wide smile. "Good morning."

The receptionist was strikingly attractive: long auburn hair framing a face that was more than pretty, with huge dark eyes, a generous mouth, and a smile that could stun even the most cynical male at fifty paces. She swung the smile at Plato; he reflected it back.

"Howdy, Marianne." Tyler touched her arm fondly. "This is a colleague of mine—Dr. Marley. How about fetching us some coffee, please?"

"Sure thing." She hurried away, then turned and flashed that winsome smile over her shoulder. "Nice meeting you, Doctor. Cream or sugar?"

"Black is just fine, thanks."

Tyler walked on down the hall and opened the door to a corner office. "Have a seat, Plato."

The office was every bit as comfortable as the man. Deep pile carpet underfoot, genuine plaster overhead rather than the hospital-standard ceiling tiles, tabletop lamps instead of fluorescents, and soft-cornered oak furniture. The walls were lined with bookshelves; the few open spaces between were covered with colorful Latino tapestries or diplomas and certificates. A surprisingly small desk was tucked into a corner alcove, while a pair of huge overstuffed club chairs huddled before a wide picture window overlooking the Veterans' Memorial Bridge.

Plato took one of the club chairs, and Cummings settled ponderously into the other. He sighed happily; the psychiatrist obviously did most of his work from the chair rather than the little desk in the corner.

"I conduct many of my therapy sessions right here," he told Plato. "It's quite comfortable, and the patients sometimes benefit from the distraction—especially during painful sessions. The view often helps them collect their thoughts."

He gestured out the window. Far below, a ponderous steel freighter was nosing its way up the Cuyahoga; Cleveland's menagerie of bridges was dutifully lifting and swinging clear of its path like huge iron dancers lifting their skirts in stately curtsies.

"Of course, I don't see my *agoraphobics* in this room."

They both chuckled. Here above the river, the elevation was more like ten stories than eight. And the hospital's position here on the banks of the Cuyahoga created something of an optical illusion; Cummings's window actually seemed to be leaning out *over* the river. Plato felt an irrational desire to clutch the arms of his chair.

"Rather unsettling at first, I know." The psychiatrist nodded; his ability to read Plato's thoughts was even more unsettling than the view. "But the patients grow accustomed to it."

"Good thing *Francine* isn't agoraphobic," he replied. "On the other hand, she probably ends up counting the freighters."

"Exactly." Cummings shrugged. "Luckily, we don't see more than a couple every session."

Just then, Marianne appeared with two steaming mugs of coffee—*real* mugs, not styrofoam cups—on a tray. She handed them to Plato and Tyler, then paused. "Doughnuts this morning, Ty?"

"Sure." He took a noisy sip and smiled. "Perfect, as usual. Thanks, Marianne."

She flashed that stunning smile again, then patted his

shoulder fondly. "I'll run down to the corner—back in a flash."

He nodded, and she whisked out the door.

"Nice service," Plato said after she was gone. He took a sip and nodded. "This is *fantastic* coffee."

"Hazelnut-mocha blend. Marianne grinds the beans fresh, right here in the office."

Plato sighed enviously. "I've got a temporary receptionist now—and I can't even get her to answer the phone."

Tyler gave a shy, almost embarrassed grin, flashing a glance over at his desk. Plato looked over, and saw a familiar face. *Two* familiar faces—Tyler and Marianne. A framed eight by ten photo showed the happy couple in bathing suits, on the deck of some sailing boat.

"We're engaged," Tyler admitted. "Been seeing each other for quite a while."

He stared down at his coffee.

"Hey, that's *great*," Plato told him. "Congratulations."

"Thanks." He shrugged. "Office relationships aren't exactly *smiled* upon here at Riverside."

"So what?" Plato wasn't a prude; besides, he and Cal had met at Riverside. Not that they often worked together professionally—except after Luella Huckleby's death. "Anyway, she seems like a great lady."

"She is." Tyler rubbed his fingers through his hair. "I should have seen that, a long time ago." He shook his head, seemingly dragging himself back to the present. "But you were saying something about Francine . . . ?"

"We had an interesting talk this morning," Plato replied. "I think Francine discovered some important insights about her son. She's worried about him."

"I *wondered* whether Aaron was going to factor into this." The psychiatrist nodded again, then slapped his thigh. "But let's talk about Francine later. The real reason I asked you here was to talk about Jimmy Dubrowski."

Plato wasn't surprised. He had been planning to ask Cummings about his former patient anyway. "I understand you were his psychiatrist."

"I was." His jolly face melted into a rare frown. "And I still would be, if the jury had reached the right verdict."

"Didn't they?" Plato frowned, puzzled. "Dubrowski was *convicted*—he basically confessed, didn't he?"

"Yeah. He did." Cummings shook his head. "But he didn't really *know*, Plato. He'd been off his drugs and on the run; he didn't *remember* what happened. And I still don't think Jimmy was a violent person."

He took a deep breath. "But then, what about—"

Plato didn't get to finish his question. At that moment, somebody screamed.

It was Marianne, crying for help.

CHAPTER 7

For someone shaped like a cannonball with legs, Tyler Cummings was remarkably quick. He sprinted out of the office with Plato following close behind; the hallway quivered with his thundering footsteps.

Tyler reached for the waiting room door, savagely twisted the knob, and yanked the door aside with a crash that nearly pinned Plato to the wall. They sprang through the waiting room and down the corridor to see Marianne struggling with a wizened elderly man near the elevators. Janice Hathaway was already down on the floor, struggling to regain her feet.

Cummings gathered steam and pounded toward them like a runaway freight train, scattering chairs and IVAC poles and a hospital gurney on his way to the rescue. Plato rushed to follow, dodging the flying furniture and equipment in Cummings's wake.

The patient—a shabby old man in a tattered plaid suit, battered fedora, and moth-eaten galoshes—glanced away from Marianne just in time to see the Cummings Express rolling down the line. Effortlessly, he tossed the receptionist to the floor and turned to the huge psychiatrist.

"*Goddamned-shit-eating-scum-sucking-son-of-a-bitch!*" he roared, bringing one frail arm up in an astonishing roundhouse. His fist connected with Tyler's chin with a sickening *crunch!* that would have made Evander Holyfield see stars.

The psychiatrist chugged right past the patient, his legs reflexively pinwheeling to keep pace with his semiconscious body. Finally, Tyler slammed into the flimsy wall beyond, and his body slumped to the floor in a quivering heap.

Behind him, Plato stared in slack-jawed astonishment. Like a cartoon character, the big psychiatrist had actually left a Cummings-shaped imprint in the corridor's flimsy drywall.

The pause was probably what saved him. The old man glared at Plato but turned away disdainfully, shifting his attention to his left, back to Janice Hathaway. The nurse flashed a winning smile, and the man stepped closer— like a sailor fascinated by a siren's song.

"Nobody's going to hurt you, Mr. Albretto." The nurse's voice was a velvety soft whisper, the quiet, wary purr of a nervous kitten. She was still smiling, charming him into range. Behind her back, she uncapped a syringe.

"You're damn right they're not." Mr. Albretto sneered. Apparently he didn't think much of kittens, nervous or otherwise. But he relaxed, slowly letting down his guard. A girl as stunning as Janice Hathaway *couldn't* be dangerous—and he seemed to have discounted Plato as a threat.

Mr. Albretto took another step, and Janice sprang in a perfectly timed leap, grabbing for that deadly left arm as she flew past him, and lifting her syringe for the kill. She might have made it, too—if the door to the locked ward hadn't opened an instant before she sprang. In the millisecond it took Janice to travel through the air, Mr. Albretto had already moved, twisting away to face the new threat. A pair of well-muscled orderlies charged down the hall; apparently they had heard Marianne's shriek.

The patient bellowed defiantly and tore up the hall past Plato in a fog of gin fumes. In one of the bravest moves of Plato's life, he joined the fray, jumping on the poor old man's back and riding him to the floor. On the way down, Plato threw his arm out to break their fall; he didn't want to kill the poor guy. He felt a sudden surge of lancing pain as his left wrist buckled under them. But he managed to straddle the patient with his thighs and pin one of his arms to the floor.

Mr. Albretto was astonishingly strong, thrashing about on the slippery linoleum like a terrifying cross between a python and a bucking bronco. Plato fought to keep control, locking his legs tighter around the man's thighs and ducking away as he twisted to take a bite out of his captor's shoulder. Luckily, the poor fellow only had about two and a half teeth in his head.

And even more luckily, the cavalry arrived just as Plato's grip started to slip. Marianne rushed over to grab the man's free arm—the one that had thrown the wickedly effective roundhouse—and pinned it flat. A muscle-bound orderly scrambled up and grabbed Mr. Albretto's left arm in one hand and planted his other palm between the patient's shoulder blades, pinning him neatly to the floor like a bug on a display board. Tyler Cummings had apparently come back to life; he crawled over and sat firmly on the man's legs, crushing any further resistance.

Plato was free to scramble out of bite range and watch as Janice aimed her syringeful of Thorazine and joyfully plunged it into Mr. Albretto's hip.

The patient was still howling and cursing in protest, almost foaming at the mouth. But over the next several minutes, as Plato caught his breath and Marianne stanched Cummings's bleeding lips and forehead, the man's resistance slowly faded. The shrieks faded to a mutter, then to a whisper, and finally to silence. Mr. Albretto's head lolled, his limbs slackened, and he studied the linoleum with a glassy-eyed stare.

Cummings struggled to his feet and fingered his jaw, then surveyed the damaged wall.

"Vinnie Albretto sure can pack a punch."

Glancing at the imprint, Marianne nodded. "He always could."

When Plato frowned curiously, she explained.

"Vinnie was national welterweight champ, way back in 1948." Studying her fiancé's chin, she bit her lip. "And he still packs a wallop."

"No kidding." The psychiatrist cautiously worked his jaw left and right. "I don't think it's broken. Not *quite*."

"Sorry about that." Still holding her syringe, Janice shook her head. "I thought I could handle him myself. But when he fritzed . . . I didn't want to hurt him."

That was the problem with psychotic patients—they didn't respect karate or jiujitsu, nor did they have much of an instinct for self-preservation. Janice could have restrained Vinnie Albretto, but only at the risk of causing serious injury.

One of the maxims in psychiatry was "safety in numbers"—both for the benefit of the patient and the staff. Up to a dozen hands were sometimes needed to safely restrain a particularly strong and combative patient.

"You did just fine, Janice." Tyler glanced at Plato and explained. "Vinnie lives on the streets—but he shows up at my office whenever he's about to have a psychotic break. Some kind of homing instinct, I guess. But it sure keeps things interesting."

Plato nodded.

The psychiatrist turned to his nurse. "I take it the ER didn't give him enough Thorazine?"

"I didn't check the dosage," Janice admitted. "Another patient came in just as we were getting ready to transport Mr. Albretto. Dr. Randall is still with her."

The orderly flipped through Albretto's transport papers. He shook his head. "Ten milligrams, that's all."

"They were probably worried about his age," Janice explained. "And the alcohol on his breath."

"Vinnie's got the metabolism of a teenager—and he *always* has alcohol on his breath." Cummings shook his head. "We'll need to work out a better system for transport. Something safer."

Janice nodded. "Thank goodness Dr. Marley was here."

"I know." The psychiatrist flashed a sheepish grin at Plato. "Nice tackle. You ever thought of taking up psychiatry?"

"No way." He massaged his left forearm and winced—it was starting to swell, and it hurt like hell. "It's way too physical for me. I'll take geriatrics any day."

"Vinnie Albretto *is* geriatric," Cummings observed with a sly smile. He chuckled. "I've been thinking about referring him to your office, for his medical care."

"Thanks, Tyler." Plato lifted his arm and gasped. "You're all heart."

The arm only got worse. The throbbing intensified over the course of Plato's morning office hours until, by lunchtime, his entire arm felt like it was being slowly carved away by an angry sculptor with a very dull chisel. Of course, the chiseling wasn't making it any smaller.

In fact, the arm was getting *bigger*. Lots bigger.

Sitting alone in the cafeteria, Plato rolled his shirt sleeve up and studied his wound. The skin around his upper wrist was swollen and tense, like an overinflated tire. A deep blue stain was spreading along the inside of his arm, from the knob of his wrist halfway to his elbow. His fingers and thumb refused to bend any more; aside from the pain of movement, they had swelled into five angry, inflexible little sausages.

Plato knew he should take himself to the emergency room, but he just didn't want to face the facts, didn't want to think about Cal's reaction if he really had broken his arm: *You poor clumsy dear.* And that patronizing smirk from the athlete of the family.

Plato's palm was puffed up like a softball; it reminded him of those latex-glove balloons they used to make during slow days on the obstetrics ward. Once he got back to his office, he would pack it in ice. As long as it wasn't actually *broken*, he'd be okay.

Plato didn't want to consider the possibility—the likelihood—that his arm might indeed be broken. He tried to roll his sleeve back down and button up, but the sides of the cuff didn't overlap any more. So he rolled both sleeves up and tried to finish his lunch—and to read the journal article he was supposed to cover with the family practice residents this afternoon.

The article—a lively little piece entitled *Mechanical Versus Drug Treatments for Vasogenic Impotence: A Meta-Analysis*—should have interested Plato, but it somehow failed to grip. Maybe it was the noise level in the physicians' dining room: several of the doctors had formed a betting pool, and the air was lively with speculation about this evening's Monday Night Football game. Or maybe it was the lunch itself—a deadly concoction of cold baked haddock swimming in half-congealed butter,

with wax beans and scalloped potatoes on the side. And
lime Jell-O for dessert.

What's so difficult about keeping fish warm? Plato
wondered testily. And who the hell eats wax beans and
lime Jell-O?

He spotted a cafeteria worker scurrying across the dining room, and was tempted to charge over and give her a
piece of his mind. Why in God's name couldn't they
serve *decent* food at Riverside General, just once in a
while? Once a week? Once a month?

Imagine the rise in staff morale, the decline in patient
mortality.

Plato had risen to his feet before he caught himself. He,
a physician, was about to chew out a lowly cafeteria
worker for providing a menu she probably had no control
over, and which she probably hated just as much as he
did.

In short, he had almost acted just like one of the old,
crotchety physicians he so despised.

Plato slumped back into his chair. Was he changing?
Was he getting that old, already?

"What the hell's the matter with you?" a voice asked
from above his head. It might have been the Voice of
Conscience, but actually it was Marta Oberlin, the chief
of the obstetrics and gynecology department. The feisty
woman was also one of Cal's closest friends. She shook
her head at Plato. "You look like one of the new dads—
just before he faints in the delivery room."

"Sorry." He shrugged. "Just ticked off about the food,
I guess."

"They've been serving this stuff every Monday since
Prohibition, and it hasn't bothered you till *now?*" She
pulled up a chair beside Plato and frowned sympatheti-

cally. "Hey—I heard about Cally. I've been meaning to give her a call. How's she doing?"

"Not bad. It was a hell of a shock, though." For the fiftieth time that day, Plato narrated the story of Cal's attack, their attempt to catch Jimmy Dubrowski, his disappearance outside the medical school. But like a few other close friends, Marta's interest wasn't just morbid curiosity; she was genuinely concerned about Cal.

"If there's anything I can do to help, just give me a call." The obstetrician patted his hand and gasped. "Good heavens, Plato! What the hell's wrong with your arm?"

He pulled it away defensively, hiding it under the table. "I fell on it. That's all."

"*Fell* on it?" She clucked. "The damn thing looks like it got run over by a tank."

Plato shrugged, wincing.

Marta put out a hand. "Gimme."

"You're an obstetrician, not an orthopod," he protested. But reluctantly, Plato put his hand back on the table. Even that slight movement set it pounding like a pile driver.

Marta gasped, shook her head, and gently probed the wrist. She bit her lip. "I've never seen swelling like this." She frowned up at Plato. "Most people are smart enough to be *seen* before it gets this bad."

Her long fingers danced a circle around the wrist, finally stopping at the radius—the long forearm bone on the thumb side. Gently, she prodded the radial head.

"Jesus *Christ*, Marta!" Plato bellowed in pain, jerked his hand back, and howled again as the arm whacked the edge of the table. Two dozen physicians looked up from their lunches at Marta and Plato.

Never a shrinking violet, the obstetrician stood up to make an announcement. Her voice was loud and penetrating, like a quarterback calling a last-minute play change. "Anybody here want to check Plato's wrist? I think he's got a Colles' fracture."

Half of the doctors rushed over to the table; the others simply watched curiously while they finished their lunches.

Nathan Simmons—Plato and Cal's family doctor—was one of the first to arrive. He studied Plato's hand and shook his head sternly. "It's X-ray time again, pal. You are just *so* clumsy."

But before he could lead his patient away, Rex Anderson, the hospital's hand specialist, butted in. He studied Plato's wrist closely, turning it and gently bending the fingers, then pressing the magic button at the head of the radial bone. Once again, Plato bellowed in pain. Anderson nodded sagely.

"Colles' fracture, all right." He grinned at Marta Oberlin. "Nice pickup, doc."

She nodded.

"Take a look at this, Mike." The hand specialist turned the specimen over to his lunch partner—an orthopedics resident from the Cleveland Clinic. "Classic Colles', though it doesn't look to be dislocated."

Before Plato could stop him, the orthopedic resident pressed the same spot, eliciting the same howl of pain.

"Right," the resident agreed. "No dislocation that I can see."

"It's *going* to be dislocated, if one more person examines it." Before anyone else could grab his wrist, Plato ducked behind Nathan for protection.

Reluctantly, the family physician turned to the others. "All right, folks—you heard him. Show's over."

The other doctors—orthopedic residents and internists and a family doc or two—grumbled disappointedly but headed back to their lunches. Nathan Simmons guided his case study out the door. A few minutes later, they were standing at the entrance to the emergency room, where Nathan turned Plato over to the senior attending physician.

"Colles' fracture," he said confidently. "Rex Anderson checked him out already."

The ER attending examined Plato and nodded his agreement. But that didn't stop him from having the wrist examined by the senior resident, the two junior residents, three medical students, and another orthopedic surgeon. All of them—even the medical students—touched Plato's button, waited for the howl of pain, and nodded sagely, calling it a "classic Colles' fracture."

The X-ray department seemed to agree. And so, three hours later, Plato's wrist was finally bound up in a cast, and he was free to telephone Cal at the County Morgue and deliver the bad news.

"Hi, Cally." He took a deep breath; he was already groggy with painkillers. "I had another little accident—I think you'll need to drive me home tonight."

CHAPTER 8

Deep in the bowels of the County Morgue, Cal hung up the telephone and shook her head at the body sprawled on the table.

"It just figures, doesn't it?" She sighed. "Have you ever heard of anyone so accident-prone?"

The woman—a blue-haired octogenarian with false teeth, false eyelashes, and the most astonishing set of false scarlet fingernails Cal had ever seen outside of a Halloween costume—merely stared at the ceiling with glassy-eyed disdain.

And she had every right to. After all, Ivy Brosniak's death had been something of an accident, too. The poor woman had been stabbed to death in a bungled burglary attempt on her house in Brook Park. She had surprised the thieves—a pair of kids barely old enough to vote—as they ransacked her home.

The case promised to be open-and-shut, thanks to quick police work and a bloody T-shirt found in one boy's bedroom closet. Cal had drawn a blood specimen from Ivy's vena cava for DNA typing; the specimen would be compared with the blood on the boy's shirt and the match would be presented as evidence at trial. Rumor had it that the pair was already considering a guilty plea for second-degree murder.

DNA typing had also been used for Deirdre Swanson's murder four years ago—except that time, the blood had belonged to the murderer. Deirdre was a tough kid, a psychiatric nurse in Tyler Cummings's office. She had put up quite a struggle before she died—enough to draw blood from her killer. Jimmy Dubrowski might just as well have left his signature on the body.

Once Jimmy was finally brought in, the match was found to be perfect. Blood found at the scene of Deirdre's death as well as that of the third victim—a young man named Jerry Tammerly—had matched a sample from Jimmy Dubrowski. The likelihood of error had been several billion to one.

Almost certainly, Ivy Brosniak's case would end up just the same way. Except *her* killers wouldn't be able to plead insanity; they had no excuse whatsoever. Hopefully, their verdicts would be correspondingly harsh.

Cal moved back to the body, switching her microphone back on and summarizing her conclusions. "Based on core body temperature, rigor mortis, and other physical changes, I estimate death as having occurred between eight p.m. and midnight last night. Death was caused by multiple stab wounds to the abdomen, chest, and back with laceration of major vessels, cardiac tamponade, and subsequent heart failure. The wounds were clearly the result of an attack and not self-inflicted; the manner of death is ruled homicidal. Signed, dated, Calista Marley, M.D., Deputy Coroner, Cuyahoga County."

Cal flipped her gloves in the trash and unzipped her white paper gown, then wheeled poor Ivy Brosniak into the cooler. She shook her head sadly; the morgue saw several similar cases every year. The tragedy went beyond Ivy, extending to her family, to the boys' families, and to the perpetrators themselves. A life had been taken and two more lives thrown away.

And unlike Jimmy Dubrowski, the killers had no excuse.

Cal closed and latched the cooler door and switched off the lights in the autopsy suite. She could finish Ivy's paperwork tomorrow, after the dictation was transcribed. Plato was waiting for her, and Riverside General was across town and across the river—a twenty-minute drive, at least. On days when Cal worked at the morgue, they drove to work separately.

But she had a feeling they'd be riding together for the next few weeks.

Outside, it was another ghastly December evening in Cleveland. A fog of half-frozen sleet hung in the air, dripping down Cal's face and neck and clinging to her hair and coat. Little icy driblets trickled inside her coat and blouse and skated down her spine. Water clung to her brows and lashes, smearing her makeup and ferrying gobs of mascara into her eyes. The walk to her car felt like a stroll through a giant Slushee.

Her little red Acura was buried under half an inch of the stuff—wet glop that wasn't snow or ice or rain but something in between; precipitation with an identity crisis. Not having anything better to do, the brisk December winds churned it up from the surface of Lake Erie and dumped it all around the city. Cal would have vastly preferred snow.

But the weathermen were exulting over Cleveland's mild winter—taking credit for this year's absence of blizzards in the same way they always dodged the blame for harsher winters. Despite chillier than normal temperatures, Northeastern Ohio hadn't seen more than an inch or two at a time. Much to Cal's disgust, all the ski slopes were in miserable condition, covered with a glaze of ice and artificial snow.

She turned out onto Adelbert, threaded the car through University Hospitals' endless construction projects, piloted around three accident scenes between Severence Hall and the VA hospital, and carefully wended her way through Rockefeller Park to the freeway. The Innerbelt was a sluggish old snake, slowly slithering its way through the heart of Cleveland.

Cal finally crossed the Cuyahoga and crawled up RiversEdge Drive to the old hospital, only to see the familiar flashing lights just in front of the ambulatory care center—another accident scene. She had promised to meet Plato at his office, but the accident was blocking the parking lot entrance. Cal cruised on past after making sure nobody was hurt, and parked in the hospital's main lot. The sleet was coming down even harder, but the tunnel leading from the hospital to the office building would be nice and warm.

She parked the Acura and hurried into the half-deserted hospital lobby, darting over to the elevators and pressing the DOWN button. She entered the empty elevator and jabbed the button for the sub-basement. Just then, Cal's wet purse fell from her slippery grasp and spilled its contents all over the floor.

In her haste to pick up the mess, she didn't glance up as the elevator doors closed, didn't see a tall, broad-shouldered figure in a red and blue uniform set his newspaper down and hurry over to the bank of elevators.

He stood there for a long moment, studying the indicator lights above the closed doors until they paused at the second floor down—the one marked "SB."

He whirled away and rushed over to the stairwell. Behind him, a Riverside General security guard watched the man disappear behind the closed door and shook his head.

Another pizza delivery for Pathology—the third one tonight.

The sub-basement of Riverside General always gave Cal the creeps. The tangled maze of passages and storage rooms was gloomy, dusty, and dank—a catacomb of ancient hospital annexes, endless additions and modifications, and closed wings waiting to be torn down. The walls varied from plaster to tile to cinderblock and even fitted stone, while the floors featured everything from gleaming linoleum to packed dirt.

A stroll through the basement of Riverside General was like a journey back in time. Near the main elevators, at the very center of the catacomb, the corridors were well-lit and modern-looking; not at all threatening or scary. But as you approached the tunnel entrance, the fluorescent lighting grew dimmer and faded to bare overhead bulbs, the corridors grew narrower and mustier, and the very air seemed haunted with ghosts from Riverside's past.

The only persistent elements were the battleship-gray steam fittings and electrical conduits hanging from the ceiling overhead, the parade of NO SMOKING signs posted every ten paces, the cigarette butts scattered like autumn leaves, and the roaches skittering along the walls and floor.

Near the tunnel entrance, Cal almost screamed as an oversized cockroach scuttled along the dusty floor near her feet. He paused directly in front of her shoe, probed the air with a thoughtful feeler, and moved on. Cal sighed thankfully. Down here, the roaches were as big as mice—

and she didn't doubt that the basement housed plenty of those as well.

During the entire walk from the elevators to the tunnel entrance, she hadn't encountered a single soul. No *human* souls, anyway.

Cal paused at the door to the tunnel, reluctant to open it, imagining a tide of wriggling cockroaches washing over her as she crossed the threshold. Standing in the dim light, watching and listening, picturing the tunnel walls beyond teeming with millions of the pests, Cal imagined she *did* hear something. A loud scuffling sound, like an entire insect army on the move. She leaned forward, brushed her hair back from her ears, and strained to listen.

But the sound was coming from behind her.

Cal whirled just in time to spot a huge figure lumbering up the hall. It wasn't a cockroach, or even a mouse. It was something far worse.

It was Jimmy Dubrowski.

Cal screamed, loud and long, but she knew it wouldn't do any good. Once again, Dubrowski had caught Cal at her most vulnerable moment. The sub-basement was generally deserted except for shift changes and lunch breaks; its only reasons for existence were to provide access to the tunnel system and to prop up the rest of the hospital above. And to make sure that none of Cleveland's cockroaches went homeless.

Sure, this level housed a couple of offices—and the Pathology Department—back near the elevators, but those rooms were hundreds of yards away, back through a tangled maze of twisting, turning corridors. And at this time, after normal office hours, Cal doubted whether more than one or two people were staffing the lab.

Meanwhile, Jimmy Dubrowski was still plodding

slowly and confidently up the passageway, a crazy smile plastered across his face. Cal stood rooted to the spot, utterly terrified and alone. And simply amazed at how *big* the man was. The killer had to duck his head with every other step to avoid the steam pipes jutting down from above. His shoulders seemed to span the entire width of the hallway.

Finally, Cal shook off her shock and fear, whirled back to the tunnel entrance, and yanked on the heavy steel door. She might not be as big as Jimmy Dubrowski, but she was certainly faster.

There was only one problem. The tunnel door was locked.

Cal twisted the heavy brass knob and yanked and tugged and pulled, but the door didn't budge. Apparently, during the past month or so, some security-conscious genius had decided to lock the tunnel entrance after office hours.

It made good sense; the hospital was far more accessible to the public than the ambulatory care center. But that was poor consolation for Cal.

She spun around and gasped. Jimmy Dubrowski was almost upon her, just a few paces away. Once again, she could see the glazed look in his eyes, the crazy leering grin, his terrifying habit of licking and smacking his lips—as though he was relishing this final moment of revenge.

Cal was trapped; the corridor ended here and, with the tunnel door locked, she had nowhere else to go. She vowed to fight him, to hold out for as long as she could. She raised her head to scream again just as Jimmy Dubrowski paused, gazing in horror at the floor.

Cal didn't blame him for being terrified; she gasped when she saw it, too.

Crossing the floor in front of Jimmy Dubrowski's size-eighteen shoes was the granddaddy of all cockroaches. The thing was *bigger* than a mouse—maybe even bigger than a *rat*. It was almost as big as Dubrowski's foot. It looked like something from a horror movie—*Killer Cockroach of the Cuyahoga*.

For such a huge man, Dubrowski performed a surprisingly graceful leap, bounding sideways and whirling in mid-air like a ballerina with a hormone problem, coming down again fully four feet away, never taking his eyes from the Paul Bunyan of the roach world. The little monster paused curiously, sent out a tentative feeler, and scuttled toward Dubrowski.

Apparently, it wanted to be friends.

But Jimmy wanted none of it. He bellowed in terror and performed another Nureyev, vaulting farther down the hall. The leap wasn't nearly so graceful, mostly because he banged his head on a steam fitting above and lost his balance. Dubrowski almost fell to the ground, catching himself at the last moment, just as he was face-to-face with Super Roach.

He bellowed again, utterly terrified.

Cal didn't wait for him to recover. She sprang into action, sprinting up the hallway past Dubrowski and his giant roach, gasping despite herself at the true size of the little monster. At six inches long or more, the roach looked like a small lobster. The tough little guy must have been one of Riverside General's original tenants; he had probably been around since before antibiotics—or roach motels.

Not that he would fit inside one anymore.

She pounded along the corridor, glancing back over her shoulder to see Dubrowski edging away from the cockroach and breaking into flight. The killer was fast as well as graceful; his huge legs were quickly gobbling up Cal's short lead. She ducked down a side corridor, praying it wouldn't be a dead end, made another quick left turn, and leaped through an open door.

Waiting just inside the small, dirt-floored chamber, Cal's breaths echoed in the musty silence. Cobwebs clung to her hair, and the dust she had stirred up from the floor almost made her sneeze. Dubrowski's footsteps drummed closer and closer, and Cal held her breath. He made the turn down her corridor and pounded past the open door as Cal edged further into the darkness.

And bit off a scream as a *body* tumbled into her arms, its hands clinging to her sleeves and its hair catching on the lapels of her coat. Twisting and squirming and gibbering in terror, she wriggled free of the thing's grasp, watching in horror as its head sprang loose and tumbled across the floor.

An anatomy teaching doll stared up at her with glassy-eyed reproach, as though to blame her for twisting its head from its shoulders.

Cal sighed with relief, but gasped again as she heard Jimmy Dubrowski's plodding footsteps coming back up the hall. She ducked her head out for a quick peek. The killer was pausing in each doorway, stepping inside each room and checking it out in the dim glow of the hallway lights. Apparently, the corridor had been a dead end.

He was getting closer—only two rooms away now. Thoughts racing, heart pounding in her throat, Cal ransacked her mind for a way to slow Dubrowski down. The blonde-haired teaching doll wore a smug grin, as though it knew the answer but wasn't sure if it should tell.

Blonde hair. Cal grinned back at the head and nodded.

Seconds later, she had reassembled the mannequin, propped it up in a corner, and dressed it in her coat. The height was perfect, and with its face turned to the wall and its blonde hair hanging down over the collar, it might have been Cal herself.

Except for one detail. Cal had carefully peeled away the plastic skin covering the facial muscles, arteries, and nerves. Once Dubrowski came close enough, once he turned the doll around, he would get the shock of his life. The mannequin's face was a horrifying mask—a tangled mass of red muscles and arteries, yellow nerves, and blue veins. Its mouth was especially horrifying—a web of plastic tissue stretched wide in a menacing, lipless grin.

Cal waited until Dubrowski ducked into the room next door, then silently stole out of her hiding place and back up the hallway. She turned the corner and hurried quietly away. After fifty yards or so, she broke into a run. Even then, she sprinted as softly as she could, stifling her breaths and listening for the telltale sound of Jimmy's discovery, like a commando waiting for a time bomb to detonate.

When it finally came, the blood-curdling scream was immensely satisfying to Cal. Dubrowski's panicked howl was just as terrified as hers had been, back when she had found herself trapped.

Poetic justice. She grinned at her sweet revenge, and burst into an all-out run.

Seconds later, she reached the elevators and safety.

CHAPTER 9

"You see? I *told* you this would happen."

"Don't pester the poor boy so, Fenton." Mrs. Abernathy's gentle voice held a trace of irritation. "You can see he's been through a terrible fright."

"It serves him right," Fenton replied smugly. But he shut up, just the same.

And thank goodness for that, Jimmy Dubrowski reflected. It had been a harrowing ordeal, sitting in the lobby in that pizza delivery outfit, waiting for Dr. Marley to appear, certain he'd be discovered, hiding behind the newspaper until he was just about ready to give up, and finally spotting her walking over to the elevators.

Following her downstairs, sure he finally had her trapped, when a mutant cockroach straight out of *Sleeper* started trying to eat his shoe.

Jimmy *hated* cockroaches—they had zillions of them at the Mansfield prison, but none of them were half as big as that monster. And if that wasn't bad enough, when he finally got away from the cockroach and caught up with Dr. Marley again, it wasn't her at all! It was a mannequin that looked just like her—except without any skin on its face.

God, that lady was *crazy! Crazy-crazy-crazy!*

"You should have killed her when you had the chance," Fenton jeered.

"You *should* have stayed in prison," Mrs. Abernathy scolded. "Where you belong. Where you'd be safe."

Following the maze of dusty corridors back toward the elevators, Jimmy Dubrowski shook his head. Maybe Mrs. Abernathy was right. At least in prison he got his three square meals a day. And he got his medicine, too—the Haldol that kept the voices away—*especially* Fenton.

He didn't mind Mrs. Abernathy so much, but Fenton drove him crazy.

And back in prison, Jimmy got to talk with Dr. Haverson, the nice young shrink that met with him every week. Haverson wasn't as nice as Dr. Cummings, but he was a good listener.

And a good talker, too—he had explained why Jimmy did all those killings, helped Jimmy look inside himself at the ugliness there, learn to understand his anger about his dad and channel it into healthy outlets like weight lifting and running and even painting. Jimmy hadn't known a thing about art, and couldn't have cared less, but a nice lady came to the prison once a week and taught a watercolor class. She'd said Jimmy was good, that he had real talent. It was true—when his hands weren't shaking, he did some decent pictures. Maybe someday, after he was free, he could—

"You'll never be free," Fenton interrupted. "There's nothing for you out here. Nothing but revenge, making them pay for what they took away from you."

"Shut *up!*" Jimmy whispered hoarsely. He squeezed his hands over his ears to block out the voices, but it was no use.

"You're a failure," Fenton continued remorselessly. "A murderer—a psycho-killer. The West Side Strangler." He chortled with glee. "You'll be hunted down like a dog and shot in the streets. Just like you deserve. There's only one way out."

"*No,*" Jimmy murmured. Hands still covering his ears, he trotted up the stairs to the second floor. He opened the stairwell door and peered out.

Inside his head, Fenton continued his rant. "It's no use, Jimmy. They're going to catch you."

"Oh, *do* be quiet, Fenton." Mrs. Abernathy's voice was fainter. She sounded tired, as though she was finally ready to give in. "Leave the poor boy alone."

The second-floor corridor was deserted, except for a platoon of laundry racks. The huge four-wheeled carts were heaped with mounds of sheets and towels and hospital gowns.

"*They're going to catch you,*" Fenton raved in a singsong voice. "*They're going to catch you. For Deirdre, and Luella, and Jerry.*"

"For *us,* Jimmy," a trio of voices whispered: the three victims of the West Side Strangler. They were there, inside his mind—vengeful ghosts of Jimmy's Christmas Past who would haunt him forever.

"I *trusted* you," Luella Huckleby cried.

"We *all* trusted you," Deirdre Swanson said sadly. "And look what you did to us."

For just a moment, Jimmy could see them there, at the end of the corridor. Three dead bodies, three betrayed friends. He squeezed his eyes shut, trying to block them out, trying to *think!* What was he looking for? Scrub suits.

"They'll *never* fit you," Fenton insisted. "You're trapped here. You blew it, Jimmy Dubrowski. You're just a stupid lug. You should just kill yourself—like your father did."

Jimmy ignored him, pulling open a door and switching on a light. His father was there, hanging from the ceiling—just like Jimmy had found him all those years ago.

"*No!*" he shrieked, covering his ears and shutting his eyes, blocking the sound of Fenton's voice and the sight of his father's horrible face. When he opened them again, his father was gone.

The room was full of dirty laundry hampers. Jimmy found one with scrub suits, picking through it until he found a triple-extra-large set. They weren't too dirty, just a few spots of blood on the pantleg, so he shook them out and started to change. The pizza delivery outfit had been pretty comfortable; he'd found it in the sub-basement during one of his explorations. God only knew what it was doing there—maybe it belonged to somebody that died. Jimmy had probably just traded one dead man's suit for another, not that he cared.

But comfortable or not, he needed something new. The cops would be hunting for a big guy in a pizza delivery suit. They'd never think to check someone in surgical scrubs.

"It doesn't matter," Fenton taunted. "You're too *stupid* to outrun them for long."

"Shut up," Jimmy muttered. He pulled the shirt over his head and smiled grimly. Long ago, back in high school, he had wanted to be a surgeon. A brain surgeon— so he could maybe figure out how to cut out the voices in his head. Especially Fenton.

"You'll *never* get rid of us." Fenton laughed, an insanely gleeful cackle. "We're part of you."

"*All* of us," Deirdre Swanson added, and the others chanted their agreement. "We'll be with you *forever.*"

"Leave him alone!" Mrs. Abernathy yelled.

Her voice echoed into a sudden silence. The ghosts—

and Fenton—were gone, for now. But someone else was here. Jimmy heard voices outside, in the corridor. People marching down the hallway, talking in loud voices. It sounded like a dozen cops yammering back and forth.

Jimmy cracked his door open and peered out. A single security guard was walking up the corridor toward his hiding place, prodding the clothes racks with his billy club and muttering into a walkie-talkie.

The radio screeched back in response; one voice after another reporting their positions around the hospital.

Jimmy eased the door shut and took a deep breath. Cold sweat rolled down his forehead and trickled into his eyes. His breaths came in quick gasps, and his pulse pounded in his chest. The guard was getting closer, opening closets and storage rooms to peer inside, muttering into his walkie-talkie every few seconds.

The hunter had become the hunted.

"It's *hopeless*, Jimmy!" Fenton shouted jubilantly. "He's got you now!"

"Shut *up!*" Jimmy hissed, sure that the guard could hear Fenton's shrill, penetrating voice.

"You've got to kill him, Jimmy. Strangle him, just like the others."

"*No.*" Standing there in his surgical scrubs, Jimmy Dubrowski squeezed his eyes shut again and pressed his hands to his temples, as if to crush the voices by main force. It didn't work—Fenton continued his crazy mocking chant, Luella wept and moaned, and Mrs. Abernathy argued for silence. Jimmy just shook his head back and forth, back and forth.

And that was how the security guard found him, as he jerked the door open and shone his light inside.

Apparently, the guard really hadn't expected to find anyone there, and he looked just about as shocked as

Jimmy had been just minutes before, when Dr. Marley had magically turned into a faceless mannequin. The guard bellowed something and reached for his billy club, but Jimmy Dubrowski was far too quick.

The West Side Strangler stiff-armed the guard squarely in the chest, sending him skidding across the hall and into the RIVERSIDE EMPLOYEE NEWS bulletin board. His head whacked the thin cork, shattering it into a million pieces. The security guard tumbled to the floor, unconscious.

Jimmy Dubrowski, who had only meant to push the man out of his way, was appalled. He stared down at his hand in horrified astonishment, like the owner of a Doberman might stare at his dog after he shredded the mailman.

"Oh, *God!*" he murmured.

"*That's* showing him," Fenton sighed with satisfaction.

Jimmy emerged from his storage room and approached the body. Terrifying memories came flooding back— memories of the courtroom, the pictures of the corpses, the nightmares he'd had over and over again, watching himself as he strangled those helpless people.

He was shocked, stunned. Ever since the killings, a tiny part of him had clung to the conviction that he *hadn't* done the murders, that it had all been part of an elaborate frame-up, that he had been the fall guy for some international crime ring. Maybe the Mafia, or drug smugglers. Or even the FBI—lots of guys at Mansfield had gotten framed by the FBI, practically *everyone*.

He knelt beside the lifeless security guard, tears coming to his eyes—for the guard, and for Deirdre, and Luella, and Jerry. "I'm sorry. Oh, God, I'm *sorry*."

"Sorry doesn't help," Jerry Tammerly said sadly.

"He's right," Fenton agreed. "Not much point in being

sorry *now*. You killed this guy, just like you killed all the others. Just like you'll kill that cute little lady doctor."

"He *didn't* kill them," Mrs. Abernathy insisted weakly. But even she seemed unsure now.

"Of course he did. Just look what he did to *this* poor stiff."

"And what he did to *me*," the once-beautiful Deirdre Swanson murmured. She appeared there on the floor beside the guard, her beautiful face swollen and gray, a lamp cord strung tightly around her alabaster neck.

Jimmy nodded, swiping at his tears. He deserved everything he got, and more.

"*Murderer!*" Fenton cried. His voice rose to a shrill, mocking chant. "*Murderer, murderer, Jimmy-is-a-murderer!*"

But Fenton was wrong about one thing, at least. Jimmy must have murdered Deirdre and Luella and Jerry—even Mrs. Abernathy seemed willing to concede that now—but he hadn't killed the security officer. Not by a long shot.

For even as Jimmy brushed away his tears of remorse, the guard's eyes fluttered open. He stared at the ceiling, then over at Jimmy. His gaze was unfocused, confused.

"What the hell happened?" He smiled curiously, reached up and felt the lump on the back of his head, and winced. "I blacked out, didn't I?"

The guard's amnesia—if it *was* amnesia—faded fast. Eyeing Jimmy, his smile faded to a confused frown, then to outright terror. He wormed across the floor, reaching for his billy club.

Jimmy scrambled over and kicked it out of his reach, then crushed the walkie-talkie beneath his heel.

"Tom? You'd better report in, or—" The radio crackled a few times, then was silent.

"*Help!*" the guard screamed from the floor. His voice echoed down the hall. "Second floor, laundry wing!"

"*Kill* him!" Fenton urged. "He'll tell them what you're wearing. Then they'll catch you for sure."

"No!" Jimmy Dubrowski roared. He whirled and sped away down the stairwell. Down on the first level, Jimmy opened a door and sauntered back to the front of the hospital. He knew his way around, of course; this place had been a second home to him—especially the locked ward upstairs. In seconds, he was out in the lobby again, watching half a dozen security guards thunder past.

"Second floor," one of them gasped. "Tom spotted him near the laundry."

Apparently, Tom had reached a phone—but he hadn't bothered to mention that their prey had changed clothes.

Walking out the lobby door, Jimmy nodded affably to the sole remaining security guard. In his surgical scrubs, he barely received half a glance. Seconds later, he was free.

"I *told* you he'd get away," Mrs. Abernathy gloated.

"He just got lucky." Fenton sighed, disappointed. "They'll catch him *next* time."

CHAPTER 10

"We'll catch him *next* time," Jeremy Ames vowed.

Beside him, Nina bit her lip and nodded firmly. Plato gave a thoughtful frown, and his cousin Homer looked up from his pasta for a fraction of a second before diving back in again.

Cal forced the faintest of smiles, as though Jeremy's promise had reassured her.

Actually, she was far more reassured by the huge crowds milling nearby. They were dining at the Coco Pazzo Café, in downtown's Tower City. The huge mall at the foot of the old Terminal Tower was packed with holiday shoppers frantically counting down those last shopping days until Christmas.

Jimmy Dubrowski had never attacked Cal in public; he had only approached her when she was alone. So Cal had vowed never to be alone again—at least not until the West Side Strangler was back behind bars.

And a shopping mall during the holiday rush was about as far from alone as you could get.

"Cally, I know you don't want police protection," Jeremy continued, "but I've gotten a county patrol car assigned to watch your house. Is that okay?"

"Fine." She nodded, relieved. Since the second attack tonight, her objections to police protection had dissolved.

Her concerns about privacy and freedom seemed petty now. What was privacy worth if you were dead?

Realizing this, Cal marveled at the change in herself. Over the past three days, she had turned from a ferociously independent woman into a frightened waif who didn't want to take three steps alone without a big, strong man on her arm. Or a cop in a patrol car outside her house.

Jimmy Dubrowski was responsible. The West Side Strangler had robbed Cal of her confidence.

Would she ever feel the same again?

Cal tried to summon the old anger, the old will to fight, but the flame just flickered and died. More than anything else, she just wanted Jimmy Dubrowski caught and sent back to prison. She didn't care about revenge. She just wanted to feel safe.

"Cally?" Plato was leaning close, frowning with concern.

"Huh?"

"Are you all right?"

She summoned the brittle smile again. "I'm fine. Just thinking."

The others exchanged worried glances.

"I'm sorry—did I miss something?" she asked.

"Not at all, dear." Nina leaned over to pat her arm. "I just told Jeremy I wanted to do a bit of the shopping tonight. For Jeremy—and the *baby*. Maybe we can together go, hmm?"

"Sure." Cal nodded quickly; the smile was less forced. If anything could help her feel more like herself, it was shopping. "After all, that's the whole reason we came, right?"

The others nodded. It was true; over the past few years,

the trip to Tower City for dinner and Christmas shopping had become a holiday tradition.

They had actually planned their outing for this coming weekend, but Jeremy had suggested rescheduling it for tonight. The detective had been among the first to reach the hospital after Dubrowski appeared, but he hadn't joined in the manhunt. Instead, he had sat with Cal and Plato, filling them in on the progress of the dragnet, and finally calling Nina and Homer to suggest that they all have dinner together.

Jeremy Ames—the macho nonshopper—had actually suggested the evening together at Tower City.

And it was just the right thing. The bustling crowds, the choir singing carols down in the central arcade, the holiday music and decorations were putting Cal more at ease with each passing minute. Apparently, the cop knew more about psychology than Cal had realized.

"I still have to buy *your* present," Plato admitted, waving his casted wrist and wincing. "I haven't gotten anything yet."

"I have to get something for Nina," Jeremy added.

"And I need something for my cat." Homer pulled a rumpled shopping list from his pocket and shook his head sadly. "What do you get for a cat who has everything?"

"A dead mouse," Jeremy suggested.

"Another cat," Nina countered. She nudged her husband and winked. "For the *companionship*."

"Bart doesn't want any companions," Homer grumbled. "He's a loner—he can't even stand *me*."

Jeremy paid the bill and stood. As Cal's impromptu therapist, he seemed satisfied that she was responding nicely.

Outside, the shopping mobs were just as thick as ever. Santa Claus was holding court near one end of the huge atrium. Snowflakes and reindeer and fantastic colored balloons floated overhead, suspended from the five-story glass ceiling. Candy canes and Christmas wreaths adorned every pillar and post, and you couldn't walk ten feet without bumping into an elaborately decorated—and perfect—Christmas tree.

Studying the decorations, Cal decided that Plato was right. Some Christmas trees could be *too* perfect.

Homer rushed over to his favorite spectacle: the arc-fountain in the center of the atrium. At first glance, the fountain didn't look like a fountain at all, more like a huge flat granite slab—Arthur C. Clarke's monolith tipped on its side. But the slab was riddled with baseball-sized holes. And from the holes, seemingly at random, water leaped up in perfect twenty-foot streams to pour into holes on the opposite sides. The water arcs were highlighted with colored lamps, and they danced in a gleeful frenzy—like a hundred and one Dalmation pups cavorting on the moon.

The first time Cal had seen it, she couldn't help laughing, bubbling with emotional sympathy for the sheer silliness of the fountain. But Homer's devotion went far deeper. The arc-fountain seemed to speak to his soul. The assistant prosecutor could stand beside the fountain for hours, watching the streams leap and dance.

"Come on," Plato told Jeremy. "We'll stand here all night if we wait for Homer."

The detective shot Nina a significant glance. "I think somebody needs more than another *cat* in his life."

Cal nodded. For almost four years now, Nina and Jeremy had been trying to find a woman for Homer. And for all those years, the lawyer had frustrated their every effort. The problem was that Homer looked at his work in much the same way as he did the arc fountain. Lots of nice girls had entered his life, only to walk away when they got tired of being ignored.

It would take an extraordinary woman to wake Homer up, to make him pay attention. Somebody at least as fascinating as Tower City's arc-fountain.

"Let's go, Cal." Nina touched her elbow and winked. "We need to find something for the new baby."

Cal giggled. After making plans to meet at Homer's arc-fountain in an hour, she and Nina hurried off, threading their way through the crowds, and chatting. Freed of the men, they made fantastic progress. In less than an hour, they had stopped in the Nature Company, the Museum Store, two toy stores, and the Indians' team outlet.

During their travels, they had bumped into Plato and Jeremy three times. The third time, Nina turned her husband around by the shoulders and gently booted him away.

"*Go!* Enough of this following us—you're not at work!"

Cal laughed, embarrassed. "He's probably just making sure we're okay."

"Maybe." Nina shrugged. "More likely, he's making sure I don't sneak away—to run off with another man, no?"

Cal was surprised. "Is Jeremy jealous?"

"Sometimes." She smiled. "He calls me all the time from work. 'Just checking in,' he says. And why not? Police are very suspicious."

"Plato's like that, too." Cal grinned. "I dance with another guy, and he thinks I'm having an affair."

"Women can be even worse," Nina replied. "My old roommate—"

She broke off suddenly, pointing to a shop window.

"That's *it!*"

Atop a pedestal at the very center of the window display, an antique gold pocket watch lay on a bed of crushed velvet. Its lustrous cover was elaborately engraved, its dial was picked out with tiny emeralds, and a heavy gold chain dangled from its side.

Seconds later, a salesman opened the case and put it on display for Nina. The watch was obviously the showpiece of the store—Cal drew in a sharp breath when she saw the price. But Nina flashed a sly smile at the salesman.

"This price—is it a rigid figure, or just something you *hope* to get for the watch?"

"Pardon me?" The salesman—a pink-faced high-schooler who looked like he was playing dress-up in his father's suit—merely frowned blankly. "What's that?"

The store manager bustled over and smiled at Nina. "Can I help you, ma'am?"

With his polyester suit, his broad, earnest smile, and his rigidly lacquered gray hair, the manager looked like a televangelist announcing the Good News to his audience. Nina repeated her question, and the smile faded from his face. He might have just learned that a favorite sheep had strayed from the fold.

He leaned closer, and touched his ear with a heavily jeweled finger. "I'm not sure I understand."

"Let me put it this way," Nina replied patiently. "I would like to buy this watch. But, given the scratch on the inside of the watch cover, and the missing emerald at the nine o'clock position, I would not wish the full price to pay."

She studied the watch closely and sighed, like a reluctant volunteer greeting a sick, runty kitten at the door of the animal shelter. *Sure, it's not perfect*, her look seemed to say, *but we can't just leave the poor thing out in the cold*.

"Also," Nina continued, "these are not the original hands—Breguet never used this style of hands."

Finally, she named a price—less than half of the figure listed on the ticket.

The manager sucked in his breath, insulted. He plucked the watch from Nina's hand and frowned at the cover, the hands, and the missing jewel on the face. Finally, he shook his head and clucked. "Trivial details—purely cosmetic."

"And yet, the *cosmetic* details give the watch its value, no?" Nina shrugged and gestured to Cal. "Let's go."

The manager bit his lip and shook his head as they turned; the lacquered hair waved rigidly atop his forehead like a rooster's comb. "I *could* drop the price ten percent."

Nina paused and shot Cal a secret smile. Then she walked back to the counter and returned the volley. "*Forty* percent. Plus, you replace the emerald and polish the scratch away."

"I *can't* go below fifteen."

The skirmish continued for another fifteen minutes, with the store manager steadily losing ground. Desperate, he even pulled the "I have to go call my boss" ploy, heading for the back room for a cup of coffee while Nina and Cal cooled their heels. But it didn't help—nothing helped. Nina Ames seemed to know more about pocket watches—mainsprings and fusees, bar movements and hunter cases—than Cal knew about cadavers.

Clearly, the manager was out-flanked. He knew it, the pink-faced salesboy knew it, and the small crowd of spectators gathered around the battle zone knew it as well. Finally, the poor man called a full-scale retreat and raised his flag in surrender. Nina Ames had captured the antique pocket watch at a thirty-percent discount, with the emerald and polish thrown into the bargain.

Outside the store, Cal shook her head at Nina in awe. "Wow! I'll have to go shopping with you more often. You're a *master* at this kind of thing."

"I've had a good deal of the practice." She gave that faint European shrug of hers—more a twitch of the shoulders than anything. "*Contrattare*—that is how we do things back home."

"That poor manager." Cal giggled. "You seemed to know a lot more about the watch than he did."

"Of course." When Nina saw her friend's puzzled frown, she laughed. "Didn't Jeremy ever tell you? My father is a jeweler—a watchmaker, really. I worked in his shop ever since I was a little child." She held her hand at knee height, then gestured back at the jewelry store. "Not like *him*."

Cal nodded. "It's a beautiful watch."

"A perfect gift for Jeremy," Nina gushed. She patted her tummy and winked at Cal. "When the baby comes, he must pay more attention to the time. And he will."

She flashed a Visigoth smile, and Cal understood. Jeremy Ames's workaholic days were over.

"I had just come here, to the States, when I met Jeremy," Nina said. Her face suddenly clouded. "I was to be a witness at the trial."

"Trial?"

"Jimmy Dubrowski's trial." She sighed. "Thank the good Lord, I was never called to testify." She brightened again. "But after all, that was how Jeremy met me. And asked me out—four times before eventually I told him yes."

Cal was curious. She had known that Nina was involved in the Dubrowski case, but she knew none of the specifics. Then again, Cal was a coroner, not a detective. She wasn't privy to all the police—and prosecutor's—information, no matter how curious she sometimes felt. Of course, these days, she could just give Homer a call and catch up on the latest gossip, or wait until poker nights when Jeremy spilled the beans about an investigation.

But back then, Cal hardly knew anyone in Cleveland. Not even Plato.

"You were a witness?" Cal asked, hoping for more details. "You mean, you *saw* something?"

"Yes—I saw *him*." Nina shivered. "On the porch of a victim's house—on the same night she was killed."

"Which murder?" Cal frowned, remembering that Nina had ended up needing police protection. If her evidence was so important, why hadn't they ever called her to testify?

But before Nina could answer, they spotted Homer and Plato and Jeremy. Homer was staring raptly at the fountain, standing in precisely the same spot, with the same idiotic smile pasted on his face. Plato and Jeremy rushed forward to greet them.

"Here." Plato gallantly reached for her bags. "Let me carry those for you."

"Nuh-uh." Cal snatched her parcels back and grinned at Nina. "He's worse than a little kid at Christmas. I have to hide his presents at work." She glanced at Homer. "Did he move at all while we were gone?"

"For a minute or two." Plato shook his head. "He got a scratching post for his cat."

"Where's *my* present?" Jeremy asked.

"It's coming, don't you worry."

Tower City was about to close—even the arc-fountain stopped spouting. Homer finally turned away, and they all headed down to their cars. In their hurry to leave the parking lot before the rush, Cal completely forgot to ask Nina about the Dubrowski case.

It was a mistake she would later regret.

CHAPTER 11

By Friday morning, Jimmy Dubrowski still hadn't turned up. A reward had been posted for information leading to his arrest; it had generated Dubrowski-sightings everywhere from downtown Cleveland to the Virgin Islands. Cal had offered to fly down to St. Thomas to check out that lead herself, maybe even offer herself as bait, but Jeremy turned her down.

On the other hand, at least the police protection had eased off. For the past three days, a patrol officer had accompanied her to the morgue, to the anatomy lab, to the hospital, and to the ladies' room, shadowing her every move but always stopping out of nose-shot of the cadavers. A sheriff's patrol car had been parked outside Cal and Plato's house whenever they were home. Jeremy had insisted on taking most of the shifts himself; but after three days, even his boundless energy had finally started to flag. Dark circles had grown beneath the detective's eyes, his nervous twitching mannerisms had subsided, and he actually caught the flu, spending most of Thursday in bed.

Friday morning, Cal convinced the sheriff's department to call off the protection. None of the Dubrowski sightings had been anywhere near her or the house, and Cal's omnipresent escort was starting to get on her nerves. Big Brother was watching Cal, and she felt a growing urge to give Big Brother the slip.

But there was another reason Cal felt like she could do without the police escort. Over the past few days, she had been sifting through the files from Jimmy Dubrowski's trial. Jeremy had forwarded copies of the court transcripts and psychiatric evaluations, and Cal had checked through her own files at the morgue. At first, she had been trying to figure out where Jimmy might be hiding. But as she studied the case more, Cal started looking for some kind of discrepancy.

Something was wrong, and it wasn't just that Jimmy Dubrowski was on the loose. Checking through the papers, it seemed that the police—and Cal—might have been a little too quickly satisfied with their investigations.

She was sitting in her office at the County Morgue when Jeremy Ames himself popped up at the door. He poked his snout through the half-closed door and aimed his bleary eyes at Cal.

"You busy?" His voice was a coarse rasp.

"Jeremy!" Cal hurried over to the door and helped him into a chair. She shook her head disapprovingly. "You should be home in bed."

The detective's face was pale and wan—even more emaciated than usual. Far from his usual bounding schnauzer look, Ames looked more like a stray puppy trapped on a freeway median. His long snout was red and raw, his eyes were watery and bloodshot, and even his bristly gray crew cut looked tired. His shoulders shook every few seconds with deep, racking coughs.

"I'm fine," he whispered between bouts. "I'm just fine."

"No, you're not." Cal perched on the edge of her desk

and frowned at him. "You look like you belong down-stairs."

Jeremy frowned blankly.

"In the cooler," Cal explained. "With a toe tag."

He shuddered. "Don't talk to me about cadavers. I just finished a crime scene on a murder-suicide. I'm surprised it's not here yet."

"It is. The happy couple is downstairs." Seeing his frown, she continued. "I'm not the *only* person who does autopsies around here."

"But you did the Strangler's autopsies," he noted quietly.

She leaned forward. "What's this about, Jeremy?"

"I want to find him," he replied simply. "I *have* to find him."

"Why? What's wrong?"

Jeremy frowned at the half-open door, then hobbled over and closed it. He slumped back into his chair and explained. "You're not the only person who's getting threats."

"Jimmy Dubrowski is after *you*?"

"Not me." He closed his eyes and took a deep breath, setting off another round of racking coughs. "Nina."

"Nina!" She sat back, stunned. "What happened?"

"I got a call last night. Very simple." He shuddered, remembering. "A low whisper. He asked if this was Detective Ames, and I told him yes. And then he said, 'Then you'll be interested in this. Your wife is going to be my next victim. She's gonna pay, just like you made *me* pay.'"

Cal gasped, then shook her head, puzzled. "But I thought Nina didn't testify."

"They didn't need her to," Ames replied. "But her name came up once or twice during the trial. And anyway, we're not talking about a *sane* person." He grimaced. "Dubrowski may not even remember who Nina is. I think he's trying to get back at *me*."

"Is Nina all right?" Cal asked. "Does she know?"

"Yeah." He sighed. "I told her about it, tried to get her to stay with a friend, but she wouldn't. Some women are very stubborn."

Cal smiled.

"I was hoping maybe we could hash this out," Jeremy added. "Maybe figure out where the hell Jimmy is hiding."

"They finally caught him at the library last time, right?" Cal asked.

"Right." Jeremy brushed a hand through his tired gray hair and sighed.

"Then maybe—"

"Nuh-uh." He shook his head. "Their security is a lot tighter since that happened. And we've had city cops snooping around that place every day since Jimmy escaped."

"Maybe he's left town," Cal suggested. "It's been six days—he could be in Canada, or even Mexico by now."

"I don't think so. Why would he threaten Nina if he wasn't here to carry it out? He sounded awfully convincing." Jeremy fought off another round of coughs. "Anyway, we got a pretty good sighting this morning. Somebody spotted him outside a McDonald's in Aurora."

Cal swallowed heavily. Aurora was just up the road from their home in Sagamore Hills.

Jeremy tugged his ear and studied her carefully. "I *still* think you ought to have someone watching your house. Especially now."

"I don't know, Jeremy." She fingered the file on her desk—the Huckleby case, the one that had troubled her the most. "I've been looking back through the files. Our autopsy reports on his three victims, and the files you sent me." She shook her head. "I'm beginning to wonder whether we actually got the right person."

"That's *crazy*, Cal!" Jeremy's snout twitched suspiciously. "You can't really doubt it. You're the one that performed the DNA analysis."

Actually, Cal hadn't done the DNA testing herself— she had sent the samples down to the state lab in Columbus. But she had testified on their conclusiveness, noting that the chance of the blood samples matching anyone else *but* Jimmy Dubrowski had been less than a billion to one.

"I know." She shrugged. "And at the time, everything seemed to point to Jimmy Dubrowski." She flipped through two charts—the first and third killings. "The victims both put up quite a struggle, and blood found at the scenes matched Jimmy perfectly."

"*And* he was scratched up when we finally caught him," Jeremy added. "*And* the first killing took place at his psychiatrist's office. *And* the second and third murders happened near his apartment. Eyewitnesses—including Nina—put him at both places around the same time as the killings."

Cal nodded. Jeremy was right; a pile of evidence pointed to Dubrowski's guilt. Jimmy had admitted that he was attracted to the first victim, even asking Deirdre Swanson out on a date and being gently rebuffed. He had flown into a jealous rage when he learned that Dr. Cummings and Deirdre had been dating for several months.

The nurse had been murdered on the evening after she and Cummings were engaged. The ring had been torn from her finger. Police had later found it inside

Dubrowski's apartment. He claimed to have no idea how it got there.

The next murder occurred shortly after the first—before police had even pinned Jimmy as a suspect. Luella Huckleby—a sweet old lady who lived near Jimmy's apartment building—had befriended Jimmy, cooking him dinner every Friday evening. But that particular Friday night, Luella suffered an apparently fatal fall down her basement steps.

With Plato's help, Cal had discovered that Luella's death was no accident. But nobody ever understood why Jimmy had killed his good friend; his motive had been put down to insanity.

The third murder had a much clearer motive. Jerry Tammerly—a young man who lived on the floor below Dubrowski's—had been strangled in his apartment, three days after the first killings, and just one day after the police issued a warrant for Dubrowski's arrest. Tammerly had already called the police, claiming to have information on the Huckleby case. But he never got to deliver it; he was strangled with a lamp cord before detectives arrived.

Once again, an eyewitness had placed Jimmy near the scene of the murder, though nobody understood how he knew about Jerry Tammerly's call to the police.

But the psychiatric evidence was perhaps the most damaging of all. The prosecution's forensic psychiatrist had concluded that Jimmy Dubrowski was a dangerous and violent psychopath—a paranoid schizophrenic with delusions of persecution and violent fantasies. And although Tyler Cummings had testified on his patient's behalf—claiming that Jimmy's psychosis had been well-controlled with drugs for over a year—his own laboratory tests belied the claim. Cummings had happened to check Dubrowski's drug levels on the very day of the first murder. The tests had shown that, when Deirdre Swanson was killed, Jimmy Dubrowski had no detectable antipsychotic drugs in his bloodstream.

Repeat tests performed after his arrest three weeks later confirmed the near-total absence of the drugs controlling his schizophrenia.

At the times of the murders, Jimmy Dubrowski had apparently suffered a psychotic break. With all that evidence stacked against him, the prosecution had little trouble making its case. Even Jimmy had seen the writing on the wall. Halfway through the trial, he had tried to shift his plea from not guilty to not guilty by reason of insanity. But it didn't help.

"Sure, there were some inconsistencies," Jeremy admitted. He waved it off with a gesture. "But no more than you see with any murder case."

"Like someone spotting him in Youngstown, sixty miles away, when Jerry Tammerly was killed."

"And that other psychiatrist—the one the defense hired." Jeremy shrugged. "He claimed Dubrowski wasn't any more violent than you or me. That he was perfectly harmless."

Cal nodded. There were other inconsistencies as well, like a report that someone else—a much *smaller* man— had been seen leaving the Tammerly apartment after the murder. And signs of a forced entry: if Jimmy Dubrowski was such close friends with Luella Huckleby, why had he needed to break in? The prosecution had contended that Luella had grown afraid of him, and witnesses close to the victim had seemed to agree.

But the biggest discrepancy of all had never been brought up during the hearing. Cal had only discovered it herself today, while leafing through her copy of the court records and exhibits.

"I won't pretend I didn't have my doubts," the detective concluded. "I had a funny feeling about it. Kind of a gut reaction that something was screwy." He shrugged. "But I was wrong—he did the murders."

"You're sure of that now?"

"I was sure of it by the second day of the trial," Jeremy replied. "So was Jimmy's lawyer—and the rest of Cleveland, for that matter."

"And so was I," Cal said quietly.

"But now that he's stalking you, and trying to kill you, you've changed your mind?" Jeremy buried his snout in a Kleenex and honked dubiously. "Maybe *you're* the one that needs a shrink, Cally."

"I'm going to talk to one," she agreed.

The detective just shook his head, convinced she was joking. He stood and shrugged on his coat, then touched Cal's arm as she walked him to the door. "You just take care of yourself, kid. And *call* me if you or Plato need anything."

"We will," she promised.

"I'll be easy to find." Another bout of hacking coughs shook his wiry frame. "I'll be at home. In bed."

After Jeremy left, Cal sifted through the court records on her desk once more. Although Jimmy Dubrowski's medical chart had never been successfully subpoenaed, the prosecution had dredged up copies of his drug levels from the outside lab where they were performed. Cal checked the numbers once again and shook her head.

Jimmy Dubrowski had been taking Haldol for several years before the murders; his dosage hadn't changed in over a year. And although his blood levels had been all over the board during the first years of his illness, his levels had stayed remarkably constant during the year before the killings. Apparently, he had been taking his medication very faithfully.

Dr. Cummings checked Jimmy's Haldol levels every three months. Few psychiatrists monitored blood levels anymore, but Cummings was more compulsive than most. Which was why he had checked Jimmy's Haldol level on the very day of the murder.

But Jimmy had also been attending Cleveland State to study computer science. He had applied for a job in the school's computer support department just weeks before the murders. He had been hired—and for a pre-employment physical, the school's physician had also drawn Haldol levels. By the time of the trial, the results still hadn't appeared as evidence. The blood sample had been drawn two weeks before the murders, but the tests had been run by an out-of-state lab. Only later were the results entered into the records.

Two weeks before the first murder, Jimmy Dubrowski's Haldol level had been normal: 25 nanograms per milliliter.

Even if he had stopped taking the drug immediately after his employment physical, Cal doubted whether all of the Haldol would have been cleared from Jimmy's bloodstream. But she wanted to know for sure.

So she picked up the telephone and dialed Tyler Cummings's office. Luckily, Jimmy's psychiatrist was between patients. In just a few minutes, he came on the line.

"Don't tell me, Cal. Let me guess." Tyler's voice boomed over the line. "You want to send me the bill for Plato's rehab."

"Hardly that," she replied with a smile. "I wanted to *thank* you. For keeping him out of trouble."

"Anytime he wants another broken arm, you just send him up here." The psychiatrist chuckled. "Vinnie Albretto wants to send him a card."

"Vinnie Albretto?"

"Plato's sparring partner. Vinnie was the welterweight champ back in 1948. He's still got a wicked left hook."

"Maybe he could teach Plato some of those moves." She sighed. "The way things have been going, I think he could use the lesson."

Tyler's voice dropped to a near-whisper, but it still rang in Cal's ear. "I heard about your run-in with Jimmy."

"Run-*ins*. Plural." Cal filled him in on the second attack, down in the hospital tunnel.

"That must have been awful, Cal." The psychiatrist took a deep breath. "I hope they find him soon—for his sake, as well as yours."

"Me, too. But that's not why I'm calling." Quickly, she explained her discovery from the court records: the normal Haldol level that had been drawn just two weeks before the first murders.

"Wow." Tyler whistled. "And I know what your *next* question is. How quickly is Haldol metabolized?"

Actually, Cal already knew the answer. She had looked it up in the *Physician's Desk Reference*. As she had thought, Haldol has an incredibly long half-life: six days in normal patients, as opposed to minutes or hours for most other drugs. If Jimmy had stopped taking the drug just after the first blood test, his levels would have dropped by three-quarters, but the drug still should have been detectable.

Tyler Cummings seemed to agree. He told Cal what she already knew, then sighed. "But we're only talking about a few nanograms—*billionths* of a gram. At such low concentrations, the lab tech might have read it as 'undetectable.' "

"I called your lab," Cal replied. "Their Haldol test is sensitive down to one nanogram. Even if he stopped taking the drug on the day after that pre-employment physical, the level should have been around *six* nanograms."

It didn't make any sense. Why would someone falsify Jimmy Dubrowski's Haldol levels?

"That's still well within the detectable range," she reminded him.

"I know. But that's assuming the level was correct at the pre-employment physical, and that *my* lab's level was correct. I don't think I need to tell you about lab error, Cal." For the first time, Tyler actually sounded defensive. "And remember, we're talking about two different labs."

"But—"

"Can you hang on a minute?" The psychiatrist covered the phone; Cal could hear some vague rumblings through the line. Finally, he came back on. "That was my nurse—she said my next patient is waiting."

"I'd like to talk some more later; maybe tomorrow—if you have time."

"Sure, Cal. Sure." Tyler sounded reluctant and eager at the same time, like a swimmer dipping a toe into a chilly swimming pool on a hot day. "I'd like that. I've had some thoughts of my own about Jimmy. I'm not sure that—"

Voices suddenly swelled in the background.

"Gotta run, Cal—we've got a crisis going on here. Call me tomorrow morning, okay? I've got some time open—maybe for lunch."

"I'll do that," she promised.

But Tyler Cummings had already hung up.

CHAPTER 12

"Turn it some more," Cal ordered.

She was standing in the middle of the living room, studying Plato's Christmas tree with a critical eye, trying to find the best side to face the room.

"*Again?*" Plato grumbled, his voice muffled by the tree's branches. He had wormed his way under the bottom limbs to tighten the collar of the stand and pivot the trunk. Only his blue jeans were visible beneath the thick lower branches; the Christmas tree seemed to have swallowed him whole and not quite finished the job. "I've already turned it in two whole circles."

Cal nodded. He was right; she had seen this face of the tree twice already, and all the others as well. The trouble was, *none* of the tree's sides were particularly full or shapely. It looked even worse, even more forlorn and Charlie Brown-ish, than it had on the farm.

"Okay," she sighed. "This is as good a spot as any."

Plato scrambled out from under the tree and stood. A blob of sap had stuck to his cheek, and his hair was full of pine needles. Combing them out with his fingers, he eyed his handiwork and grinned. "It wouldn't feel like Christmas if our tree was *perfect.*"

"No problem with that," Cal replied. "This tree isn't anywhere *near* perfect."

"I'll take care of it for you, kiddo." He stroked his beard, studying the tree. "You'll see."

"Oh, no." She groaned. "Not another *patch* job."

"Why not?" Plato frowned. At first, last year's Christmas tree had been similarly deformed. But Plato had gone to work—tying droopy branches to their neighbors above, drilling a few holes in the trunk and grafting extra branches to hide the worst bare spots, trimming the tree into a perfect cone before they started decorating. Plato Marley, M.D., Certified Arboreal Surgeon. "I thought it looked *great* last year."

"It did," Cal agreed. "Until your prosthetic branches came loose."

He nodded grimly. The tree had looked perfect at first, but the extra branches pulled loose after just a day or two. A week later, they had turned brown and nearly started a fire.

"Maybe I'll just tie up the droopy ones," he agreed.

"Fine." Cal nodded quickly. "And while you're doing that, I'll start the videos."

It was another Christmas tradition—decorating the tree while Rudolph and Charlie Brown and the Grinch played in the background. Plato always strung the lights according to his master plan: big seven-watt bulbs twining inside near the trunk—"to add *depth!*"—and hundreds of twinkle lights orbiting the outer branches. He was a perfectionist; Rudolph usually had faced the Abominable Snowman by the time Plato had filled in all the gaps. Meanwhile, Cal would carefully unwrap their precious boxes of ornaments, ranging from the tarnished trinkets and globes of childhood to mementos from last summer's vacation on Cape Cod.

Candles were lit all around the house, sending out wintry scents of holly and bayberry and apples and cinnamon. Cal cracked a bottle of Chardonnay; half of it was gone by the time they started hanging the decorations.

"Remember this one?" Plato unwrapped an ornament and displayed it proudly. "My very first Christmas present to you."

Cal took it and chuckled. The "ornament" was handmade by Plato himself—a tiny plastic troll taped to an itsy-bitsy cot, complete with sheet and toe-tag: another body for the morgue.

"Hang him high," she advised. "Aunt Thelma nearly had a stroke when she saw it last year."

"Aunt Thelma has no artistic sentiment," Plato sniffed. But he complied, climbing on the ladder and hanging it up near the top.

"I don't know what we'll tell our children when they see that," Cal fretted.

"We'll just say their mom cuts up dead people." He grinned. "They'll love it. Imagine how much fun you'll have on Take our Daughters to Work Day."

Our children, Cal mused happily. Picking up another ornament, she smiled. With any luck, they might have their first by next Christmas.

The thought sent a warm tingle up her spine; she reached out and gave Plato a hug.

He smiled back, surprised. "What's that for?"

Cal told him and he laughed.

"If we're going to have a baby, we'd better get to work."

He pulled her close, wrapping her up in his arms and giving her a long, lingering kiss. Nuzzling her neck, he swept his hands along her spine, down to her hips, slipping under her Cleveland Indians T-shirt and fondling, caressing. Cal leaned closer into his embrace, pressing her lips to his again, holding him tight as her desire started to build.

Finally, she pulled away and grinned. "But if we keep this up, we're never going to finish the tree."

"There's always tomorrow," Plato murmured dreamily.

"No, there isn't," she replied. "We've got a ton of Christmas shopping to do. And the big Christmas party is tomorrow night—remember?"

"Okay, okay." He stopped her with another kiss. "We'll finish the tree *first*. And then . . ."

"And then we'll get to work on that baby," Cal agreed.

Plato poured more of the Chardonnay while Cal switched videotapes. As they hung more decorations, all the Who's down in Whoville sang their Christmas songs and the Grinch plotted his evil schemes.

They were on the top half of the tree now; Cal unwrapped the last box of ornaments and handed them to Plato up on the stepladder. One of the last decorations was a yellowing plastic picture frame with a metal hook and a tiny photo of one of the oddest-looking kids Cal had ever seen.

"Who's the heck is *this*?" she asked, frowning at the photo. The poor kid looked like a startled possum: his eyes were huge and close-set, his nose was long and skinny, and his chin receded into his neck. One front tooth was missing, but the other more than made up for it. "I never saw this ornament before."

Plato studied it and chuckled. "That's me—I found that last summer, when I was cleaning out my old boxes."

"Wow." Cal stared from her husband to the photo and back again. Unspoken thoughts of ugly ducklings ran through her mind. She wondered just what was underneath that beard. "You were, umm, a *cute* kid."

"Yeah, sure." He plucked the photo from her hand and

hung it up in the Alpine heights of the tree—even higher than the cadaver ornament. "Now you know why I grew a beard."

"It's not that bad," she consoled. "I wasn't exactly a beauty queen, either. I had braces and pigtails."

"You couldn't have been *this* bad." Still standing on the stepladder, Plato squinted at his younger self. Finally, he shook his head at Cal. "You still want to have kids with me?"

"Certainly."

He gestured at the photo. "Knowing they might end up like that?"

"Of course."

"You're a very brave woman." He climbed down from the stepladder. "Either that, or you're really in love with me."

"Actually, both." She shrugged. "Besides, we're both doctors—we'll get a bargain on plastic surgery."

Frowning in mock anger, he wrapped her up and nuzzled her neck with his beard: Plato's Revenge. He kept it up until she giggled and gasped and shrieked for mercy, then reached down and tickled her ribs until she was breathless. Finally, he scooped her up and tossed her over his shoulder with his uncasted arm, carrying her up the stairs.

"And now, wench, Brownbeard will have his way with you!" He tossed her onto the bed, then sprawled over her, still frowning menacingly. "You'll never get away."

"I don't *want* to." She reached for him, tenderly pulling him down into a soft embrace, nuzzling his neck, then turning for a long, slow, passionate kiss.

Their lovemaking was lingering and deliberate and delicious: the product of years of experience. Each knew the other's tastes and needs and desires, and they were comfortable enough to express their own wants without shyness or reserve.

Even more sweet for Cal was the sheer naturalness of the act: no pills or barriers barred the way: each encounter really *could* be the start of a new life—a union more profound and lasting than anything they had ever experienced before. Making love without her pills was like skinny-dipping for the very first time, or sailing on the open sea, or skydiving. Anything could happen.

And Cal felt closer to Plato than she ever had before.

They came together in a surging crescendo, like the crash of a tidal wave, feeling an intimacy that went beyond physical passion—a closeness that seemed to tie their very souls together.

Lying beside her, Plato finally caught his breath and spoke. "I think that did it."

"Did what?"

"I bet we've started a baby."

She smiled quietly. He was right. It was completely silly and illogical and unscientific—but that moment of closeness, of shared passion, had been too special for anything else. Lying there in the afterglow, Cal felt their bond linger—as though part of Plato was still with her, had become a part of her.

Perhaps it had.

He wriggled down the bed and rested his head on her tummy, patting it fondly. "Anybody home?"

"You're crazy."

Her muscles tensed as she giggled; Plato lifted his head and exclaimed, "See? It's already kicking."

"Eggs don't kick," she reminded him, tugging him back up beside her. "You'll have to wait a few months for that."

"Oh, yeah." He sighed, then moved closer to rest his head on her breast.

Cradling him with one arm, Cal reached across to stroke his beard, his hair, his forehead. His breathing slowly faded away into soft snores of contentment. Plato was asleep.

Cal lay awake for a long while, thinking of the future, of the baby that might be on the way, of the man she loved so dearly. And in her quiet, satisfied happiness, she didn't think once of Jimmy Dubrowski before she fell asleep.

But Cal made up for it in her dreams.

It was the sub-basement all over again: Cal was fleeing through the catacomb beneath Riverside General Hospital, chased by a panting, sweating, snarling Jimmy Dubrowski, so close that she could feel his hot breath on the back of her neck, so thirsty for revenge that she could hear him grunting and snarling like a wolf once thwarted, and determined to bring down his prey in one final, ferocious chase.

And the hospital basement really *was* a catacomb: walled with crude brick, floored with dirt, and dripping water from the crumbling arch of a ceiling overhead. The passage meandered through the ground like the hovel of some gigantic and slovenly earthworm. The tunnels were dark and dank and musty, lit with just the faintest of glows from some hidden light up ahead. Cal was lost, and alone, and terrified.

And Jimmy Dubrowski almost had her in his clutches. But with each staggering lunge, each fumbling grasp, Cal managed to tear free at the last second.

Still, she couldn't hold out much longer. Her breaths came in ragged, sobbing gasps, her legs cramped as though banded by twin tourniquets, and her head pounded like an anvil to her hammering pulse. And still Jimmy Dubrowski came closer, and closer.

Cal finally burst out into the open, into the light. Into the familiar corridor near the Pathology Department—Cal's home ground over these past four years. Sobbing with relief, she blundered through the door of the autopsy suite, hoping to find a telephone, a weapon, a *friend*.

What she found was more appalling, more terrifying than even Jimmy Dubrowski.

Cal had found her friends. The morgue was filled to overflowing with gray-faced and white-sheeted bodies on carts: rows and rows of bodies waiting for autopsies. And every single one was a friend—Homer Marley's hulking body sprawled across an oversized gurney, Nina Ames elegant even in the repose of death, Jeremy finally at rest after all these years. Department chiefs and comrades, fellow doctors and nurses and medical students, even Ralph Jensson—the Cuyahoga County coroner.

But closest to the door was the most appalling sight of all: Plato himself spread-eagle on the autopsy table like the victim of a medical crucifixion, his broken body split open in the classic Y-incision of a postmortem. . . .

Cal was paralyzed. Her breath choked in her throat. She felt the terror clutching at her neck, strangling her more thoroughly than any murderer could. She whirled as the double doors flew open behind her, as Jimmy Dubrowski spotted his final prey, his most treasured prize, and stretched his lips in a cruel smile of victory.

He came closer, and closer. Enormous hands reached up and clutched her throat in a final death grip. The Strangler squeezed slowly, relentlessly, savoring the sound of Cal's final gasping breaths, the quivering death throes of his victim, the final agonizing twitches as consciousness waned.

Cal had struggled and fought in vain. Her last vision, as consciousness finally faded, was of scarlet trails of blood seeping through the joints of the cinderblock walls.

But somehow, Cal gathered her breath for one final, choking scream.

"Cally—*Cally!*" It was Plato's voice, somehow coming from the autopsy table. "Wake up!"

She whirled—kicking, punching, screaming. The killer had her in a bear hug; his hot breaths in her ear, his bearded chin scraping her neck.

But Jimmy Dubrowski didn't *have* a beard.

Cal's eyes blinked open in confusion. Plato was lying beside her in bed, in the darkness of their room. It had all been a nightmare, a horrible, awful dream.

"It's *okay*," Plato was whispering. "It's all right, Cally. You're safe, nobody's going to hurt you."

His voice was so soft, so tender—like a father soothing a frightened child—that she couldn't help sobbing. With relief, with fear, but most of all with gratitude for the dear man who shared her life, kept her safe and warm and loved. She would never be alone again.

"I'm sorry," she told him. "It was a terrible dream."

"Tell me all about it," Plato murmured.

He released her arms and rolled over to lie beside her, cradling her head in the crook of his arm and stroking her hair gently. And she told him about her dream, from the chase through the catacomb to the awful finale in the autopsy suite. Plato shook his head sympathetically and held her close.

"It's okay," he told her. "It's all right. Just a bad dream."

He sniffed loudly, and for the first time, Cal noticed that he was holding a Kleenex to his nose.

"What's wrong?" she asked suddenly. "Are you getting another cold?"

"Just a runny nose," he replied. But his low, offhand tone told her that he was hiding something.

"Lemme see," Cal insisted. She pulled the Kleenex away and gasped. Plato's nose was raw and red and swollen. Already, the skin beneath his eyes was puffy and dark. The Kleenex was sodden with blood. "Plato! What *happened?*"

"I had a little accident," he confessed. He shrugged, embarrassed. "See, you were kind of struggling and I tried to calm you down, but I can't use my arm, and your hand got free and—"

"I *punched* you?"

"Wicked left jab," he said admiringly. "You and Vinnie Albretto ought to duke it out some time."

"Oh, Plato—I'm *sorry!*"

All thoughts about her dream were forgotten. Cal rushed downstairs for an icepack and more Kleenex; seeing the two nasty shiners developing, she brought up a steak for good measure. Not that she knew of any medical justification for putting steaks on black eyes, but it couldn't hurt.

Plato accepted her ministrations with bemused good humor, perhaps content to see her distracted for a while. Finally, the bleeding stopped and he started complaining of frost-bite, so Cal allowed him to drift off to sleep.

But she couldn't sleep herself. It was three a.m., that limbo time between night and morning, between drowsy and wakeful. Between dinner and breakfast.

After tossing and turning for a sold half-hour, Cal finally admitted that she was *hungry.* Maybe it was the steak on Plato's face, or maybe the fact that she'd hardly done more than pick at her take-out pizza last night.

Regardless, Cal would never get back to sleep on an empty, growling stomach. So she resigned herself to her fate, and to the leftover Papa John's sausage and double-cheese pizza. The leftover pizza was calling to her from the kitchen, singing a siren-song in Italian, an opera of mozzarella and oregano, tomatoes and onions and a crisp, flaky crust.

Cal tossed on her robe and ran down the stairs. Five minutes later, she was sitting in the kitchen, digging into a piping-hot slice fresh from the microwave, and staring outside at the trees in the courtyard.

It was a funny thing: in the flickering moonlight, the nearest fir tree seemed to be covered with snow. Huge, ungainly blobs dangled from the branches, like gobs of wet snow, or wisps of cotton candy.

The crazy thing was that they *moved* in the fitful breeze, swinging and swaying more than branches should. And it hadn't snowed much tonight . . .

Cal scrambled to the back door and flicked on the light. At first glance, her eyes seemed to be tricking her, or maybe it was just another dream. Another horrible, terrifying dream.

Dangling from the limbs of the fir tree were dozens, maybe even *hundreds* of blonde-haired Barbie dolls. The medical kind—"Dr. Barbie"—dressed in long white coats with tiny little stethoscopes around their necks.

And something else. Dozens of little nooses tied neatly to the branches. The Marleys' fir tree had been transformed to a Christmas tree of murder, a Tannenbaum of death.

The breeze kicked up again, stirring the lifeless Barbie dolls in a grisly dance, a hundred noosed victims of a lunatic's rage. And a promise of revenge.

Cal screamed.

CHAPTER 13

"The coroner says your department will pay for a hotel," Jeremy told Cal the next morning.

They were all sitting at the kitchen table—Jeremy, Plato, and Cal—drinking coffee and pretending not to watch the team of detectives dissecting one of the most bizarre crime scenes in recent Cleveland history. In the courtyard just outside the window, one cop was making a cast from a huge boot mark in the frozen ground while another shot pictures of the ghastly Christmas tree. A Trace Evidence technician was carefully freeing the noosed Dr. Barbies from the branches and bundling them in brown paper sacks. One Dr. Barbie per sack, as though each was a victim of some horrific crime, of a serial killer of plastic blondes.

Cal shuddered.

"I really think it would be the best thing," Jeremy urged softly.

Plato touched her hand. "He's right, Cally. Your safety is more important than being home for Christmas."

"And *your* safety too, pal." Jeremy frowned at Plato's black eyes. The shiners were developing nicely; together with his brown beard and nervous frown, he looked like an anxious raccoon. "We can try to protect you from Jimmy Dubrowski, but we can't protect you from *her*."

The joke was lost on Cal; she wasn't listening at all. They had been around this block several times this morning; Cal was adamant about staying here for Christmas. Ralph Jensson, the county coroner and Cal's boss, had even promised to spring for the Ritz-Carlton downtown. But Cal wasn't buying it—she wasn't going to spend the holidays hiding in some hotel, no matter how nice.

Instead of considering Jeremy's and Plato's arguments, she was frowning out the window, at the growing stack of paper bags, piled on a plastic sheet in the snow. Row upon neat row, like the pitiful aftermath of a bombing incident.

Except that these Barbies weren't killed or even injured. None were even *scratched:* the killer had taken remarkable care in stringing them up by their pencil-thin necks. The only difference between these Barbies and the ones in the store was their hair: the West Side Strangler had carefully trimmed each Barbie doll's hair to shoulder-length. To the same length as Cal's.

"What are they going to do with those?" she asked absently.

Plato and Jeremy exchanged glances and raised eyebrows and nods of their heads, as if to say, *She's worse off than we thought.*

"*You* know, Cally," Jeremy urged. He coughed and honked into a Kleenex; slowly but surely, he was recovering from his cold. "Trace Evidence will check them out in the lab, looking for fibers, bits of clothing, maybe fingerprints—anything to indicate the identity—"

"But that's *silly!*" She spread her hands. "Examining *Barbie dolls?* It's not like he *killed* them or anything. And we already know who did it."

Jeremy and Plato exchanged those glances again.

"Don't we?" Cal asked.

"Sure we do," Plato agreed. He shrugged, and fidgeted, and tried not to stare out the window. The technician was up on a ladder now, taking down the last and loftiest Barbie. He swayed, and wobbled, and nearly fell before finally freeing his prize.

"But what difference does it make?" Jeremy asked. "We still need them as evidence."

"Of *what*?" Cal gave a hollow chuckle. "Doll mutilation? Poor taste in tree-trimming?"

"Cally—" Plato began.

"All I'm thinking is, maybe we should *donate* them." She glanced outside, watching as the last Dr. Barbie was carefully slipped into her paper sack. "You know—to the Salvation Army or something."

"Toy Central already said they didn't want them back," Jeremy agreed.

Toy Central, a storefront shop in Northfield, had been robbed sometime last night. The flimsy back door lock had been chiseled open and the burglar had crept inside, leaving the store completely intact except for a pyramid of three dozen Dr. Barbies stolen from a window display.

With surprising care, Jimmy had even managed to chisel the lock back into shape on his way out.

"What do you think, Jeremy?" Plato was smiling now—with relief, perhaps, grateful that his wife wasn't headed for a rubber room. Not just yet.

"If it's okay with the coroner, it's okay with me." He shrugged. "I think we've got enough with the picture and that boot-cast. It's Jimmy's size, by the way."

"You'll still be able to keep it quiet?" Plato asked.

Jeremy had used his influence to keep the story from the newspapers and television stations. So far, anyway. Only a few people in the sheriff's department and the coroner's office had heard the story. By the time it leaked, the evidence would be long gone and Jeremy would "neither confirm nor deny" the incident.

"We can say they're a donation from the Cops for Kids fund," he agreed. "We do this kind of thing all the time."

Plato nodded gratefully, and Jeremy hurried outside to announce their plan for the Dr. Barbies. The Trace Evidence technician nodded, handing his bundle to the two sheriff's deputies on the scene. Soberly, like two pallbearers carrying a host of fallen queens, they marched from the scene with their cargo slung between them.

Back inside again, Jeremy turned to Cal. "Now, we just have to decide where you're going to stay."

Cal shrugged. "I don't think there's much to decide."

Jeremy and Plato exchanged one last glance—a look of relief, even triumph: the little lady had finally come to her senses.

"I'm staying right here." She nodded resolutely. "No matter *what* Jimmy Dubrowski thinks—I'll be home for Christmas."

"You're the most stubborn person I've ever met," Plato told Cal later that afternoon.

They were riding the elevator up to the eighth floor of Riverside General. Today was Saturday, a blessed day off for both Plato and Cal, a day when they should be staying as far away from the hospital as humanly possible. But Cal had telephoned Tyler Cummings earlier that morning, and stubbornly pressed him for a luncheon date. And stubbornly dragged Plato along with her.

Afterward, they would return home—to the house that Cal had stubbornly refused to leave, when they might instead be vacationing in an all-expenses-paid suite at the Ritz-Carlton. A *safe* suite at the Ritz, with a sheriff's deputy parked outside the door to fend off further Barbie doll attacks. Or worse.

"Why couldn't it wait until *Monday?*" Plato pressed. "Tyler Cummings sure didn't seem to think it was this important."

"But I *do*," Cal replied simply. "I have an idea that—"

She didn't finish her remark. Just then, the elevator doors slid open and their whispered quarrel was drowned in a torrent of angry shouts.

The shouting echoed up the corridor from the right— from behind the closed door leading to Tyler Cummings's reception area. Cal rushed down the hall and yanked the door open with Plato following close behind.

Inside the waiting room an elderly gentleman was berating the quivering receptionist, rapping his cane on the frosted glass window in time with his words. He was impeccably dressed and coifed, with a three-piece suit, a Rolex watch, and an impressive mane of stiff silver hair. Combined with his silver mustache, silver eyebrows, and silver-rimmed glasses, he looked like the victim of an industrial accident in a tinsel factory.

In point of fact, he was Thorson Grummond, sportscaster and commentator for Cleveland's top television network: he had covered the Tribe, the Cavs, and the Browns for as long as Plato could remember. He was a Cleveland legend; Plato's memories of Indians and Browns games were inseparably linked to Grummond's voice, a slow, methodical, and warbling delivery—an improbable cross between Howard Cosell, a bishop intoning the list of saints, and an overexcited hamster.

Right now, the hamster element was winning out: Thorson Grummond's voice was high-pitched and sniping. But he still spoke with that classic measured delivery, punctuated by the metronome of his cane.

"I made my a-*point*-ment for eleven *thirty!*" the sports-caster squeaked, hammering the window in a slow cadence. "I've been *sit*-ting for half an *hour*."

"I'm sorry, Mr. Grummond—"

"I've been *see*-ing Dr. Cummings for *twen*-ty years now," he sniffed. "His record was *flaw*-less until to-*day*."

"I don't know what to say," Marianne stammered. She had rolled her chair some distance from the window, well out of cane-reach. Her voice was a faint bleat, like an apologetic sheep. "Dr. Cummings just left for the moment—"

"And *that* was half an *hour* ago." Grummond gave the window one last firm rap and grunted, apparently disappointed at the toughness of the glass. "Per-*haps* he can *call* me when he's ready to per-*form* again."

Grummond spun on his heel and spotted his audience for the very first time. The vast silver eyebrows fluttered, then he shook his head at Plato and Cal.

"No *point*, folks." He shrugged one shoulder back at the window, then stomped his cane on the floor. "The *doc*-tor, it seems, is not *in*."

He marched off, and Cal and Plato hurried to the window. The receptionist scooted her chair closer, then peered warily over their shoulders as Thorson Grummond slammed the door behind him. She sighed, relaxing visibly, then smiled at them.

"Can I help you?" She glanced over at Plato and gasped at his black eyes. "Dr. Marley—what *happened?* Did Vinnie Albretto hit you, too?"

Plato almost told her the truth, but he caught Cal's steely gaze and changed his mind.

"I . . . uh . . . had a little *accident*." He shrugged off Marianne's concern. "My wife and I were supposed to have lunch with Tyler today."

"I know." Marianne nodded and explained: Tyler had told her about his luncheon plans and asked her to remind him after his last appointment. Unfortunately, Tyler had *missed* that appointment—as they could see. The gentleman had been very upset.

"We saw," Plato agreed. He frowned. "Why would Tyler take off, if he was seeing patients this morning?"

"He had an opening—a cancellation," the receptionist explained. "A half-hour slot at eleven."

She batted those long eyelashes at Plato, and Cal edged closer, castling her king.

"He said he was going for a walk—Tyler always does that whenever he has a break." Marianne tossed her hair back over her shoulder; it fell slowly into place, like a shower of autumn leaves. "The walks help him think, to change gears between one patient and the next." She shook her head and smiled wistfully. "The only trouble is, sometimes he gets *too* relaxed. And he ends up being late for an appointment."

"Did he tell you anything else?" Cal asked. "Had he gotten any phone calls beforehand? Besides mine?"

"There were a couple," she replied, sifting through pink slips on her desk: carbons of the messages she had taken. "One from a drug rep—a guy that keeps bugging him. And another from Aaron—" She broke off suddenly, remembering her patient's confidentiality. "From another patient. Or a patient-to-be. He took that in his office."

"Nobody else called?" Plato persisted.

"No . . . wait. Tyler got *paged* once this morning; he answered that in his office." She frowned thoughtfully, then plucked a familiar black plastic object from her desk. "I tried paging him a few minutes ago, to remind him about Mr.—about his last patient, but he'd left his beeper in his office."

Cal shot a glance at Plato: a mixture of worry and concern and outright *fear*.

"Where does Tyler usually walk?" Plato asked, trying to keep his voice as level, as casual as he could.

He must not have quite succeeded, because Marianne suddenly sat up, her eyes widening with fright. "You don't think anything *happened* to him—?"

"I think we ought to check around, just to be sure," Plato soothed. "Maybe call hospital security."

"He takes his walks down by the river," the receptionist replied. Her voice was quivering, but she shook her head briskly: everything would be all right as long as she didn't let herself *think* anything was wrong. "That river trail, between the hospital and the shore. It's so safe, right here on the hospital grounds. . . . Isn't it?"

Cal whirled and sprinted through the door with Plato following close behind. He knew just what she was thinking.

After her experiences, she knew that Riverside General wasn't a safe place any more. Not at all.

CHAPTER 14

"God-*damn* it all!" Cal savagely punched the DOWN button and folded her arms, fuming. "I had a *feeling* that Tyler was hiding something. He *hinted* that he knew something this morning, but he said he'd know more by *lunchtime*."

As she drummed her foot on the linoleum in time with her words, Cal's tirade sounded not unlike Thorson Grummond's. Plato sighed thankfully—at least she didn't have a cane.

"Tyler'll be all right," he murmured soothingly. What could have happened? Tyler was a big guy—almost as big as Jimmy Dubrowski. And besides, Jimmy didn't seem to have a grudge against *him*. "He's forgetful—*I* know that. He's always missing meetings and rescheduling appointments."

"Hmmph."

The elevator finally slid open and they rode down to the first floor, rushing out the door like a pair of fresh young interns dashing to their first Code Blue. But Plato and Cal were running *away* from the patient floors, heading instead toward the employees' entrance at the back of the hospital. Their footsteps pounded on the polished gray linoleum and echoed from the sickly yellow walls and rows of lime-green lockers marking the employees' area; it hadn't been remodeled in at least thirty years.

They burst out through the back door, almost knocking down a pair of nurses returning from a restaurant lunch. Cal gestured to the right and Plato followed her around a corner, to the brick-paved courtyard at the back of the hospital.

In better weather, the plastic picnic tables and benches were usually packed with Riverside's staff, taking their lunch outdoors to enjoy the sunshine and the river breeze, or watch five-story-tall freighters threading the Cuyahoga.

But not today. The past week had brought a serious cold snap, and it was snowing again, a fitful shower of tight white pellets that bounced like the styrofoam filling of a bean-bag chair. The pellets clung to Plato's hair and beard and rolled down his coat and shirt to melt into steam. He was sweating and panting, fighting to keep pace with Cal as she streaked effortlessly through the maze of tables and chairs and benches.

Finally, she paused to wait for him at the foot of the river trail.

It was more of a boardwalk, really—a sort of dike built up when the last hospital president had tired of repairing the flooded basement every spring. A concrete retaining wall was built up several feet higher than the courtyard; a brick-paved walkway was built atop the wall. A short wooden stairway ascended to the walk, which was lined by a heavy hemp railing and featured heavy stone benches every few yards.

The trail stretched all the way from Siegel Medical College to Riverside General's parking lots on the other end of the hospital: fully three or four blocks. But for most of the distance, the trail was elevated and open to the full view of traffic near the hospital or school. Plato was sure that Tyler Cummings was safe—even on a Saturday, the area was hardly deserted enough for Jimmy Dubrowski to risk coming out in the open.

He pointed this out to Cal, but it didn't help much.

"We're not exactly dealing with a sane, rational person," she reminded him grimly.

Plato nodded and they walked upriver, along the path toward the medical school. The river wasn't frozen yet, but the sluggish eddy bordering the dike was packed with a jumble of thick ice. A brisk Erie wind whistled up the Cuyahoga and across the ice, urging the snow into a crazy dance: a dozen tiny white tornadoes spinning along the shore.

They walked all the way up to the medical school and turned around. The clouds overhead were getting lower and heavier. Already, the skeletal arch of the Veterans' Memorial Bridge was blurred by the belly of a snow cloud. Close at hand, a defunct jack-knife railroad bridge rusted patiently on the riverbank like a dinosaur caught in another Ice Age.

Cal slowed down and finally stopped, shaking her head. She and Plato had surveyed the entire length of the trail and found nothing. Either Tyler Cummings was safe or he had been spirited off.

And though Plato was willing to believe the West Side Strangler might risk a daylight attack, he couldn't imagine even Jimmy Dubrowski being crazy enough—or *strong* enough—to abduct someone as big as Tyler Cummings in broad daylight.

"Tyler's probably back in his office by now," Plato suggested cheerfully, "waiting for us."

Cal shrugged.

"A hundred things could have happened," he continued. "Maybe he got sick. Or maybe he really forgot about his last appointment, just like Marianne said."

"Maybe." She turned back toward the hospital. "I feel like such an idiot—running out of his office like that." She glanced at Plato and grimaced. "I was *sure* Tyler had found out something. That maybe he had figured out how to reach Jimmy."

"Maybe he has." Plato shrugged. "But I'm sure Tyler's smart enough to tell the police about it."

"I don't know. He's very loyal to his patients—you know that." She frowned. "And he *still* doesn't seem quite convinced that Jimmy Dubrowski was guilty."

"Now, that *is* crazy."

They walked along past the rusting steel dinosaur. Plato paused to marvel at its impressive length and weight: perhaps a hundred feet of interlaced steel girders rising into the air. Cables and pulleys and wheels and counterweights had once balanced the bridge as it gently descended to kiss the other side of the river. But the railway on the opposite shore had been replaced by a neatly paved street. The only indication of the structure's original purpose was a pair of steel rails running up the length of the bridge to puncture the sky: a railroad to heaven, the St. Peter's Express.

Turning away, Plato caught a glimpse of tan fabric fluttering in that brisk Erie breeze. He turned back and looked closer. Down near the edge of the pylon, clinging to a rusted reinforcement rod, was a tattered shred of cloth. Just beyond it, Plato could see a length of taut rope.

He stepped between the railing and the bridge structure and paced along the outside of the rope. Turning back, he glanced down at the bridge pylon and nearly lost his breakfast.

Dangling near the water's edge at the base of the

bridge, twisting gently in the breeze, was Tyler Cummings. His feet were embedded in the ice. The rope stretched straight up to one of the bridge supports, one of the girders piercing the sky.

The psychiatrist had bought his railway ticket to heaven.

Tyler was long past dead, but they still had to try. Plato scrambled down onto the ice, half-expecting to plunge straight through into the river. But the ice was solid here; his fall didn't even crack the surface. He hustled across the jumbled, jagged wastes until he reached Tyler's body. Overhead, Cal had rushed along the edge of the bridge pylon and whipped out her trusty Swiss Army knife. She glanced down at Plato.

He waved her off for a moment and studied the corpse thoughtfully. If Cal cut him free, Tyler might very well plunge right through the crust and into the river. Tyler's feet had punctured ten inches of solid ice; he was sunk to his knees in gray slush. Carefully, Plato spread his feet apart to plant them on a solid surface, reached for Tyler's thighs, and heaved.

It was easier than he expected. Out here in the cold air and frozen water, rigor mortis still hadn't set in. The psychiatrist's knees flexed easily, and his legs lurched free of the slush. His sodden shoes were planted on the ice now, and his knees were bent at right angles, as though he were sitting on an invisible chair, giving therapy to a spectral patient.

Plato finally nodded up at Cal, then put his arms around the corpse's torso. Cal cut the cord and the three hundred pounds or so that had once been Tyler Cummings tumbled to the ice; Plato barely broke the psychiatrist's fall.

"I'll run for help," Cal called. She tossed her knife down to Plato and tightroped back to the river walk.

"Don't bother running," Plato advised quietly. When Cal poked her head over the edge, he continued. "Tyler's long past help."

Cal took a long look at the body lying below her and nodded soberly. "Just wait with him—I'll be back soon."

Plato carefully cut the rope away, leaving the knot intact just as Cal would have advised. But it didn't help; nothing he could do would help Tyler Cummings in this world. The psychiatrist's face was swollen and dusky blue; his eyes ballooned and his tongue bulged from an appalling mask of death. He was a picture-perfect illustration of a hanging victim, or a strangulation victim, or perhaps a little of both.

Or maybe something else. Turning the psychiatrist's head to study the ligature mark, Plato spotted a pinkish smear in the snow. He looked closer; sure enough, Tyler had a swollen, sticky lump just over his left temple.

Plato stood up on the ice and frowned at the bricks of the river walk, which was now just at eye level. He glanced up at the other half of the rope, whipping in the breeze like a flagpole runner, then studied the bricks again.

The snow and ice of the trail showed signs of a scuffle near the bridge support. Had Tyler been hit on the head and *dragged* to the river? How? Who could possibly be *strong* enough?

Plato could think of only one person.

He hurried back to the victim and eased the body onto its side. Tyler Cummings's tan coat was frayed and torn, streaked with dirt and damp snow. Plato recalled the shredded piece of cloth he had spotted up on the bridge support—had it torn loose from the coat when Cummings was dragged to the edge and pushed off?

Or was the whole thing a product of Plato's imagination, of his desire to believe that a man as successful and competent and pleasant as Tyler Cummings would never kill himself? After all, Tyler might simply have snagged his coat on the bridge support before he jumped, and then hit his head on the way down. The dirty streaks on the coat could have easily rubbed off from the concrete bridge pylon.

But if not, and if Jimmy Dubrowski were still around . . .

Plato suddenly wished he hadn't let Cally run off alone. What if she—

He hadn't gotten past an initial shudder of fear before Cal herself poked her head over the edge of the river walk. Breathlessly, she pointed back over her shoulder.

"They're coming," she panted. "With a stretcher."

Tom Brunelski, one of the ER attending physicians, poked his head over the edge of the walkway. He measured the drop, then hurdled down to the ice with practiced ease, as though he did just that sort of thing every day. He was wearing a National Ski Patrol jacket; maybe he *did* do that sort of thing every day.

But even Tom wasn't a miracle worker; one quick check of the victim and he simply shook his head.

"Tyler's gone. *Long* gone."

A nurse and a pair of orderlies appeared just a few moments later. They handed a stretcher down to Tom and Plato, then scrambled down to help load the body aboard. After lifting the body up onto the sidewalk they started to wheel it back to the hospital, but Cal shook her head grimly. She would examine the body here.

The orderlies shrugged and drifted back toward the hospital empty-handed.

"I didn't know Tyler very well," Tom confessed later. Cal was examining the body and the crime scene while he and Plato and the ER nurse sat on a park bench and watched. "Was he depressed?"

Plato shook his head. "I don't know."

The emergency room doctor shrugged it off. For Tom Brunelski, this was just another unsolved mystery, one of many he might encounter in a typical day. It was the nature of his job. ER doctors did their best to handle crises, to stabilize patients until their transfer, to diagnose life-threatening conditions. But many of their patients were discharged before the answers ever arrived, or were sent up to the hospital floor—or down to the morgue—after only a brief encounter.

Of course, this case was different. Tyler Cummings was a member of the hospital staff. And Tom Brunelski was more curious than the typical ER doc.

"How did you guys ever know where to *find* him?" Tom finally asked. He combed a hand through his wavy blond hair and flashed a smile at Plato—an odd combination of reluctance and polite curiosity.

Plato filled him in, telling Tom about their luncheon date, about Tyler's missed appointment that morning, the receptionist's suggestion about the river trail.

"That's right," Tom agreed. "I've seen him out here before—walking along the river or sitting on one of these benches." He chuckled. "You've got to admire a guy with that kind of free time."

Plato shrugged; it was an old argument. The emergency room at Riverside was a zoo—Tom put in just fifty hours a week, but they were *hard* hours. He'd only been out of residency for five years, but his face was already lined and creased with strain and his blond hair was streaked with gray.

On the other hand, Tyler Cummings might have had less stress in the average patient visit, but he had also worked longer hours. And some of his patients could be very challenging. Plato glanced down at the cast on his arm and shook his head: a psychiatrist's work could be every bit as stressful as an emergency room doctor's.

"I saw Dr. Cummings heading outside this morning," the nurse told them. After seeing the patient onto the stretcher, Jane Ebbins had lagged behind with Tom. Sitting farther down the bench, she frowned and shook her head in disbelief. "Just after eleven o'clock."

"Did you talk to him?" Plato asked. "Was he walking with anyone?"

Jane gestured back toward the hospital, now lost in the snow. "No—I just saw him heading out the back door there. I had just come out on my break. To have a cigarette."

She hunched her shoulders and shot a guilty glance over at Tom, but the attending physician shrugged. He was a smoker, too—and he rarely bothered to go outside to indulge his habit.

"Did anyone leave *after* him?" Plato asked.

"Not that I could see. But I wasn't out here for more than a few minutes."

They sat for a long moment, waiting for the police to arrive. And watching Cal sniff around the scene, studying the piece of rope Plato had freed from Tyler's neck, and checking the other end, which was still attached to the bridge support. Peering at a railing farther down the bridge, closer to the ground.

"Is she always like this?" Tom asked, studying Cal curiously.

"Yup." Plato nodded. He recognized the signs. Cal had gone beyond shock, perhaps even beyond fear. Her mind and senses were working in high gear, registering the crime scene, laboriously gathering each tiny detail, assembling traces and suggestions to form a scenario of what had occurred, a theory which she—or someone else—might confirm in the lab.

All that thought, all that observation, helped keep her emotions on ice.

She had told Plato about it once long ago, back when they first met, when she was working on the original Dubrowski case. Back when Jimmy Dubrowski was still at large, when he had called her at home, and stalked her at work, and frightened her nearly senseless. But Cal's logical mind had taken over—the same rigid self-control she had learned even earlier, at her mother's death.

Later there would be time for sadness, for the inevitable recriminations over her supposed role in Tyler Cummings's death. For the fear. But not yet.

Finally, Cal drifted back over to the little group.

"Jane says he came out here alone," Tom told her. He squinted at the bridge and shook his head. "But it seems like an awfully funny place to commit suicide."

Plato felt a surge of déjà vu—another psychiatrist, another apparent suicide just last spring. Another serial killer.

He had a feeling Tyler Cummings's "suicide" was just as false as the other incident.

"Did he really hang himself?" Plato finally asked Cal. "Or was he murdered?"

"Both," she replied simply.

CHAPTER 15

Later, Cal showed Plato exactly what she meant. Tom Brunelski and Jane had left after giving their statements to the detectives, and Tyler Cummings was neatly zipped up inside his body bag. The scene was still cluttered with technicians from the police department and the coroner's crew, taking a few last photos and finishing up their work.

"Somebody knew Tyler was coming here," Cal said. Her tone was brisk, clipped and precise—the same voice she used when testifying in court. "They were either familiar with his habits, or they had lured him out here. Maybe both."

She led Plato to the edge of the bridge pylon, pointing to the scuff marks he had noticed in the snow. She gestured at the gap in the rope railing near the edge of the bridge: a three-foot space, easily wide enough for a person to walk through.

"The killer had tied a rope to that crossbar up there, before Tyler ever came outside." She gestured to a rusting but sturdy steel brace overhead, the one which had held the noose. A coroner's assistant had climbed up to cut the rope free, but it was easy to mark the rod that had been used. It was bent in the middle, like a flattened V. Cal pointed down to the gap in the rope railing. "The killer probably paused right here with Tyler, slipped the noose over his head, and pushed him over the edge.''

Plato studied the scuff marks again, the bent crossbar, and the open space beside the bridge pylon. He frowned.

"It's kind of hard to believe, Cally." He pointed up at the crossbar. "First of all, wouldn't Tyler have noticed a rope dangling up there?"

"*We* didn't," she pointed out. "Not at first, anyway."

She led Plato along the edge of the concrete pylon and pointed through a square hole in the bridge structure. Plato realized he was looking through a window, at the inside of the bridgekeeper's shelter. Most of the dials and switches had been ripped away or crumbled to ruin, but the back wall—the side near the river walk—still held three long cast-iron handles. Two were covered with shards of broken glass and flecks of rust, the fallout of decades of decay. But the third had been wiped almost clean.

Cal pointed to a wisp of white fiber hardly thicker than a human hair clinging to the handle's rough surface. "The killer probably anchored it there to keep it hidden. Wound it around once, then yanked it free at just the right time."

She moved back out to the sidewalk and reached her hand inside, showing that the rope's end would have been within easy reach.

"But that doesn't make sense, either," Plato protested, following her back to the walk. "You're saying somebody slipped a *noose* over Tyler's neck and pushed him over?" He shook his head. "Tyler Cummings wasn't a little guy, not by a long shot. I doubt if even Jimmy Dubrowski—"

He didn't get to finish his sentence. In a flash, Cal had tossed something over his head, cinched it tight, and given it a gentle tug.

"*Graak!*" Plato murmured hoarsely. He tiptoed back

from the edge of the walkway and tugged at the strap around his neck. "*Oh-khay.*"

She released the strap—an extra cord that the orderlies had left behind when they hoisted Tyler Cummings's stretcher up from the ice. Beside her, a coroner's assistant smirked at Cal.

"An excellent demonstration, Dr. Marley." Bentley, one of the dieners at the morgue, had come along to help gather evidence. He smiled at Plato. "I would be very careful around this lady."

"I always am," Plato replied soberly. He watched as Bentley leaned inside the controller's shelter and tweezed the shred of fiber from the handle.

"Match it with the cord from the victim," Cal instructed.

"Of course, ma'am."

Bentley tucked the fiber inside a bag and carried both over to an open case lying on the ground. Whether gathering evidence, or opening skulls, or carrying organs off to be weighed, Bentley always moved with the solemn and dignified grace of an English butler. His looks and deportment matched the part as well, he was plump and distinguished and always impeccably dressed. And like an English butler, the diener didn't seem to have a first name; everyone always just called him "Bentley."

"We're almost finished, ma'am," he told Cal. "Just a few more pictures."

Cal nodded and tucked the strap into her coat pocket, then turned to Plato. "Most people don't realize how easy it is to be strangled. Once that cord's around your neck, it's all over."

Plato shuddered.

"Even if Tyler did struggle, Jimmy just had to pull it tighter. Tyler probably passed out before Jimmy tossed him over." She leaned on the bridge support and watched the photographer taking a few more pictures of the hole Tyler had left in the ice. Her voice suddenly grew quiet. "That's just the same thing he did to Jerry Tammerly— strangled him first, then tried to make it look like suicide."

"How can you tell the difference?" Plato asked.

Cal led him over to the stretcher where Tyler Cummings was waiting inside his body bag, all set to go.

"A bag for everything, and everything in its bag," Cal muttered. She unzipped the sack and pulled the plastic down over Tyler's head, then lifted and turned his neck. Only now was it starting to stiffen. With her finger, she traced a narrow parchment-colored line diagonally around the neck, angling upward from just below the chin to disappear at the very back. She gestured at an empty space at the back of the neck where the line didn't quite meet itself. "That's where the knot was tied—less pressure here."

Cal then traced another thin, barely-visible mark encircling the neck half an inch below the first. Although it was the same width, this line ran horizontally around the neck rather than tilting up at the back. She lifted Tyler's chin and pointed to a spot just above his Adam's apple, where three or four dark scratch marks crossed the line.

"Fingernails," she said bluntly. "Tyler struggled a bit, trying to get the cord off his neck."

Plato swallowed heavily, watching his wife. Sometimes, Cal seemed like a total stranger to him, as though he had hardly begun to understand her in the four years since they met. Every other doctor he knew—all the friends and colleagues he had trained with, practiced with, and learned from—saw death as the enemy, as a shocking and unwelcome interloper in their work.

But Cal's specialty *was* death. Rather than fearing its presence, or denying it, or doing everything in her power to halt its progress, she stared it straight in the eye, studying it with the dispassioned calm and curiosity of an etymologist dissecting a black widow spider.

Plato couldn't help imagining *himself* in Tyler's position, struggling with the cord around his neck, scraping his own flesh away in his desperation to get free, to breathe, to *live*, watching the world go black as he finally lost consciousness, perhaps feeling the sudden fall and *snap!* as the cord tautened and he plunged toward the river.

"Fingernails," Plato muttered softly. "So that's how you know he was strangled first?"

"That, plus the duskiness of his face, and the scleral hemorrhages." Still coldly clinical, Cal lifted the victim's eyelids; the whites of Tyler's eyes were dotted with telltale reddish pinpoints. "Blood could get *into* the head, but it couldn't get back out. Of course, once he fell, the arteries were closed off as well."

"He hit his head, too," Plato pointed out, recovering slowly. "Maybe on his way down."

"I know." Cal nodded, tucking the body back inside his bag and closing the zipper. She gestured for Bentley to take him away, then led Plato back to the bridge support. "He smacked his head on the edge, *here*."

She showed him the spot: a tiny red streak on the concrete was outlined with a chalk circle.

"They already took a scraping." She pointed to the reinforcement rod, where Plato had spotted the piece of tan fabric. "Between that mark and the piece of his jacket you spotted, we can see how he fell. How he was *pushed*."

Plato nodded. The rod and the streak outlined a logical

arc, the pendulum of Tyler's body as he swung down through the last seconds of life.

"But even with all this evidence, a good defense lawyer could probably claim suicide." She shrugged. "They might even say Tyler changed his mind and tried to get the noose off, then fell to his death."

"Pretty far-fetched."

"I've seen crazier things work in court." Cal smiled tightly. "But there's one piece of proof that *nobody* can dispute."

She bent over to open Bentley's precious box of evidence. Donning a pair of gloves, she pulled out the upper half of the rope—the part which had been tied to the bridge support. "Take a look."

Plato did. He had been surprised when the technician had sawed through the steel cross-brace to free the knot, rather than cutting the rope loose or simply untying it. But now Plato understood why. The knot had been hacked with a dull knife: several cuts were obvious, though only a few fibers had separated.

"Jimmy Dubrowski probably wanted to make it look like a suicide again," Cal concluded. She pointed back to the river. "But when he saw the hole in the ice, he had a better idea."

Plato remembered Tyler's legs, buried up to the knees in icy water. If the knot *had* come free, the body would have fallen through the ice. It might not have been found for months, if ever; Tyler's body could have ridden the river's undercurrent clear out into Lake Erie.

"I wonder why he stopped cutting."

"Maybe someone came along and interrupted him." She closed her eyes and took a deep, shaky breath—the first emotion Plato had seen her display since they found Tyler's body. Her eyes shone with a sudden glint of fear, but the icy control returned almost instantly, like a snow-ball dousing a match flame. She took Plato's hand. "Let's head back inside and see what Jeremy's up to."

"Not a clue, not a hint," Jeremy told them. The sheriff's detective had accompanied Cleveland police to the scene. Officially, the case would be under the city's jurisdiction, but the hunt for Jimmy Dubrowski was a cooperative effort crossing several city boundaries. The two city detectives on the scene had seemed glad of Jeremy's help.

After only a few minutes outside, all three had come inside to interview Tyler Cummings's office staff and anyone else in the hospital who might furnish some hint about what had happened.

"We've talked to the receptionist, to his nurse, to half the people on this floor. Even some of the nuts over in the locked ward." Sitting in the reception area, he scowled at the office window and shook his head. "Haven't talked with his partner yet—she's been seeing patients all afternoon. Couldn't spare a minute to talk about the poor guy."

Marianne seemed to have overheard Jeremy's comment; she poked her head through the window and sighed. "Dr. Randall is just finishing up; she'll be with you in a minute."

Tyler's fiancée had undergone a remarkable transformation: her dark eyes were red-rimmed and bleary, her makeup was smeared, and her perfect auburn hair was a bedraggled mess. Even her voice was different—just this side of a sob.

And understandably so. Plato was surprised that Marianne was still here. She disappeared from the window again; Plato heard faint whimpering and a soft, dismal toot into a Kleenex.

The door to the therapists' offices opened and a young woman scurried out, grabbing her coat and dashing off into the hallway, staring down at her feet the entire time, as though she didn't quite trust them to carry her in the right direction. Behind her, still standing in the doorway, was a tall, thin, gray-haired woman. Joan Randall pursed her lips and studied her inquisitors sternly, like a grade-school principal eyeing a group of truants. Finally, she spoke.

"Detective Ames?"

"Yes, ma'am." Jeremy jumped to his feet, self-consciously straightening his tie and brushing doughnut crumbs from his pants.

Joan Randall had that effect on people, Plato knew. He had only met her once or twice before, at hospital gatherings where she always reminded him of a chaperone, glaring severely at people who laughed too loudly or drank too much or told off-color jokes. At medical staff meetings, she often complained of the immaturity of the interns and residents. She pronounced *immaturity* with a hard "t" sound: immah-*tour*-ity.

In both form and manner, she was the precise opposite of Tyler Cummings. Between the two of them, they might have made two perfectly average-sized, happy but earnest psychiatrists. Instead, Tyler had gotten all the weight *and* all the cheerfulness. Joan Randall didn't look like she had smiled since Freud died.

She wasn't smiling now. She was staring down her nose at Jeremy with an eye that—as Tyler Cummings had once put it—could sear a steak at ten paces.

"I suppose you'll want to interview me, too?"

"That's the idea, ma'am," Jeremy agreed. "Just a few

questions, nothing formal. We can talk out here if you'd like."

"If I must . . ." Her shoulders lifted in a bony shrug. She was wearing a stiffly formal black dress that accentuated her gaunt frame, a pair of opal earrings, and a paisley scarf of purple and black, like a cloth bruise. It was the perfect outfit for a funeral, as though she had somehow known her partner would die today. She leaned back inside the door and spoke. "Marianne, we're finished for today."

The receptionist took the hint, rocketing into the waiting area just a few seconds later, bundled up in a trendy black woolen overcoat and red scarf and clutching an entire box of spare Kleenex. Jeremy stood as she walked past.

"Take care, Marianne." He touched her arm. "Sure you're okay?"

"K-kay." She nodded, hiccuped, and vanished through the door, barely containing a fresh bout of noisy sobs before she reached the elevator.

"Friend of the family," Jeremy muttered as he sat again.

Joan Randall sighed heavily and shot him a meaningful glance. "Marianne and Tyler were very . . . *close.*"

"So I understand." Jeremy hitched himself up in his chair. "Would you like to talk here, or inside?"

She fired a glance at Plato and Cal. "Is this to be a *group* interview?"

"If you have no objection," Jeremy replied smoothly. "Dr. Cal Marley is, as you know, a deputy coroner. And Plato discovered your partner's body. They both had plans to meet with him today. Of course, if you object—"

The psychiatrist tossed off another bony shrug. "*Hardly* that—I certainly have nothing to hide." She studied Jeremy for a long moment, then sat down primly in a chair opposite the trio. "I just hope this isn't going to take very long . . ."

"I don't think so. Just a few preliminary questions." The detective frowned at his hands. "Dr. Randall, you don't seem terribly upset by your partner's death—if you don't mind my saying so."

"Whether I *mind* it or not is hardly germane to your investigation, is it?" She took a deep breath and sighed. "If what you mean is, am I upset by Tyler's death, of course I am."

Her statement gave birth to a dubious silence.

"Tyler Cummings was an excellent clinician," Joan finally continued. "I had no complaints about him as a partner, or as a colleague. His absence will be deeply felt by his patients and by the other doctors throughout the hospital."

The pronouncement was oddly atonal, devoid of emotion: the sort of statement a corporate CEO might deliver to describe the loss of a valued but obscure employee. Plato was shocked—surely even Joan Randall should have been able to scrape up a hint of regret if not grief at the loss of her partner.

If nothing else, Tyler's death must have been a shock. But Joan spoke as though it were merely another irritating interruption to her busy day.

"Then you respected Tyler Cummings?" Jeremy asked, dashing something down in his notebook. The detective had some psychiatric expertise of his own. Jeremy never actually wrote much of anything, he had once confided to Plato. He kept it all in his head and dictated it later—transcribing it himself. But the act of writing tended to put witnesses on their guard, to make them recall and respond more precisely. "Your working relationship had no problems or difficulties?"

"I would hardly say *that*." The psychiatrist glanced over at Plato for assistance. "*You* know how partnerships work, Doctor. The typical squabbles over holidays, weekend call, billing and reimbursement."

Plato nodded.

"Of course, Tyler and I had a more difficult situation than most people," Joan continued. "After all, he *was* my ex-husband."

The silence following this pronouncement was even more empty and prolonged than the first. Plato had been at Riverside for almost a decade—as a medical student, a resident, and a geriatrics fellow. He had known Tyler Cummings for years, but they had never really been more than acquaintances.

Still, he would have never imagined that Tyler was capable of such a . . . well, such a *bizarre* act. Joan Randall had all the romantic appeal of a freshly opened bar of Ivory soap: hard and sharp-edged and utterly undefilable. Plato would have rather married Sister Gertrude Aloysius, his austere and dinosauric grade-school principal, not that the question had ever come up.

Jeremy was understandably the first to recover from the shock; he had no idea how different Tyler and Joan really were.

"You're divorced?"

"That's generally how it happens," Joan agreed acidly. She gave a bitter laugh. "Of course, there *is* annulment— Tyler tried that. He was Catholic and I'm, well—"

Puritan, Plato couldn't help thinking.

"Atheist, with an option on agnosticism." The thin ribbons of her lips twitched at the corners; it was either a smile or a facial tic.

"I can understand how it would be hard to work to-gether," Jeremy agreed quickly. He certainly could; the detective was a veteran of three divorces himself, though Plato didn't think he had actually *worked* with any of his wives.

"It was difficult, at first," the psychiatrist admitted. "But we've been divorced for five years, now—and sep-arated a while before that."

"And yet, neither of you—?"

"Wanted to leave here, to give up our patients and our practices? Hardly." Her lips twitched again—a momen-tary flicker, like Morse code flashing from a signal lantern. "I think Tyler expected *me* to, at first. But ulti-mately, he ended up moving much of his practice to the clinic."

"The Cleveland Clinic?"

She nodded. "He still worked here two days a week, but he was planning to move out altogether next spring."

"And leave the practice to you?"

"Not really—most of his patients were following him to the clinic." She shrugged again. "I'm planning to hire another partner; I'm really doing very little general psy-chiatry anymore. My specialty is sex therapy."

It was time for another pause, for another gathering of scattered wits. Poor Jeremy obviously had no idea what to say; he just made a few gurgling sounds and retired. Cal was staring at the psychiatrist with slack-jawed as-tonishment. If Sister Gertrude Aloysius herself had head-lined at Tiffany's Nightclub in the Flats, Plato couldn't have been more surprised.

But he was the first to recover. He smiled and nodded. "That's right—you gave a Grand Rounds on impotence last spring."

Not that Plato had attended. As a geriatrician, what he

didn't know about impotence could have been printed on a page torn from Sister Gertrude's *Pocket Catechism*. But he remembered the flyer advertising the conference.

"It was very good," he continued. "Very informative."

"Thank you." The Morse-smile flickered again. "I don't get as many elderly patients as I would like."

It was a hint, a cast for referrals. But Plato didn't take the bait; he just nodded and smiled. "Building a practice takes time."

"How would you characterize Dr. Cummings's relationship with the other members of the staff?" Jeremy asked, apparently dropping Joan as a subject for now.

Her upper lip curled in disdain. "*Here*, or after hours?"

"Both."

She sighed. When she spoke, her voice carried a note of resigned disappointment, like a mother discussing an errant child.

"Tyler saw our divorce as a sexual liberation," she began. "Of course, he had an extremely repressed childhood—a deeply religious father and a sexually frigid mother. His feelings about sex and relationships were very confused, guilt-ridden and repressed. And yet, he had a warmth of personality and a need for intimacy which were bursting to be expressed."

Jeremy blinked.

Plato wasn't surprised. Obviously, Joan Randall had spent a lot of time analyzing her ex-husband. Very few of Plato's friends were psychiatrists; it was hard to resist the temptation to bring work home, to psychoanalyze your family and friends. To express every argument or disagreement as an expression of a repressed id, a conflict between an unfulfilled oral stage and an improperly developed superego. Or whatever.

"Naturally, he remained a child in many ways, a very

needy child," she continued. "And when I failed to fulfill his—well, his *insatiable* appetites, he sought satisfaction elsewhere."

"Elsewhere?"

"I should say, *everywhere*." Her steely gaze shot from Jeremy to Plato and back again. She scowled over the receptionist's window. "Marianne was only his latest in a long string of . . . companions."

"She led me to understand that they were engaged," the detective noted.

"Of course they were," she agreed. "Tyler was *engaged* to at least half a dozen women since our divorce—including, of course, poor Deirdre Swanson."

Plato frowned, but then remembered: Deirdre Swanson had been the West Side Strangler's first victim. She, too, had worked in this office—as a nurse. Jimmy Dubrowski had apparently fallen in love with her during his visits; he hadn't realized that Deirdre and Tyler were a couple.

Judging from Tyler's latest fiancée, Plato supposed that Deirdre Swanson must have been quite a temptation for the Strangler. The news of her attachment to Tyler had obviously been quite a disappointment.

Having apparently gathered enough background details—or perhaps reluctant to encourage a further psychiatric dissection of the victim—Jeremy moved on to the facts: had Joan seen any strangers in the office, had she overheard any of Tyler's last telephone conversation, had she seen him leave the office for his walk, and so on.

But the psychiatrist was singularly unhelpful. No, she had not seen any unexpected patients or visitors that morning. She had been busy in her office, writing up a research paper for presentation at an upcoming conference. Tyler always answered his telephone messages in the privacy of his office, and she certainly had no wish to listen in or even incidentally overhear his telephone conversations—for both professional *and* personal reasons. And no, she hadn't seen him leave the office for his walk; she had spent virtually the whole morning in her office.

Finally, her impatience began to show again.

"I really don't see the point in all this questioning." She hitched herself up and pulled her skirt down over her knees for the fourteenth time that hour. "It's obvious that Jimmy Dubrowski somehow lured Tyler to the bridge and strangled him there. Instead of questioning me, you should be out looking for Jimmy."

"We have two dozen officers doing that right now," Jeremy assured her.

"Then you should have three dozen. Or four." She frowned. "Jimmy Dubrowski is a *very* unstable young man, and very clever. As you must have discovered by now. I'm not surprised he escaped."

"That's *right*." Jeremy's face lit up with a sudden recollection. "You testified at his hearing, didn't you? For the prosecution."

"So did Tyler—for the defense. He was convinced his patient was innocent." She stood and folded her arms; the interview was over. "Obviously, he made a very big mistake."

CHAPTER 16

"She was merciless," Cal recalled later. "She tore Jimmy's defense to pieces."

They were rolling down I-77 south of town. Behind them, Cleveland's skyline had disappeared in a squall. Not much snow had accumulated yet, but the weathermen were cheerfully predicting a possible blizzard by Monday or Tuesday—just in time for the start of the work week.

On the way out of town, Cal had stopped at the morgue to check on Tyler's autopsy. As expected, it was already finished. Ralph Jensson, the county coroner, had performed it himself—both because of the stature of the victim and because the morgue staff Christmas party was tonight. Poor Jim Cartwright, another deputy coroner with such a miserable outlook and rotten luck that he was known as Eeyore, was on duty this weekend. And, as usual, the morgue's fridge was stacked floor to ceiling with unexamined corpses—two late-night stabbings, a shotgun suicide, and Tyler Cummings, in addition to an unexpected flurry of pre-blizzard traffic fatalities.

Cartwright's rotten luck had even gained him fame *outside* the morgue; the county sheriff had joked that Cleveland's homicide rate might drop by a quarter if only Jim Cartwright didn't have to take weekend call.

The backlog was so severe today that Cal had pitched in too, doing a quick MVA autopsy while Plato had a cup of coffee. By the time she was done, Tyler's autopsy results were in, and they were no surprise. Ralph Jensson agreed with Cal about the strangling-hanging method of murder and the gash on Tyler's head. The wound to the temple was slight and probably incidental to his final fall; the skull showed no signs of fracture and the brain had no visible contusions or hemorrhages. Either finding could have meant that Tyler was clubbed unconscious *first*, then strung up and heaved off the river walk.

And of course, the strands from the bridgekeeper's control handle had matched with those from the noose. Cal's competence was sometimes uncanny, even intimidating to Plato. Compared with her, he sometimes felt like a complete bungler: his elderly patients could be so complex and confusing that he got lost in a maze of diagnoses and medications. For those patients, there were rarely any simple or clear answers.

At least Cal seemed to have brightened up a little, to have relaxed in the familiar surroundings of the morgue and her colleagues. And of course, nothing lifted Cal's spirits like a quick autopsy—except shopping.

"Tyler did a good job of testifying for Jimmy," Cal continued. "But not good enough. Joan Randall made him look like an idiot."

"How?" Plato asked, bewildered. "Tyler Cummings was very sharp, very competent."

"Maybe a little *too* competent," she pointed out. "Tyler was generally positive about Jimmy, but he naturally had some uncertainty. The same uncertainty *anyone* would have—psychiatry isn't an objective field." She shrugged. "But Joan made it *sound* objective—and she made Jimmy Dubrowski look like Hitler's first cousin."

"I take it Jimmy had an 'extremely repressed childhood'?" Plato guessed.

"Worse. His father committed suicide when Jimmy was six or seven. Guess how?"

"Hanging."

"You got it. That gave her plenty of ammunition: posttraumatic stress, a tremendous burden of guilt, an Oedipal complex about his mother—who seemed like a perfectly nice person to me, by the way." She shook her head sadly. "I felt pretty sorry for his mother during the hearing. For *both* of them. She passed away just a few weeks after Jimmy was sentenced."

"Hold on a minute." Plato frowned. "I thought Joan Randall was a *sex therapist*. How did she get appointed as the prosecution's star witness?"

"She was just a general psychiatrist back then. At least, she didn't mention sex therapy on the witness stand." Cal sighed. "Plus, she wasn't the *star* witness—just another so-called expert called in to testify about Jimmy. There were a few others, including a pretty sharp forensic psychiatrist, but Joan stole the show." She paused for a long moment. "Back then, I got the feeling there was something *personal* involved in her testimony. But I didn't know just how personal it was."

"I wonder if she had more than a vested interest in making Tyler look bad," Plato mused.

"What do you mean?"

"Something Jeremy pointed out, after we finished talking to Joan just now. None of the detectives had mentioned exactly *where* Tyler was found."

"So?"

"Joan Randall said Jimmy must have 'lured Tyler to the bridge and strangled him there.' How did she know about the bridge?"

"Maybe she could see it from her window," Cal guessed. She shook her head, wincing at his bizarre implication. "Don't tell me you're thinking Joan might have *framed* Jimmy Dubrowski for all those killings."

"Well-l-l." Plato smiled lamely and shrugged. "She *did* have it in for Tyler—I think she had some *repressed* feelings of her own. Like a lot of anger."

"And how about Deirdre Swanson? And Luella Huckleby, and Jerry Tammerly?" She squinted at him, astonished at the thickness of his head. "And what about how Jimmy stalked *me*, before they finally caught him? Jesus Christ, Plato—he tried to *kill* me last Saturday!"

"I know. Sorry." He shrugged. "I guess I didn't like Joan Randall."

"*Nobody* likes Joan Randall." She softened, chuckling. "Can you believe she and Tyler were ever married?"

"I've spent most of the afternoon trying to understand it."

"Sort of like Bud Abbott marrying Queen Elizabeth." Cal laughed again.

Her icy wall was finally starting to melt. They chatted about Tyler and Joan, about poor Jim Cartwright's rotten luck, about the upcoming party tonight. About anything but the murder itself; they were like two hikers walking along the edge of a cliff, instinctively avoiding the precipice beside their feet.

Plato turned off the freeway at Sagamore Hills and crossed the Cuyahoga before turning onto County Road 142. The snow was falling thicker and faster here, frosting the farmhouses and barns and old country estates into a giant Currier and Ives print. Veering into their own driveway after an isolated patch of forest, Plato turned to Cal.

"Are you going to be okay?" he asked. "Do you still want to go to the party?"

"I think so." Cal took a deep breath and nodded slowly, then stared up at their century-old home crowning the driveway ahead. It was an impressive structure, a rambling Victorian wreck being gradually and painstakingly rescued from ruin during weekends and vacations and long summer evenings. Octagonal turrets, balconies, ornate latticework, and half-moon windows: a giant moldering dollhouse Cal had fallen in love with on their very first visit just before the wedding.

It was home.

And yet, even home had grown unsafe, had become a dangerous territory rather than a safe harbor. They hadn't expected to come home this late in the day; dark windows stared out into the gloomy twilight, and the house itself looked lonely and abandoned. Rather than taking pleasure in the old Victorian architecture and spacious grounds, Plato now saw only hazardously far-flung rooms, easily broken windows, and isolation from the watchful eyes of neighbors.

Cal seemed to feel the same way. She reached for Plato's arm. "Just one thing. From now on, let's keep some lights on all the time, okay?"

"Sure—I'd been thinking about putting some floods up near the roof, anyway. Those motion-sensitive ones, you know?"

"And that tree." She didn't seem to be listening. "The one in the courtyard. I think maybe you should cut it down."

Plato nodded soberly. He understood: neither of them could ever see that fir tree again without picturing those Barbie dolls—and, by extension, a corpse dangling from the bridge. A corpse that easily could have been Cal's instead of Tyler's.

"Sure, Cally. Sure."

The morgue Christmas party kicked off at six o'clock, but the Marleys didn't make their appearance until nearly seven. Plato had cut the fir tree down that very afternoon and dragged it away, dropping it down into a steep ravine deep in the woods. And while Cal showered, he made a complete tour of the house again, checking windows and doors, sifting through the basement and even climbing up into the attic. He found no signs of forced entry or even of an attempt.

Still, he wished he could board up the windows, and bar the doors. Or better yet, pack up a suitcase and move into the Ritz until the Strangler was captured again.

But Cal was still adamant on that point. Jimmy Dubrowski wasn't going to force her out of her home, no matter what. She wasn't going to spend her Christmas in a hotel room.

So it was long past dark by the time they hit the road. And as usual, they got lost trying to find Ralph Jensson's house.

The coroner lived in a beautiful old mansion in Cleveland Heights, just off Fairmount Boulevard. The whole neighborhood was an architectural showcase, a monument to Cleveland's first exodus to the suburbs around the turn of the century. And the Fairmount area was at its finest during the holidays; many of the homes were trimmed with wreaths and pine roping, or decked out with lights and lawn displays, or floodlit like showpieces in a museum. The gently falling snow was piling up on roof peaks and garlands, porch tops and fountains, accentuating the lines and curves of the brick and granite and marble dwellings.

Unfortunately, it was also piling up on the street signs; a brisk northwest wind had plastered a coat of snow onto the faces of the markers. It didn't help that all the streets had similar-sounding anglophilic names that tended to end with "e": Shelburne, Claythorne, Sherbrooke, Traymore. And the neighborhood itself was rather confusing, full of gently winding streets that subtly carried you off in a different direction than you expected, or meandered down to half-familiar intersections that you were sure you had seen before.

The trouble was, Plato and Cal had seen it *all* before. They had gotten lost every single year so far, had always taken themselves on an accidental tour of Fairmount's residential museum before finally blundering down Ralph Jensson's street. And this year was no different.

But finally, just as even Plato was ready to throw up his hands and phone for directions—or at least shin up a pole and scrape off a street sign—Cal spotted a familiar steeple in the distance. Plato backed the car up and turned down the street; sure enough, Ralph Jensson's home, affectionately know as the Monastery, hove into view.

The coroner's house was more of a cathedral, really: gaudy Gothic in style, fashioned with everything from huge blocks of granite to intricate bits of stained glass, featuring steeply sloping rooflines, soaring peaks, towers crowned by jagged spires, and even a pair of flying buttresses roofing a portico at the side of the house.

The front porch and door felt less like a home than the entryway to a church: the wrought-iron gate opened to a marble porch and huge lancet-arched doors. The doorbell chimed like a carillon; Ralph Jensson answered the door with a pipe in one hand and his wife Althea in the other.

Like the late Tyler Cummings and his ex-wife, or Plato and Cal, for that matter, Ralph and Althea were poorly matched for size. Ralph Jensson was a plump and burly Scot, while Althea was tall and elegant—the cream of Cleveland's post-war aristocracy.

But they complemented each other perfectly in every other respect. Both were tops in their field—Ralph in forensic pathology and Althea in pediatrics; she was capping a long and distinguished career by retiring as Chief of Staff at Rainbow Babies and Children's Hospital. Both balanced wisdom and experience with humor and wit and a taste for practical jokes. In conversation, they had a tendency to finish each other's sentences, perhaps even each other's thoughts.

They simply fit together; they were as comfortable and companionable as a pair of old shoes.

And, of course, they shared a love of entertaining. The Jenssons' parties were legendary, especially the annual morgue Christmas bash. Unlike most medical gatherings, the professionals and other staff members weren't segregated; Ralph invited *everyone* who worked at the morgue—from doctors and dieners to fellows and floor-sweepers. Tonight, the Monastery would be packed with a riotous and rollicking crowd.

It was a party Cal wouldn't miss for the world.

"Come in, come in!" Ralph boomed in his slightly nasal brogue. He waved his pipe toward the living room, already swarming with revelers. "The party's just getting into gear." He winked at Althea, then leaned over to swoop Cal into his arms and give her a fatherly peck on the cheek. "Merry Christmas, my lass!"

"And Happy New Year, Ralph." Cal giggled as he set her gently down again.

Ralph really *was* like a father—a visiting lecturer at

Northwestern's medical school, he had learned of Cal's interest in forensics and taken her under his wing, sponsoring a rotation in Cleveland during her senior year, keeping in touch and encouraging her career, and finally offering her a position when she finished fellowship. He had been a teacher and a mentor, a guiding light and a true friend.

He had given Cal away at the wedding.

"Just be careful near the fireplace, dears," Althea warned. Her eyes sparkled with mischief. "There's been a slight . . . *accident* there."

She was right. Part of the vast living room was marked off with bright yellow police tape. A typical crime scene was laid out on the slate floor before the hearth, including a very high-profile victim.

He was lying facedown on the slate beside a roaring fire; the toes of his boots pointed inward, and his neck was bent at an odd and unnatural angle. He was heavily bearded and white-haired, wearing a red suit with white trim, a broad black belt, and a pair of polished black boots. Beside him, a large placard read, WE FOUND THIS POOR MAN IN OUR CHIMNEY; CAN YOU HELP US?

It was a standard Jensson party game, one that had been repeated every Christmas for years. Only the placement of poor St. Nick varied, along with the cause and manner of death. Last year he had been found, apparently drowned, in one of the huge bathtubs upstairs; a crafty Scrooge-type had actually electrocuted him with a hair dryer. The year before, he had popped up under Ralph's Ford Bronco. The coroner himself had been suspected, but his name was cleared when party guests realized that Nick's head injury didn't fit the presumed accident.

Plato grabbed the case summary and studied it with interest. Cal merely looked on, surveying the scene and scanning the report but not contributing any suggestions. The cases—whose correct solution was always rewarded with a bottle of Macallen's single-malt Scotch—were always off-limits to deputy coroners and forensics fellows. It was no great loss; few of them, including Cal, really wanted to work on another case anyway. But the rest of the staff and spouses loved them.

"Come on, Sherlock." Cal led her husband through the crowd, exchanging holiday greetings and hugs with the support staff, the dieners, and the other deputy coroners. Even Jim Cartwright had managed to break away from the morgue, though he was warily keeping his pager in his hand like a man holding a live hand grenade.

"I made it, Cal," he said, flashing a rare grin. Jim was a nerd, but a lovable one: Bryl-creamed hair, black plastic-framed glasses with duct tape on the bridge, button-down shirts and polyester pants, and the inevitable pocket protector—even at Ralph's Christmas party. Jim dreamed of being the next Patricia Cornwell; he was forever scribbling his thoughts in little notebooks and losing them all around the morgue for the dieners to chuckle over before returning. But one day, he would assemble them all into a fantastic novel—a medical thriller, or maybe a gory forensic mystery.

If he could ever find the time.

He leaned over to give Cal a self-conscious peck on the cheek, then gravely shook hands with Plato. Jim's manner with Plato was always that of a gallant loser in a joust for the fair maiden's hand, which was probably how he saw himself. Before meeting Plato, Cal had grudgingly accompanied Jim Cartwright on a couple of dates. But for Jim, the flame apparently still lingered; he was blushing like a third-grader caught stealing a kiss during recess.

He tore his gaze away from Cal and glanced at Plato, who was furtively studying the case.

"I'll give you a hint, Plato." Jim smiled impishly. "It's not what you think it is."

She chuckled. "You're nasty, Jim."

"Aww, Cal. He *knows* I'm just teasing. Don't you, Plato?"

He looked up from the case study. "Huh?"

"Let's move along, Plato." She rolled her eyes. "I'd better settle you in a quiet corner and let you finish reading. Before you embarrass yourself again."

"Again?"

"Never mind."

The party was just as wild and wonderful as ever. Althea had outdone herself with a tableful of hors d'ouerves, canapes, crepes, and cookies. The Jenssons' perfect twelve-foot Scotch pine was trimmed in a matter of minutes by a horde of chattering, kibitzing partygoers. Beer and wine and Ralph's menagerie of single-malt Scotches flowed like embalming fluid. Even Bentley dropped his customary reserve: he and Jim Cartwright waltzed around the kitchen to Jimmy Buffett's *Ho Ho Ho and a Bottle of Rhum*; not much later, Ralph tucked them both into taxis for home.

And Plato actually managed to solve the case first, concluding that Nick had been the victim of a simple but tragic occupational accident: Santa had fallen head-first down the Jenssons' chimney after imbibing a bit too much reindeer grog. His blood alcohol level was 0.09— legal for sleigh-driving, perhaps, but far too hazardous for chimney descents in the dark.

Ralph and Althea came over to present the award: a bottle of eighteen-year-old Macallen's and a silver dissecting probe, engraved: CORONER OF THE YEAR.

"Well, Plato." Ralph handed over the prizes; he gestured to Cal. "It looks like you've learned a lot from this lass."

"Taught me everything I know," Plato agreed. He squinted at the probe, then waved the Macallen's with a happily lopsided smile. "Like how to drink Scotch—never used to touch the stuff before. Great stuff, Macallen's."

Ralph flashed a knowing grin at Cal. "Apparently, you've taught him quite well."

"No kidding." Plato patted her shoulder with all the gentleness of a grizzly bear. "Great girl, Cally."

She sighed; Plato had sampled a bit too much of the coroner's Scotch collection. "Don't worry, Ralph—I'm driving home."

"Oh, I'm not anxious about you getting *home,* dear." The coroner flashed a worried frown at Althea, then leaned closer. They were sitting in a remote corner of the family room; most of the crowd was back in the living room or heading out the door; the party was winding down. "It's your safety once you get there that has me concerned."

"Oh, Ralph—"

"I'm not kidding, Cally." For once, the jolly coroner's voice grew stern. He shook his head sadly. "I've had a word with Sheriff Givens, and he feels the same way. Your house is just too isolated and too sprawling to properly protect. He would need a half-dozen deputies to do it right, and he doesn't have them. Especially now."

"If you don't want to stay in a hotel," Althea offered with a motherly smile, "we'd love to have you *here* for the holidays. Timothy is visiting his in-laws this year; our house will be practically empty."

"That's awfully kind of you, Althea." Plato had

sobered suddenly; he was staring down at his hands. "Maybe you're right."

He glanced over at Cal, but she looked away quickly. Cal was fighting tears—at Althea's kindness and Ralph's concern, at the prospect of being forced out of their home for Christmas. But it would be awfully nice to spend the holidays here, almost like being home.

"We'd need a couple of days," Cal finally replied. "To arrange boarding for Ghost and Dante, to pack and close up the house . . . You're sure it's okay?"

"Of *course*, dear." Althea leaned over and gave her a hug and a Kleenex. "You just come on over as soon as you're ready."

And so it was settled. They headed for home just a few minutes later with Cal driving and Plato sitting quietly in the passenger seat. He was probably thinking about their decision, about spending the holidays with a couple who—for Plato, at least—were comparative strangers.

"I really think it's the best thing," Cal said finally.

Plato didn't reply. Cal glanced over at him as they passed under a streetlamp. He was fast asleep, snuggled into a ball against the window with his coat for a pillow.

Cal smiled and shook her head. He was sleeping off Ralph's Scotch. Feeling more alone than ever, she turned off the freeway and piloted the car down the back roads of northern Summit County. Sheriff Givens was right, she decided. Their house was isolated, nestled deep in one of the few undeveloped areas left in the county. Thick forest encircled it on all sides; the nearest subdivision—and the closest neighbors—were half a mile away.

And the house itself was a sprawling monstrosity, a Victorian relic that shone in the fitful glow of her head-lights like a haunted mansion. A county patrol car was parked in front of the carriage house; their guard was restored. Before leaving Ralph's, Plato had called a number at the sheriff's office to let them know they would be home soon.

Just like last week, a guard would be posted here all night. The deputy climbed out of his car as Cal parked, following them inside and checking through the house before taking up a post in the living room. He would be there for half the night, touring the house every hour, and trade places with another deputy at four a.m.

But Cal knew that one deputy wasn't enough. Even with half a dozen men, Jimmy Dubrowski might somehow penetrate their net. After all, he had somehow managed to string all those Dr. Barbies up last night without so much as a bark from Ghost. The West Side Strangler was devastatingly clever and tricky; four years ago he had eluded the police for almost a month before they finally brought him in.

Climbing into bed beside her, Plato said exactly what she was thinking.

"It's a relief—going to Ralph's." He shook his head sadly. "I don't feel *safe* here any more. Even with that deputy parked downstairs."

"I know." Cal switched off the bedside lamp. Now that the decision was made, she couldn't wait to leave, to go somewhere safe. "If we pack tomorrow, I'll call the kennels first thing Monday morning. Hopefully, we'll be moved into Ralph's house by Tuesday."

"At least the drive will be shorter."

Cal nodded and closed her eyes, thinking about the Monastery—a place of safety with neighbors close by, an electronic security system, *and* a twenty-four-hour guard. It would be safe enough, she was sure.

As long as they got there in time.

CHAPTER 17

They spent all day Sunday doing laundry and packing
and calling friends to let them know about their temporary change of address. Homer was relieved but disappointed; he had been counting on spending Christmas
with Plato and Cal. Plato assured his cousin that Althea
was every bit as good a cook as Plato himself, and
promised to cadge Homer an invitation to Christmas dinner. Jeremy and Nina gallantly offered to put them up, but
the detective lived in a microscopic two-bedroom ranch
in Lakewood; he was still paying alimony to two of his
three ex-wives.

By Monday morning, Plato and Cal were almost set.
Their favorite kennel still hadn't gotten rid of all its
weekend guests, but they had openings for both Ghost
and Dante starting Tuesday. Plato and Cal would spend
one more night at Marley Manor, then head to Ralph and
Althea's after work Tuesday evening.

Walking into the hospital, Plato felt more relaxed than
he had in weeks. Riding the elevator up to the psych ward
on the eighth floor, he had almost put Tyler Cummings's
murder behind him.

But the atmosphere of the ward brought it home almost
instantly. Janice Hathaway, the head floor nurse, buzzed
him in but barely managed a mournful nod of greeting.

The other staff walked the halls and went about their duties mechanically, like the stunned survivors of an earthquake.

Even the patients were quieter: the hushed activity room felt more like a viewing area in a funeral home. A funeral home after an arson attack, perhaps; the dozen patients scattered around the room seemed to have burned a tobacco pyre in memory of Tyler Cummings. Two paranoid schizophrenics huddled over a checkerboard in one corner, blowing filterless Camels and quiet insults at each other. The old man with the knitting needles sucked on *two* cigarettes as he frowned at a half-finished bootie. A young woman on a bit too much Thorazine snored in an arm chair, her head lolling and a droopy-ashed cigarette dangling from her lower lip. Plato hurried over and crushed it into an ashtray.

About the only person who wasn't smoking was Francine Pryce. She was sitting in her old window spot, staring out at the parking lot and counting, constantly. And dry-washing her hands.

"Hi, Francine." Plato pulled up a chair beside her.

Slowly, she pulled her gaze away from the parking lot to peer at him. Her eyes were swollen and red with tears, her face and lips were chafed and chapped, and her mouth was cast in a permanent frown.

"Oh, *Plato*," she sobbed. Francine leaned over to put her head on his shoulder, whimpering into his white coat and mustering a fresh wave of tears. Plato awkwardly patted her shoulder, muttering soothing words of comfort until she pulled herself away again. She patted her eyes with a Kleenex, suddenly embarrassed. "I'm sorry."

"Don't be."

"I just can't believe he's *gone*." She shook her head,

bewildered. "After all these years. And everything he's done for me. It's so *awful*."

"I know."

"And I've been worried about *you*, too!" Francine bit her lip, her eyes shining with concern. "And your wife—are you all right?"

With the news of Tyler's death, someone had leaked the story of the Barbie dolls as well. In that morning's *Cleveland Post*, Otto Browning had written a sidebar about Cal, focusing on her key role in Jimmy's conviction and the repeated threats since his escape. After describing the Barbie doll incident in surprising detail, Browning hinted that the case was still unfolding, that "certain facts" hitherto unrevealed would shed a blinding light on the true story of the murders. Right.

"We're fine, Francine." He patted her arm. "Cal has a police guard and everything; she can't even *sneeze* without a sheriff's deputy offering her a tissue."

"Good." Her shoulders relaxed, and the hand-washing ritual paused.

"Anyway, I came here to talk about *you*." He smiled gently. "How're you doing?"

"Okay . . . I guess." She sighed. "Aaron and I had a wonderful talk last night. He telephoned me from Princeton—he's coming home on Friday."

"That's great news!" Plato cheered. "You think you'll be ready to leave by then?"

"I don't know." Francine shook her head. "I *thought* I would be heading home today."

"I know." He nodded. Before the weekend, Francine had been almost back to normal; Tyler's death had triggered a relapse. "I heard Tyler's partner came to visit."

"Ohh, that woman," Francine spat. She grimaced. "I

told her to go away, that I'd be seeing Dr. Bernstein from now on. You'll give me a referral?"

"Of course." Plato made himself a mental note. After Tyler Cummings, Vicki Bernstein was the best psychiatrist Riverside had to offer. He had planned to recommend Vicki anyway, but he was surprised that Joan Randall had made such an awful impression. "I'll be glad to; I'm sure Dr. Randall will be happy to transfer the records."

"Would you believe I used to see her almost as much as Tyler?" Francine grunted. "Before their divorce, I was just as happy to see Joan—I sometimes *preferred* her. But the break-up changed her. She seemed to become a totally different person."

"I didn't know her before the divorce," Plato admitted. Actually, he hadn't known her before *Saturday*. Not that he really knew her very well now. Not that he wanted to.

"She was a wonderful person. Warm and caring, just like Tyler. They were really very similar, very well-matched." She sighed. "But after the breakup, well . . ."

"I know," Plato murmured, uncomfortable discussing a colleague with a patient, no matter how much he disliked Joan.

"She's cold, and aloof, and distant. And *clinical*—God! Talking with her is like talking to a psychiatry textbook." Francine frowned at her raw, chapped hands. "Lord knows *I'm* not a picture of perfect mental health, but that lady's got some problems. Keeping all her emotions bottled up inside can't be healthy; it's a wonder she hasn't had a nervous breakdown or something."

"Well—"

"Oh, just *listen* to me!" She chuckled, embarrassed at her outburst. "Prattling on like the town gossip. But I really do think she needs help. 'Psychiatrist, heal thyself,' you know?"

Exactly, Plato thought. But he just nodded and turned the conversation back to Francine. Aside from the setback last weekend, she really was doing much better. She had already met Vicki Bernstein once before when she had covered for Tyler, so Francine wasn't too apprehensive about changing psychiatrists. And with her worries about her son Aaron largely resolved, Francine was back on the road to recovery.

But she was still grieving over Tyler's death.

"I really wish I could go to his funeral tomorrow."

"Why not?" Plato asked, surprised.

"Well, naturally, I—"

"It's not like you're *committed* here, Francine. You can leave any time you want, you know that." He made another mental note. "I'll write an order for them to set you free tomorrow afternoon, in plenty of time for Tyler's funeral. Okay?"

"Thank you." She sighed, relieved. "I really want to go—he's done so much for me. I owe it to him."

"Then it's settled." Just then, Plato's pager vibrated to life; he kept it on silent mode in the psych ward. He glanced at the number and nodded. "That's Hilda—my nurse. I've got to run, okay? I've got patients stacked up across the street."

"Then go right ahead." Francine leaned closer, and gripped his arm with surprising intensity. Gazing deep into his eyes, she murmured, "And you take *care* of yourself, okay? Promise?"

"I promise."

It was a promise Plato knew he would keep. Tomorrow evening, he and Cal would leave home to stay with the Jenssons. And they would be safe.

Unfortunately, Plato was dead wrong.

CHAPTER 18

By that evening, Riverside General was battening down for the storm. Many of the hospital's nine-to-fivers had left early: administrators, secretaries, and transcriptionists. The direct care workers—especially the nurses—were asked to stay late, work double shifts, or come in on their days off to cover for the inevitable absences.

The city itself was preparing as well: grocery stores were packed with last-minute squirrels, a battalion of salt trucks was rumbling out onto the highways, and television stations were running trailers updating the weather forecast every ten minutes. The storm system had pummeled Chicago early this morning; it was only gaining force and moisture on its trip across Lake Erie. Weather radar showed the blizzard as a giant white swirl engulfing half of the midwest. As one excited weatherman had put it, this system had it all: subzero temperatures, high winds, and the biggest snowfall Cleveland had seen in a decade or more.

By eight o'clock, the blizzard was parked just offshore of Sandusky and plodding slowly and relentlessly southeast. It would smash into Cleveland sometime tonight.

And naturally, it was Plato's turn for evening office hours. Already the snow was falling thick and heavy, choking the streets with drifts. Cal was sitting out in

Plato's empty waiting room, working on tomorrow's anatomy lecture and watching the snow pile up on the deserted streets outside. She was wearing a heavy wool sweater *and* her winter coat. The heating system in the old office building, never really adequate, couldn't keep up with the falling temperatures. Outside, the wind screamed across the waiting room windows and the snow fell sideways. Incredibly enough, a tiny drift had accumulated *inside* the window, sifting through a hairline crack in the metal frame.

Plato had sent his nurse and receptionist home at four o'clock. Only one of his patients had shown up since then, a woman who lived just three blocks away from the hospital. Plato would have canceled his evening and left early, but his last patient of the night—a 7:30 appointment—wasn't answering his telephone.

Acting as his receptionist, Cal had been telephoning every fifteen minutes since 6:00 without any luck. She had left a message on Abe Fensterman's answering machine, but Plato was adamant about staying until he was sure his patient wouldn't show. Abe was one of Plato's more demanding patients, she knew—a retired engineer from NASA's Lewis Research Center who had apparently wanted to be a doctor instead. Abe was pretty healthy for his age, but not healthy enough—he subscribed to the *New England Journal of Medicine* and the *Journal of the American Medical Association*, among others.

"Abe is positive proof that a little knowledge is a dangerous thing," Plato had told her. "He comes in at least twice a month, along with his *PDR* and a laundry list of vague problems."

It seemed that Abe was a classic "problem patient"— he had run through dozens of Cleveland-area doctors before finally settling in to roost in Plato's practice. If his doctor didn't give him a prescription, Abe felt slighted. But if he *did* get a scrip, Abe thumbed through his *PDR* and fretted over the possible side effects.

Cal prayed that the old man wouldn't show; if he did, Plato would be forced to spend an hour with him.

She crossed to the receptionist's desk and called Abe's number one last time. It was already 7:40; Abe was ten minutes late. If he didn't answer, she would make Plato leave anyway.

The telephone rang eight times, nine times, ten. Just as Cal was ready to hang up, Abe answered.

"Who is this?"

"This is Dr. Marley's office," Cal replied. "Mr. Fensterman?"

"Right."

"We've been trying to reach you, to cancel tonight's appointment."

"I just got back from the grocery," Abe replied. "Good God! Don't tell me Dr. Marley is seeing *patients* on a night like this!"

"Most of them canceled—"

"I should *think* so. Who would see a doctor on a night like this? I mean, I could see if you were maybe having a heart attack or something, but otherwise, it's far healthier to stay at home. Am I right?" He didn't wait for an answer. "Already the snow is piling up in my driveway, I almost got stuck on my way in, praise God I *didn't* or I'd have had a hell of a time getting that Lincoln Town Car out of the ditch, especially with my lumbago hurting like this; did I tell you about my lumbago—it hits me right down *here*—"

Thankfully, Abe paused to point to the spot, as though Cal could somehow see through the telephone.

"Mr. Fensterman," Cal said quickly, thankful to get a word in edgewise. Abe had an astounding ability to speak without pausing for breath; no wonder Plato had such trouble handling him. "I take it you're not coming to your appointment."

"Of course not—you think I'm *nuts*?" Abe chuckled. "I told that other lady at your office just the same thing— only a crazy man would want to be on the street in this kind of weather—am I right?—and naturally right after that I notice I don't have any bread so I run down to the corner grocery and *they're* ready to close up early—"

Cal frowned. "You left a message with the other receptionist?"

"You don't think I'd cancel without *telling* you folks, right?" He paused thoughtfully. "But you know something? Talking with that other girl—Tammy, I think her name is—I wonder if maybe God left her behind the door when he was passing out the brains. She doesn't seem any too bright. Am I right?"

Cal nodded. It was true. Tammy was a temporary fill-in while Plato's full-time receptionist had her baby. Cal hadn't been very impressed with Tammy's work habits; she seemed more interested in caring for her spectacular fingernails than answering the telephone. "Thanks, Mr. Fensterman."

"Tell that Dr. Marley you should be sent home, if he knows what's good for you. Am I right?"

"You're right." Cal grinned. "I'll tell him."

But before she told him, Cal walked around to the receptionist's desk to look for the missing message. It was empty except for three bottles of nail polish, a hairbrush and compact, and a tattered copy of *Love's Deepest Hunger*; its cover featured a Fabio lookalike ravaging a Frederick's of Hollywood model on the deck of a burning frigate. Cal smiled and shook her head, flipping through the novel. The pages were dog-eared and highlighted and underlined; *that* was how Tammy spent her time when she wasn't answering the phone. One of the pages was marked with a pink slip of paper. Cal snatched it out and groaned.

It was a telephone message form: ABE FENSTERMAN CANCELING 7:30 APPT.

Cal took a deep breath and sighed. If only they had known, they could have left at six o'clock; she and Plato would be safely home by now. The way things were looking outside, they'd be lucky to get home at all tonight.

"All set?" Plato asked from the doorway. "I guess Abe isn't going to make it."

"You guessed right." Cal waved the slip of paper. "Tammy could have told you that at four o'clock, if she had bothered."

He studied the form and grimaced. "I need a new receptionist."

"No kidding."

"Hey," he said, snapping his fingers. "I wonder if Marianne would want to transfer."

"Marianne?" she asked blankly.

"Tyler's receptionist." He frowned thoughtfully. "She seemed pretty competent—and I bet Joan's not going to keep her."

"No *way*."

"What?"

"With a girl that pretty around, you'd never get any work done."

"I've already *got* a girl that pretty." He slipped his arm across her shoulders. "Prettier."

He kissed her forehead, her cheek, the tip of her nose, then moved down to her neck.

"Right." She giggled. "And look how much work you're getting done now."

"Workday's over, kid."

"I know. And we'd better get moving." She pointed at the window: the snow was coming down so hard that the hospital across the street had disappeared in a pall of white. "Or we're not going to make it home."

"I know." He picked up Tammy's telephone. "Hang on—I'll call the sheriff's office."

It had become a nightly ritual: telephoning a number at the county offices, telling the dispatcher they were heading home and asking them to send the guard along. With the manhunt still going on, the sheriff couldn't afford enough deputies to watch the Marley house around-the-clock.

He hung up a minute later, frowning.

"What's wrong?" Cal asked.

"They're shorthanded tonight," Plato replied. "Too many accidents around the county. Plus, one of the deputies crashed his *own* car on the way in. Mike—our favorite guard."

Mike Rawlings had served as their protection on six of the seven nights their house was under guard.

Cal gasped. "Is he okay?"

"Yeah—he just banged his head on the steering wheel. He's over at Metro getting stitched up." Plato shook his head. "But he's going to be late."

"He shouldn't come at *all!*" Cal rushed to the telephone. "Here—give me their number."

After a short but intense argument, she was patched in to the lieutenant on duty. And after a longer discussion, Cal won her case: once he was stitched up, Mike Rawlings would be sent home. Another deputy would be sent to their house later this evening, once the weather situation was under control.

"The weather situation may not be under control until *tomorrow* night," Plato pointed out.

Cal nodded. "But we couldn't very well have Mike coming tonight, with stitches in his head. He should be home, resting."

"I know." He gathered his briefcase and coat and looked around the office one last time before switching off the lights and locking up. "Besides—if the cops can't get to us, then neither can Jimmy."

"That's what I love about you." Cal grinned and hugged his arm. "You're always looking on the bright side."

But the storm wasn't as bad as they had expected—at least, not yet. The interstate was snow covered but still passable, and wrecks and spin-outs only popped up every half-mile or so. Plato followed a friendly salt truck all the way from the center of town to Brecksville, just an exit shy of their own. The salt was probably eating their paint and underbody, but looks were no longer an issue with the old, crumbling Corsica.

County Road 142 was a different story. The snow was muffler-deep already, and drifted even higher in spots. Plato alternately gunned the engine, spun the wheel, and tapped the brakes to keep the car on an even keel. They didn't see a single other car on the road; even the *tracks* were buried. That was the trickiest part—plowing blind through the virgin snow, trying to gauge distances from telephone poles and street signs and reflectors in order to avoid the ditches close at hand on either side.

But they finally made it. The lights of home beckoned through the trees as Plato spun the wheel, keeping his momentum and gunning the car up the driveway. They got stuck only once, near the little bridge over the creek, but Plato scrambled out to push them free as Cal downshifted and rocked and gunned the car loose. He trotted behind the car as Cal plowed through the rest of the driveway, sliding to a stop just inches from the carriage house door.

"We *did* it!" he exclaimed as she climbed out.

Only then did Cal realize how tense she was, how firmly she had been gripping the door handle and the dash as Plato piloted the car home. Her arms were sore, and her back ached from sitting up in that watchful, nervous position—pressing her nose against the dash to help direct him toward the center of the unplowed roads.

But Cal couldn't pause to stretch; a bitter cold wind shrieked through the trees, bombarding her with ice and snow. It was like sticking your face in the outlet of a snowblower. She and Plato dashed up to the shelter of the porch and tumbled inside, slamming the door and shutting out the snow and the cold and the howling wind.

"I hope the roads are better tomorrow," she said with a weary sigh.

"Who cares?" He shrugged. One side of Plato was plastered with snow—half of his beard, half of his coat, one leg of his pants. The other side was perfectly clean and dry. He looked like a powdered doughnut that had only been dipped on one side. "I doubt if we'll make it to work anyway—the worst of the storm still hasn't hit yet."

He pulled his coat off and frowned at the pattern.

"A day off." Cal shook her jacket over the mat and tossed it onto a chair. "Just like the snow days we used to have in school."

Plato smiled wistfully. "Sleeping in."

"Cross-country skiing."

"Hot chocolate by a nice warm fire."

Cal nodded; it was almost enough to make her forget Jimmy Dubrowski. Almost, but not quite. Having seen the roads, she was pretty sure that their guard wouldn't make it tonight. But tomorrow—first thing—they would set out for the kennel and for the Jenssons' house. She didn't want to stay here without protection.

They gave the house a quick once-over, checking the doors and windows, prowling through the hallways and bedrooms, the basement and attic, the kitchen and living room and gazing out at the courtyard. Ghost followed them around the house with a puzzled frown; he seemed to think that they were marking territory, but they never actually *did* anything. Dante took his owners' eccentric behavior in stride; the flame-orange tabby just napped on the landing, watching the others from the corner of one slitted eye as they moved from room to room. All the while, Cal held the cordless phone in her hand, one finger on the 9 key—their speed-dial code for the police.

But she and Plato found no signs of tampering, no indications that the West Side Strangler had come to call. Feeling safer, they changed clothes and headed downstairs to start making dinner. Perry Como sang "The Twelve Days of Christmas" from the portable CD player.

"See?" Plato asked finally. "We're perfectly safe. Everything's just fine."

"As long as the power doesn't go out," Cal replied.

And oddly enough, at that precise moment, it did.

The lights flickered once, twice, then gave it up as a lost cause. The furnace motor wound down to an ominous and very cold silence. The refrigerator stopped humming, and Perry Como suddenly lost his voice.

"Thanks, Cal." Plato's voice was a sour note in the darkness.

"It wasn't *my* fault." She felt her way blindly across the kitchen, to the magnet flashlight stuck to the fridge, then switched it on. "Anyway, who needs electricity? We've got the generator, remember?"

Plato nodded. They had bought the gas generator last summer, after a run of nasty thunderstorms knocked their power out three times in four days. And of course, the same storms that killed their electricity usually brought enough rain to flood the basement. The generator was powerful enough to run both sump pumps at once *and* cook a tasty microwave meal.

"I'll get it started."

A few minutes later, Cal heard the noisy rumble of the Honda generator out in the garage; the machine was awfully convenient, but its powerful engine sounded like a jackhammer. Even inside the house, the noise shook windows and rattled walls.

But at least they had power. Plato came back inside, bearing the thick orange electrical cable; minutes later, Cal was microwaving yesterday's chicken parmesan and spaghetti while Plato dug up the space heater and a few table lamps. They even had a special cable hooked up to the well pump so they wouldn't run out of water.

"It's already getting cold in here," he noted as he plugged the heater into the extension cord. "This won't be nearly enough."

Cal nodded. The old manor house featured aluminum-cased windows, installed sometime back in the '50s, when they were all the rage. They were about as effective against drafts and moisture as pieces of waxed paper. Already, their interiors were blanketed with thick coats of frost.

And the brave little space heater put out just a few

thousand BTU—barely enough to warm a good-sized closet in this blizzard.

Cal shivered. "We'd better start the fires."

Plato nodded. Along with the fireplace in the living room, they had just installed a wood-burning stove in the kitchen. The generator wasn't powerful enough to run the furnace; the stove and fireplace were a cheaper solution to the inevitable power outages.

And even during the blizzard, the fires and space heater would keep this corner of the house passably warm. By the time the Marleys sat down to their dimly lit repast, warm log fires were crackling in the hearth and the stove, the space heater glowed toasty red, and the kitchen and living room were positively cozy.

"I just hope we have enough gas," Cal fretted.

"No problem." Plato dug into his chicken with gusto: the mozzarella cheese was just barely melted, the sauce was rich and savory, and they had even cracked a bottle of Merlot to ward off the winter chill. "We've got two five-gallon tanks—enough to keep us going for a couple of days."

"I hope we won't be here *that* long."

They finished their meal and Plato did the dishes while Cal unrolled the futon in front of the fireplace. Dante and Ghost were curled up side-by-side on the brick apron; old grudges and rivalries were forgotten in the interests of warmth. The Christmas tree was unlit, of course; Cal wished they could turn it on one last time before they left. And once again, she felt a momentary twinge of bitterness, of righteous anger at being forced out of her home by a serial killer.

But thinking of Tyler Cummings, she was suddenly ashamed of her feelings. Jimmy Dubrowski had caused others a lot more pain than just the inconvenience of not being home for the holidays.

Cal couldn't help picturing that look on Tyler's face as they cut him down, the horrible mask of a strangling victim. And those others four years ago, the unlucky casualties of a very sick man. Cal was glad the jury hadn't bought the insanity plea at the trial. Even if the West Side Strangler *was* insane, irrational, should that vindicate him from criminal responsibility?

Ignorance of the law wasn't a valid defense for *rational* people, was it?

Cal realized she was letting her personal feelings blur her professional judgment, and her ethical beliefs. But she couldn't help it. She couldn't help wondering where Jimmy was, hoping that the West Side Strangler was stuck outside right now. Freezing to death in the middle of the blizzard.

It would serve him right.

CHAPTER 19

The rack of dinner trays smelled like heaven.

Standing in the deserted stairwell just outside the hospital kitchen, Jimmy Dubrowski peered through a crack in the doorway and took a deep breath, trying to guess what treasures were beckoning from the steel-covered plates. Salisbury steak, it smelled like. With rich, dark gravy flowing over piles of mashed potatoes. And lima beans, maybe—Jimmy *loved* lima beans, especially with lots of butter and salt. And bread, and butter, and *coffee!* And chocolate cake for desert, with chocolate frosting.

Yup, you betcher!

If he was lucky. Yesterday at lunch, the elevator doors at the end of the hall had opened just as Jimmy was reaching for a tray. He'd been forced to grab one at random—and he ended up with a diabetic's tray—postoperative. Clear chicken broth, no salt, unsweetened grapefruit juice, and a couple of Saltine crackers.

Awful. Jimmy had done the poor guy a *favor* by stealing his tray.

Out in the corridor, the cafeteria attendant pushed the cart toward the elevator, and Jimmy heaved a disappointed sigh. Only once a day at most was any cart unguarded long enough for Jimmy to steal a tray. Some attendants left their charges in the hall while they snuck off for a quick smoke, while others hurried back into the kitchen for a missing dish or a piece of paperwork.

But on some days, the meal carts were never left alone for a single instant.

"It's just as well," Mrs. Abernathy pointed out. "If too many trays went missing, they'd catch you for sure."

"They'll catch him for sure anyway," Fenton muttered sullenly. "It's just a matter of time."

It made no difference, Jimmy reflected. It would be just a matter of time before he starved to death. Living on just one food tray a day, he was wasting away to nothing. After almost two weeks of hiding out at Riverside, the triple-XL scrubs hung slack and baggy on his frame, but he was way too tall for double-XLs. His round belly was melting away to nothing, and the muscles of his once-brawny shoulders were as loose and flimsy as tired old rubber bands.

He was ready to turn himself in, just for a decent meal.

"You won't *have* to turn yourself in," Fenton sneered. "They'll just track you down by your scent."

"It's true, dear." Mrs. Abernathy sighed. "You really could use a shower."

"He could use a *fumigation*."

They were right. Jimmy's home away from home lacked warm water; the best he could do was rinse his grimy face once or twice a day. But he wouldn't be here much longer. No matter what happened, this was his last night at Riverside General.

"That's the spirit," Fenton said. "Once you get your hands on that lady doctor—"

He broke off as another tray clattered through the double doors. Even Fenton was hungry now, easily distracted by the prospect of a decent meal.

And the prospects were good. This cafeteria attendant

was a smoker; Jimmy knew that from past experience. A chain-smoker, it looked like; his fingers were stained yellow and his hands shook as he checked up and down the corridor, then rushed toward the men's room. The door squealed open and closed again.

Jimmy bounded out of his hiding place and onto the cart like a wolf taking down a stray lamb. He had made his decision—if tonight was his last night at Riverside, he'd steal *two* trays, and to hell with the consequences.

"Damn right," Fenton declared. "Damn straight. And you'll need your energy, if you're going to—"

"I must agree with Fenton," Mrs. Abernathy interrupted. "I'm concerned about your nutrition, sweetheart . . ."

But Jimmy wasn't listening. He was pulling trays and lifting lids—he wasn't going to get stuck with another sugarless, salt-free diabetic meal. The pickings were disappointing, though—soup, salad, some kind of weird soufflé thing, eggs—for *dinner?*—fish . . .

Aha! Jackpot!

Jimmy snatched a tray filled with Salisbury steak *and* chocolate cake and set it on the floor, then sifted through the other racks. Time was running out; the attendant was probably down to his last few puffs and someone else was bound to appear with the next cart at any minute. Chili . . . Brussels sprouts . . . fried chicken . . . a *hamburger!* Jimmy pulled that tray and snatched a chicken breast off the other one for good measure, stacking his prizes and hefting them toward his hiding place.

And just then, the men's room door squealed open. Jimmy dashed for his stairwell and crashed through the doorway. Luckily, he had been smart enough to jam a cigarette butt in the striker, so the bolt hadn't engaged.

Jimmy slid inside, setting the trays on the floor and swinging the door back to the jamb.

Heart pounding, he squinted back through the crack. The attendant was trotting up the hall toward his door—he must have seen him! In just seconds, he would make it to the stairwell. What was better—to run, or to wait and confront the attendant?

"Wait here," Fenton advised confidently. "You can take him, easy. You'll never get away, otherwise."

"Violence never solved anything," Mrs. Abernathy scolded.

The attendant was just a few strides away. Jimmy eased back from the door and held his breath, waiting. If he caught the guy with a quick one on the chin, maybe he could knock him out—just like the cop last week.

The attendant paused just outside the door, planted one hand on it, and paused.

Out in the hallway, the kitchen's swing doors had opened again. Another cart rattled through, crashing into the first. Somebody cursed.

"What the hell are you *doing*, Lucas? Taking another butt break?"

The answer was indignant, defensive. "I—I had to hit the john, that's all."

Lucas moved away from the door and hurried back to his cart. Seconds later, Jimmy heard it rattling up the hall, accompanied by the second. Lucas and the other attendant were arguing about his smoking habits.

Jimmy breathed a sigh of relief.

"He got lucky again," Fenton grumbled. "I can't *believe* his luck."

Carefully balancing his treasure, Jimmy took the stairs down to Riverside's sub-basement. After getting the food, this part of his journey was the most dangerous; the corridor led to the hospital's various tunnels and was pretty well-traveled at shift changes. But it tended to be deserted around dinnertime.

Like that time last week, when he had almost caught Dr. Marley. Jimmy still couldn't believe that little lady got away; she seemed to know the sub-basement even better than Jimmy did. She was one smart girl, that was for sure.

"Smart enough to put you in prison," Fenton jeered. "But she won't be smart enough to get away again. And then . . ." He chortled gleefully. "You'll have her. I just can't wait until we—"

"That's enough," Mrs. Abernathy huffed. "We've been through this before. Jimmy's not going to harm her."

"Just like he didn't *harm* Dr. Cummings?" Fenton challenged.

Mrs. Abernathy didn't have an answer for that.

Grateful for the silence in his head, Jimmy opened the stairwell door and peered down the sub-basement corridor. The coast was clear; he dashed up the hall and through another door, into a gloomy stairwell that might not have been used for years before Jimmy came. Hardly anyone seemed to know about it, not even the security guards, since it was never locked. The steps led down half a flight, discharging into a gloomy tunnel lit only by a pair of window-wells on either end. This late in the evening, the only light came from the fitful glow of streetlamps in the doctors' parking lot overhead. And tonight, even that light was gone; the windows were buried under a thick blanket of snow.

Jimmy blundered into the wall of the tunnel once or twice, dishes and silverware clattering in the darkness. But he finally made it—into the basement of an abandoned apartment building across the street from the hos-

pital. The building hadn't been used in years; the old furniture inside was covered with a thick coating of dust, the
rooms were heated with ancient, cantankerous steam ra-
diators, and there wasn't any hot water in the taps.

Jimmy guessed the building was waiting to be torn
down. It was probably an old dorm for nurses or medical
students, maybe even condemned, but it suited him just
fine. He panted up five flights of stairs to the top floor—
his penthouse suite—then walked down the hall to the
corner dorm room. He turned up the steam, set his tray on
the old desk, and slumped into the bottom bunk.

Jimmy was finally home.

Ten minutes later, he finished the very best meal of his
life. Salisbury steak and a hamburger, chicken and succo-
tash and french fries, milk and juice and coffee, and *two*
slices of chocolate cake. And *butter*—four pats of real
butter! Jimmy might have gobbled it down even faster if
only he had his medicine. The Haldol and Cogentin
worked together to fix those funny movements—the ones
that scared people so. Things like smacking his lips and
wiggling his tongue around and making weird faces; he
couldn't help it, but lots of folks thought Jimmy did it on
purpose.

It didn't matter here, of course; there was nobody
around to complain. But all those funny wiggles and
twitches sure made it hard to get the food in his mouth
and chew. Jimmy had scratched his face more than once
with the fork—gashing his chin and his left cheek and almost poking his eye out.

But finally, he was finished.

And not a minute too soon. Sitting back in his chair
with a contented belch, Jimmy heard footfalls echoing on
the stairs of the empty dormitory.

"You here, Jimmy?" The voice was a soft, conspiratorial whisper. "It's me. Stan."

Jimmy pushed his tray away and walked to the door. Stan Grigsby was shuffling up the corridor, a vapid smile plastered on his face. The same smile he had been wearing last Thursday, when he had blundered on Jimmy's hiding place.

"Anybody see you?" Jimmy asked.

"Naw." Stan sniffed disdainfully. "I took that back stairwell, just like you told me to."

"Great. Fine, fine, Valentine."

"It's all right, Jimmy? Isn't it?"

"Sure, Stan, you betcher." Jimmy led him back to the dorm room and slumped onto his bunk. "Come in, come in, let the games begin."

Stan Grigsby followed him inside and sat on the chair. He studied the wreckage of Jimmy's meal and whistled. "Been eating, huh?"

"No—I just brought the dirty dishes up here to look at."

Stan's thick eyebrows narrowed in a frown, then the dull smile returned. "Aww—you're just joshing me, Jimmy. Hur—hur—*hee*. You shouldn't ought to do that."

"Shouldn't do that, shouldn't, shouldn't," Jimmy echoed. He was doing that a lot lately—couldn't help it— but Stan never seemed to notice. Stan Grigsby was dumber than a box of rocks. He was a courier and mail clerk at Riverside General, but Jimmy was amazed that he could even handle that job, since he could barely read.

Which must have explained why Stan hadn't screamed for security the first time they met. Anybody who read a newspaper—or saw a television, for that matter—knew about Jimmy Dubrowski. His picture had made the front page of the *Plain Dealer* twice in the last two weeks. On the other hand, they had used the photo from Jimmy's first arrest, back when his head was shaved, so maybe it wasn't so surprising that Stan didn't recognize him.

Thank goodness for that. It all happened right after Jimmy had stolen last Thursday's dinner tray. He had gone down to the basement, taken the tunnel over to the dorm, and climbed all the way up to his room without realizing that he'd been followed.

Stan Grigsby had popped up at his door just as he sat down to dinner, wearing that friendly, clueless smile.

"So you snitch food sometimes too, huh?" Stan had asked.

Jimmy learned that he wasn't the only one who snuck food trays up to the dormitory. Stan Grigsby had been doing it for years. He just assumed that Jimmy was another hungry Riverside employee.

Taking advantage of his surgical scrubs, Jimmy played along, telling his new friend that he was an orderly in Riverside's OR. Stan had bought the story hook, line, and sinker, even though Jimmy was starting to sport a heavy beard and smelled like something you might fish out of Lake Erie. Stan was no supermodel himself, with a shiny bald head, Coke-bottle glasses and a droopy mustache you could strain soup with. But at least he didn't smell.

And he was awfully nice to Jimmy. Every night since last Thursday, Stan had snuck away during his breaks to visit Jimmy. And he always brought along some little treat he'd picked up during his mail rounds—like the newspaper from the hospital lounge, or Christmas candy from the nurses' stations, or a couple of cans of Pepsi from one of the vending machines.

Today, he had a special treat: two Snickers bars and a *PC Computing* magazine.

"I snitched the magazine from the Cardiology waiting

room," Stan confessed. He smiled hopefully. "You said you're going to computer school, so . . ."

Jimmy had told him that he was studying programming at Cleveland State. It was half-true; technically, he was still on the student rolls there. Of course, his studies had ended four years ago.

"Thanks, Stan. That's great, great, great. Great, great, appreciate."

He cradled the magazine in his hand and took one of the Snickers bars. They ate them together and Stan told him all about his day—the secretary up in Administration he had a crush on, the way his boss kept ragging on him all the time, the dollar he had found in an elevator that evening.

"Here, Jimmy. I want you to have it."

"Have, it, have it, have it." Jimmy shook his head. "No way, nope."

"*Really.*" He tucked the bill into the pocket of Jimmy's scrub shirt. "It's okay."

"Thanks." Jimmy shook his head, embarrassed. And wishing he didn't have *another* favor to ask—a really big one. But he had to try. "Stan, I've kind of got a problem. I'm in a real fix. Trouble, trouble, on the double."

"Trouble, Jimmy?" Stan frowned anxiously. "Is there anything I can do?"

"See, I don't have a car; I always just hop the bus to work every day . . ." He told Stan the whole story, the one he'd cooked up this afternoon. How his mother lived in Sagamore Hills and her car had broken down, and how she had a doctor's appointment tomorrow morning. He could fix it, if only he had a way to get to Mom's house . . .

"No problemo, Jimmy old pal." Stan slapped him on the back and chuckled. "I'll just take you after my shift is over. I live right out that way myself. Now you'll finally get to see the Bronco—hur—hur—*hee.*"

Aside from the secretary in Administration—who ran a distant second—Stan's Bronco was his only true passion in life. He had saved his money for years and bought it cash down, then put all kinds of fancy gadgets and trim on it—a hood scoop, mag wheels, rally trim, and fog lights. He carried a picture of it in his wallet; he'd shown Jimmy the photo five minutes after they met. The jacked-up Bronco looked like a drag racer on steroids.

"Thanks, thanks, thanks." Jimmy smiled. "I can't *wait* to see it. Bucking Bronco, you betcher."

"Bullshit," Fenton growled in his ear. "You don't give a damn about his car, or about him. Maybe you should just *kill* him and *take* his car. What's the difference?"

"Shut *up!*" Jimmy hissed.

"What's that?" Stan asked.

"Nothing." Jimmy shook his head back and forth, back and forth. He was starting to get nervous, starting to worry that he'd screw this up. He had to ignore the voices while Stan was here, stay in control, in control.

"You're going to blow it," Fenton whispered.

"You'll be caught," Deirdre Swanson murmured in her sweet voice. "They'll make you pay."

"They'll *hang* you," Luella Huckleby cackled.

"Just like your father," Jerry Tammerly added.

"*No!*" Jimmy hissed, covering his ears.

"You okay?" Stan asked, touching his arm.

"Okay, okay, okay." Jimmy squeezed his eyes shut; he was blowing it. Stan was going to spill the beans, and he'd be caught. Tonight. "Just a headache. Headache, backache, stomachache, piece of cake."

"Ate too much, huh?" Stan patted his shoulder sympathetically. "Happens to me sometimes, too."

To Jimmy's relief, Stan finally had to get back to work.

And late that night—after Stan's three-to-eleven shift—Jimmy donned the coat he had borrowed from an employee locker and met the black Bronco outside the hospital's service entrance. Thankfully, the voices had left him for now. Jimmy made all the right admiring noises, fawning over the glistening new paint job— "Twelve hundred *bucks!*"—the black leather interior, and the fuzzy green dice hanging from the mirror.

"For good luck," Stan had told him. "In case I ever get Cindy in here."

They rode down to Sagamore Hills with Stan prattling all the way about carburetors and ground clearance and brake pads and mud tires. The roads were all but deserted—snow-covered and icy and almost impassable. But the big jacked-up Bronco was like a tank, plowing through drifts and across ice, rolling rock steady through the squalls and buffeting wind. Jimmy directed his friend up County Road 142, then into a generic subdivision, a street, and finally a house.

"Stop here," he said, pointing. "No—don't pull in. Mom doesn't sleep too well; I don't want to wake her up."

"Then you don't have to ask me inside," Stan whispered.

Jimmy smiled. He certainly hadn't planned to ask his friend inside, since he didn't have the slightest idea who lived there. He opened the door and swung a leg out when Stan spoke. The mail clerk's voice was quiet—and not just because he was afraid of waking Jimmy's nonexistent mom.

"You don't really work at Riverside, do you?"

Jimmy turned and peered back inside the car. Stan's face was filled with curiosity—and concern.

"*Kill* him!" Fenton screamed. "*Now!*"

"No," Jimmy finally replied. "I don't work there."

"I didn't think so." Stan looked away, staring at his fuzzy green dice, then continued. "I think I saw your picture in the paper today."

Jimmy gasped. Inside his head, alarm bells were clanging.

"*Do it!*" Fenton cried.

Jimmy pictured it happening—jumping across the seats and throttling his friend. Stan was a weakling; it would be over in an instant. At this hour, in this sleepy neighborhood, nobody would see.

"And then you'll have a car," Fenton pointed out helpfully.

"They say you killed that nice head shrinker from the hospital." Stan frowned thoughtfully. "Did you?"

"Yes," Deirdre Swanson murmured.

"Yes," Luella Huckleby and Jerry Tammerly echoed.

"No," Jimmy replied. "I didn't."

"*Liar!*" Fenton yelled.

Jimmy winced, sure that his friend must have heard Fenton's voice, must have guessed the truth. But Stan Grigsby's face lit up with a wide and knowing smile. Maybe he wasn't quite as dumb as a box of rocks.

But his next statement wasn't any too bright.

"I didn't think you did. But I just wanted to be sure."

He left Jimmy standing on the curb, swung the car around in a neighbor's driveway, and sped past with a wave and a wise smile.

Once his friend was out of sight, Jimmy pulled up the hood of his borrowed coat, buried his chin under the lapel, and glanced up the street. The wind and snow whipped his face like a thousand icicles. In seconds, his skin was chapped and raw. He was grateful for his beard now, and for the borrowed coat; he wondered if it had goose down inside. Goose down was supposed to be really warm; Jimmy's mom had made him a goose-down blanket once, when he was a little kid. Not long after Dad died. He loved that goose-down blanket; it had kept him warm when the shivers came, when the memories had threatened to drag him under . . .

But mostly, he was wondering about Stan's words, playing them over and over again in his head. And thinking.

He kept wondering about them as he ducked his head into the wind, plodded down the street and across the deserted county road, and headed cross-country toward the isolated mansion in the woods.

CHAPTER 20

"Plato." The voice on the telephone was annoyingly insistent. "You've got to get out of there."

Plato rubbed sleep from his bleary eyes and tried to listen, to think, to wake *up*. What was he doing here, on a futon sofa, in the middle of the living room?

God, but it was *cold!*

And then Plato remembered. The snowstorm—the *blizzard*. Coming home and having the power knocked out. Starting the generator and lighting the fire, having dinner by lamplight. Falling asleep on the futon with Cal, and promising he would toss a couple of logs on the fire every hour.

Apparently, he hadn't. The fire had burned down to a sullen pole of embers. Plato glanced at his watch. One a.m.

"Plato?" The voice in the receiver was Jeremy's. The detective was wide awake and hyper-alert, as usual. "Did you catch a *single* thing I said?"

"Not really." Plato scratched his head sleepily. All he could remember was the telephone jangling him out of a deep dream. A nightmare about giant alarm clocks filling the streets outside Riverside General, pealing and clanging until the hospital itself trembled, walls crumbling and ceilings tumbling to the sound of the horrible bells.

Bells that turned into a telephone. A telephone on an end table beside the futon, right next to Plato's ear.

"We got a call," Jeremy repeated patiently. "From the Sagamore Hills cops. Someone in your neighborhood says they saw Jimmy Dubrowski getting dropped off— half an hour ago."

"But we don't *have* a neighborhood—"

"That subdivision across Route 142." The detective brooked no interruptions. "The caller was hoping to claim the reward."

Plato nodded. The victims' families had put up ten thousand dollars for information leading to the West Side Strangler's re-arrest.

"Somebody dropped him off; a guy in a black Ford Bronco," Jeremy continued. "He let him off right outside the caller's house; I doubt if the driver knew it was Jimmy."

Beside him, Cal was starting to stir.

"So Jimmy Dubrowski broke into somebody's *house?*" Plato frowned; this wasn't making any sense. "Why don't you guys just arrest him?"

Cal sat up quickly, watching Plato with wide-eyed apprehension.

"We *can't.* That's what I'm trying to *tell* you." Jeremy's voice was beyond exasperation; he was pleading now. "Dubrowski didn't break in—he just walked away down the street, into the snow. Toward 142—toward *your house*."

"Oh, shit."

"All three Sagamore Hills patrol cars are handling accident scenes; they'll never get there in time."

Plato wasn't surprised. Sagamore Hills was a sleepy little town with a tiny police force; the blizzard probably had them swamped.

"And *we* sure can't get someone down there fast enough," the detective continued. "You've got to get out of there, *right now*."

Ten minutes later, they were dressed and ready to go. Plato had switched off the generator, locked up the house and slung the suitcases into the car while Cal bundled Dante into his carrier. They were taking the Acura this time; it was a little heavier, far more reliable, and much easier to drive in deep snow. Ghost would ride in the car without a carrier; the Australian shepherd had saved Plato's life once before, and he might very well get another chance tonight.

Plato started the Acura and opened the garage doors while Cal hustled the animals out to the car. Ghost got loose, barking and prancing around in the snowdrifts at Plato's feet before finally allowing himself to be rounded up. The Aussie *loved* playing in the snow, but this wasn't really the time.

Plato pulled the car out of the garage and dragged the doors shut behind them, then scrambled back in. The Acura had just been tuned up; it purred like a kitten. With Ghost glaring over their shoulders and Dante curled up in his cat carrier, Plato shifted into low gear and stepped on the gas. The Acura bounded forward, then almost stalled as it slammed into a knee-deep snow drift just beyond the turnaround.

Plato revved the engine. The wheels spun and finally bit into the snow, jerking the car forward again. Beyond the drift, the snow wasn't quite so deep, but the car still bottomed out every few yards. The powder was piled in random wind-carved heaps, like sandbars at low tide. Plato had to drive faster than he wanted, just to keep the low-slung Acura from getting hung up on a snowbar. It was a harrowing ride, threading the car through the trees at high speed, spinning the wheel and pumping the brakes long before the turns, frantically guessing at the boundaries of the driveway based on dim memories of summer days and a clear yard.

The driveway was a full quarter of a mile long; the little stone bridge over the creek marked the halfway point. It was also the lowest spot on the property and so most likely to drift; Plato and Cal had gotten stuck there dozens of times in winters past. This year, it might just be impassable—the snow piles could be hip deep. Their only hope was the pair of reflectors Plato had planted last fall.

He was waiting for it, planning his strategy of attack long before they reached the creek: Plato would spin the wheel hard left, wait until the car began to skid, then gun the engine. If he timed it just right, their momentum would carry the Acura sideways toward the foot of the bridge. Then the wheels would bite and push them into the turn and over the bridge. After that, it was clear sailing—a straight shot up a little hill, to the road and safety.

It almost worked.

Plato was ready when the bridge finally hove into view. Or, rather, when the *reflectors* hove into view; the creek was buried and the little stone bridge was just a vague lump in the snow. Even the reflectors, three feet tall, were nearly buried: just the top halves of their faces gleamed above the snow. Another half hour and they would have been gone.

Plato did it just like he had planned—spinning the wheel, timing his skid for the gap in the reflectors like a slalom skier threading a gate, gunning the engine and aiming the car at the lump in the snow. A second later the tires gripped, the car sprang forward and they were on the bridge. Incredibly, the entire *hood* was buried under the snow, shouldering the drift aside like a snowplow as their momentum carried them forward and off the bridge.

They hit the little hill on the other side with plenty of speed; Plato started to relax as the Acura dug its way up to the crest.

But he hadn't counted on the *next* drift—the one piled up on the tiny hill. Climbing up on the leeward side, they slammed into another huge mound of snow even deeper than the one beside the bridge.

They just didn't have enough speed. The car valiantly nosed into the drift, thrust half of it aside, and finally stuck tight. Plato stomped on the gas pedal but the Acura only spun its wheels, wedging itself in more firmly. He shifted into reverse, rocking back for an instant and then surging ahead again.

But the snow only packed itself more tightly.

"We'll have to shovel out," Cal murmured.

Her voice sounded odd. Plato glanced over to see her clutching the trusty Eastman T-ball bat in her mittened hands. Shoveling snow was the farthest thing from Cal's mind. Her eyes were brimming with tears, but she was bravely fighting to stay composed.

"It's okay, Cally." He reached over and squeezed her shoulder. "We'll still make it."

She nodded.

"I've got a plan," Plato told her, reaching in the back seat for the shovel—and his hat and gloves. He was already wearing a ski bib and down jacket, along with a pair of tall hiking boots and "gaiters," the nylon calf-sheaths that kept deep snow from falling into his boots.

"I'll back us down to the bottom of the hill," he continued, gesturing toward the little bridge behind them. The Acura had cleared a fair-sized trail; he wasn't worried about getting stuck there. "Then I'll come up here and shovel some of the snow clear, just enough for us to get through. You'll drive, and I'll help push us up the hill."

"I'll dig too," she amended, pointing to an extra shovel in the back seat. "You can't do much with that arm."

And so, just a few minutes later, Cal was in the driver's seat waiting to start. They had shoveled a decent-sized clearing at the top of the hill, and Plato was poised at the back of the car with his shoulder to the trunk. He would have a hard time pushing with his casted arm, but a stout tree just behind him offered plenty of leverage. Farther up the hill, another would do the same.

"Okay," he shouted. "Fire it up."

Cal stepped on the gas and Plato pushed. After their two passes over the driveway here—up and down the hill—the snow was packed and slick. The Acura's tires spun, blasting Plato's face with a spray of ice and snow. But the car made steady progress, slowly climbing the little hill as Plato heaved. It finally rolled away on its own, gaining speed as it climbed the hill. He trotted ahead, darting up to the next tree and waiting for the Acura to pass.

As the car jittered and chugged up the hill beside him, Plato braced himself against the tree trunk, reached for the rear bumper, and shoved. The Acura rammed the half-cleared drift and slowed, but kept moving. They were going to make it! He ran up a little farther, wedging himself between yet another tree and the Acura's rear bumper, and heaving with all his might.

But the car stuck fast once again, jamming hard into the drift. Worse yet, the Acura settled backwards before Plato could move. It lurched downhill, trapping his leg between the bumper and the tree, a tall maple with a stout and unyielding trunk.

"Cally!" he cried desperately. "Hit the gas—I'm *stuck!*"

Plato groaned, more from exasperation than from pain. He could almost hear Cal's patronizing voice: "Oh, you poor clumsy dear." His leg was wedged just above the knee. The wind whipped through the trees, burying the Acura's hood in an avalanche of snow. They had come so *close*—what else could possibly go wrong?

Looking up, Plato had his answer. A huge figure was plodding across the snow toward him—a giant of a man in a hooded coat and green surgical scrubs. Not that the green scrubs were very visible; most of the figure was covered in white. The man was plastered in powdery snow from head to foot: the Abominable Snowman of Sagamore Hills. The wind howled like a deranged banshee, blasting the man's face with snow and ice, but he didn't even flinch.

Plato wrestled with his leg, but it was hopeless. Besides, Jimmy Dubrowski was almost upon him. The West Side Strangler pulled his hood down and flashed an insane smile. Ice and snow clung to a scraggly beard; red streaks—scratches from his latest victim—crisscrossed his cheeks and forehead. His mouth was twisted and deformed; his tongue played over his lips like a tiger marking its prey. His eyes glittered with malevolence, a crazy, violent gleam.

Cal opened the door and stepped out. She spotted Plato and Jimmy, then screamed. Ghost bounded out of the car to the rescue, but disappeared into a snowdrift, whining and whimpering—no help there.

Jimmy Dubrowski came closer, closer. Cal ducked back into the car and reappeared with her trusty T-ball bat, but she couldn't reach them in time; the snow was just too deep. Screaming with Amazonian rage, she raised the bat and hurled it at Jimmy's head. He ducked it easily and turned back to Plato, then frowned down at the car.

Instantly, he perceived that his victim was trapped, that Plato was at his mercy, utterly defenseless. He flashed that same evil smile again, then cocked his head.

"You stuck?" he asked softly. Plato couldn't make out the words; they were snatched away by the wind. But Jimmy nodded to himself as though his question were answered. He bent down, lifted the bumper of the Acura, and heaved.

The car settled forward in the snowbank. Jimmy nodded with satisfaction, brushing his hands together; he might have been moving an inflatable rubber raft.

He turned to Plato and grinned. "There. Is that better?"

CHAPTER 21

"You'd better go get your puppy," Jimmy advised. "I think he's stuck, too."

It was true. Poor Ghost had buried himself in a snow-drift. Only his tail was visible—a tiny black flag waving frantically above the snow. Plato struggled to move but his leg was hurt worse than he realized. Cal was just standing there, staring open-mouthed at Jimmy; she seemed to be in a state of shock.

The man-giant shrugged and paced over to the trembling lump of snow. He reached down and heaved; Ghost came loose in a shower of white, wriggling and squirming in Jimmy's arms. After shaking some of the snow from his coat, he twisted around to lick his rescuer's face.

Jimmy carried Ghost over to Cal. "Nice doggy. Not very tall, though. What kind is he?"

"Australian shepherd," she replied numbly.

"Shepherd, shepherd, spotted leopard." He cocked his head at Cal. "What's his name?"

"Ghost."

Plato limped over to her side. The wind was still howling across the snow; he hadn't heard a word of their conversation.

"Where you guys going to in such a hurry?" Jimmy asked. "You shouldn't drive in this weather, you know, it's awfully dangerous. Lucky thing I caught you before you left or you'd be gone, huh? Know what I mean? Jelly Bean?"

Cal shook her head with an effort. None of this was making any sense. Jimmy Dubrowski was supposed to be trying to *kill* her, wasn't he?

He squinted down at the Acura, still buried in the snow. "You guys sure aren't going anywhere tonight, no way, nope, nuh-uh. Roads are awful—snow, snow, hear the wind blow. This little car sure won't get far, you know?"

"Maybe it would," Plato replied smoothly, "if you *helped* us."

"I don't know." Jimmy frowned. "Maybe. But you guys might get *hurt*." He licked his lips and glanced at Cal. "Besides, I came down here to talk with *her*."

"Just to talk?" Cal asked softly.

"Yeah." He frowned. "Fenton says I should kill you, but he's just like that—he wants to kill everyone."

"Who's Fenton?" Plato asked.

"One of the folks that talk to me—Dr. Cummings says they're not real, that they're sort of like static in my brain. . . . But *they* sure as hell think they're real." He leaned closer to Cal, squinted at her face. "Can we go inside? I gotta go pee."

Standing there, in the middle of a blizzard at one o'clock in the morning, Cal looked back at Jimmy Dubrowski. The wind and snow whipped her face mercilessly. It was bitter, bitter cold—the kind of subzero wind chill that sent frostbite victims to the hospitals by the dozens. The huge man was obviously suffering from some level of frostbite; his cheeks were chapped and raw, and a glaze of salt tears had frozen at the corners of his eyes. His nose looked like a single giant blister, with two icicles trailing beneath it. The corners of his mouth were cracked and bleeding, but the blood was frozen solid, flaking off onto his scraggly beard.

Jimmy's cheeks were scratched, too; Cal had first mistaken the lines for fingernail marks, perhaps from a struggling Tyler Cummings. But the lines were too close together, and too familiar to her forensically trained mind. They were *fork* marks, centered around his mouth; he even had a few on his lips. The poor man had stabbed himself in an effort to eat.

Cal saw that his hands were trembling, that the contorted movements of his face came from his tardive dyskinesia, not malice or even insanity. And his eyes shone with fear and pleading, not with anger or malevolence.

"I'm kind of cold, too," Jimmy finally confessed.

Cal glanced up at Plato. He nodded gravely.

"Come on," she told Jimmy. "Let's go inside."

"See, I broke out of Mansfield just to see you," Jimmy told her later.

They had left the Acura in the snowbank. Plato's leg was massively bruised; the poor clumsy dear was barely able to walk. And so, at Jimmy's insistence, Cal had led them back to the house while Jimmy Dubrowski—the notorious West Side Strangler—acted as a crutch for Plato.

Dante had taken to their guest instantly; when Jimmy freed him from the cat carrier and tucked him inside his coat, the male Jezebel had instantly broken into contented purrs. Ghost had gleefully accepted Jimmy as another houseguest, then bounded along the tracks in the driveway, scooping snow onto his nose and leaping over the drifts.

By the time they finally made it back to the house, poor Jimmy was weakening. His flimsy jacket was crusted with ice, his clothes were wet and frozen stiff, and his face was cracked and bleeding. Luckily, the power had come on again while they were gone; the lights had shown a warm welcome through the snow, and the furnace was slowly restoring the house to a habitable temperature. Cal took Jimmy into the bathroom and held his hands under cold running water, gradually raising the heat like a housewife defrosting a roast. Then Plato took their guest upstairs and showed Jimmy how to do the same thing in the shower. He had to stay and supervise; to the poor frozen man, even lukewarm water had felt scaldingly hot.

But Jimmy seemed to have suffered no permanent damage. Plato had helped him shave and bandaged up a few of the bigger cracks on Jimmy's cheeks, then dressed him in a T-shirt and his biggest pair of sweats. They were still two sizes too small, but they were better than the pungent surgical scrubs now residing in the garage trash can.

"I remember you from the trial," Jimmy continued in his dull monotone. "How the lawyers all listened to you when you talked, more than they listened to anyone else, because you're so smart. . . . I figured you're about the smartest lady around, you know what I mean, Jelly Bean?"

Cal nodded, absently wishing he would stop calling her a jelly bean.

"Is that why you had that scrapbook?" Plato asked. "The one with articles about her?"

"Articles, articles, articles," Jimmy echoed. It was a habit of his—probably a result of his illness. Half the time anyone spoke or asked a question, his only reply was an echo, like a record skipping a track. "Articles about her."

"Yes."

"Uh-huh." He lowered his gaze to stare at his hands. "I guess I'm sort of a fan, you know."

"You're not *angry?*" Cal asked. She wanted to be very clear on that point.

She had tried to phone Jeremy while the men were upstairs, but the line was busy. So Cal had tried the sheriff's office, only to hear the irritating message: "*Due to telephone service interruption, your call cannot be completed as dialed. Please try again later.*"

Apparently, the blizzard had knocked out some telephone lines as well as the electrical service.

"Angry? Angry?" He shook his head. "Nuh-uh. No way. Nope."

"I'm glad."

"Glad, glad, glad." Jimmy shrugged. He was a pretty good-looking guy, now that he was all shaved and spruced up. He smiled at Cal. "*Fenton's* mad. Colossally pissed—he says you put me in that prison, you and Dr. Randall . . . but I don't listen to Fenton, not much, nope, no way, nuh-uh."

Cal was glad to hear it.

"I came down here last week, just to talk, hitched a ride on a truck, but nobody home." He fingered one of the bandages on his cheek and frowned with apparent surprise. "Doors locked, half-cocked, sticker shock."

"You tried to get in?" Plato asked, glancing at Cal. The mystery of the footprints on the porch roof was solved.

"Yeah—I was cold, always cold." He beamed at the fire in the fireplace. "Warm now. I'm *inside*."

"What did you want to talk about, Jimmy?" Cal asked.

"Talk, yeah, talk about, yup, you betcher. Talk . . ." He paused and closed his eyes, rocking back and forth on the sofa; he seemed to be phrasing a particularly profound statement. "Oh, yeah. I figured if you *put* me in jail, maybe you can get me *out*. You know how it is. You know?"

Cal and Plato exchanged astonished glances.

"See . . . I didn't kill those people—I didn't, didn't, *didn't!*" His eyes widened, and his mouth twisted into an angry frown, as though Fenton were coming to the surface. "No matter what those lawyers said, no matter what FENTON says!"

He was breathing hard, rocking back and forth more violently, hammering his fist in his lap. Plato edged protectively closer to Cal.

"Bull shit, Fenton! No way, nuh-uh, nope!" He glared at a spot in the corner, as though Fenton himself were sitting there. He shook his head back and forth, back and forth. "I got framed—I was a patsy, a fall guy, a dupe. Patsy fall guy dupe, the FBI did it, figure I'm too stupid to fight but I'll show them, they'll see. Yup. You betcher."

Cal smiled cautiously. "Jimmy—"

"*You* think I killed them, too." His eyes swiveled to Cal. They were wild with anger—and fear. "Don't you."

"I want to stop the killer," she temporized. "If you didn't do it, then it must be somebody else."

"Somebody else," he echoed, frowning. "Somebody else."

"That's right."

He cocked his head at her, squinting suspiciously. But his breathing started to slow. The violent rocking calmed, the massive fists unclenched, and the beatific smile returned like the sun peeking out from behind a cloud.

"Mrs. Abernathy said you'd understand, she thinks you're great, she said all I've got to do is explain it to you, that's all, yeah. You betcher."

"Of course I understand," Cal lied. Right now, she

would say anything he wanted just to get them all to safety. Cal didn't want Jimmy to get hurt anymore, but she was still afraid of him. Hopefully, they would be able to stall him until the police came, keep him happy and unsuspecting until he was behind bars again.

And maybe, after that, she would look into the case. Not that Cal believed the verdict was wrong by any means—the DNA evidence had been rock solid, and the testimony of the witnesses was convincing. And having met Jimmy here now, face to face, Cal felt more pity than anger.

Poor Jimmy Dubrowski was a very sick man. He needed help.

Plato glanced at her, then over at Jimmy. Their guest was still rocking back and forth on the couch, muttering to the voices in his head. As he carried on his private conversation, his shoulders twitched, his feet wriggled, and his enormous hands fluttered in his lap like trapped birds. He was a medley of nervous movements and involuntary wiggles, most of them probably resulting from the withdrawal of his medication.

He had been the same way when he was arrested four years ago: off his drugs for three weeks while hiding out from the police, and who knew how long before that. Cal wondered what Jimmy was like when he was taking his medication. Apparently he could function pretty well; he had been close to graduating from Cleveland State. Doing pretty well that is, until the murders.

Jimmy suddenly looked up at them. His conversation seemed to be over. He tilted his head, squinted across the room behind them, and suddenly smiled broadly. It was the first real emotion he had shown since arriving—the first thing besides anger, anyway.

"Wow! You've got a train set? An *American Flyer?*"

He sprang from the sofa and rushed across the room, crooning happily. Cal had plugged in the tree while Jimmy was in the shower; it sparkled magically, lighting the corner of the room. Beneath it, the relic of Plato's childhood rested on the tracks.

Smiling cautiously, Plato followed him over. "You like it?"

"Like it, like it, *love* it." He beamed. "Had one when I was a kid—big old 4-6-2 loco, yup, you betcher."

Plato flashed a smug grin back at Cal.

"Old *Flyer*—New York and New Haven, wonder where that went." His voice trailed off as Plato handed him the locomotive. He frowned. "You gotta clean this, man, take care of it, you know? Got rust on the wheels and dust in the engine. And the track is a mess—mess, mess, S.O.S. Nice loco, though."

Cal was astonished at the rapid mood swing; in less than a minute after Jimmy's angry outburst, his sullen mood had completely turned around. He was still smiling, a trace of animation had replaced the flat monotone of his voice. Now he seemed almost normal—less like a paranoid schizophrenic than just an overgrown kid.

While Jimmy admired the rest of the train set, Cal headed to the kitchen to try to call Jeremy. To her surprise, the light was flashing on the answering machine. She hadn't seen it before; her other calls had been made from the upstairs bedroom. Curious, she pushed the PLAY button.

"Looks like I didn't catch you kids in time . . ." (The voice was Jeremy's.) "Too bad, because you didn't have to leave after all. That caller must have made a mistake, it *couldn't* have been Jimmy Dubrowski—not since we just got another threatening phone call ten minutes ago. I hope you're both okay; this guy sounds totally nuts . . ."

He paused for a long moment, then resumed in a low whisper:

> "It was the same threat as last time—Jimmy said he was coming here, that he was going to kill Nina . . . I'm taking her away to stay with a friend . . ."

The machine beeped, and the message ended.

Cal glanced over at the giant beside the Christmas tree, bewildered.

Jimmy Dubrowski was right—he *had* been framed. Obviously, he hadn't made the threatening telephone call; Plato or Cal had been with him the entire time since they met outside. And so, he hadn't planted the dolls in their courtyard, or made the other threatening phone calls. Or killed Tyler Cummings.

All of which led to a very important question. If Jimmy Dubrowski wasn't the West Side Strangler, who was?

CHAPTER 22

"Snow, snow, snow," Jimmy Dubrowski muttered from the back seat.

"You said it," Plato agreed.

They were carefully navigating the back streets near Riverside General. The pink glow of dawn was breaking on a sleeping city—a *hibernating* city that just wanted to roll over and go back to bed until spring. The freeways were reduced to one barely passable lane, while snow-drifts still covered most of the downtown streets and side-walks, and parked cars were just random dunes in the snow. High winds had ripped signs away and tumbled trash cans; litter rolled across the virgin snow like tumbleweeds in a desert, and an enormous pair of golden arches blocked one of the roads leading to Riverside General.

And this wasn't the worst of it. As usual, the eastern suburbs had borne the brunt of the snowfall; supposedly Kirtland had almost three feet of snow. But the southern suburbs weren't far behind; Plato and Cal had risen early this morning to find their little Acura completely buried under a snowdrift, its antenna providing the only clue to the car's location.

They had decided to return to the hospital as quickly as possible. The roads were treacherous, but at least they weren't crowded yet. Only a few intrepid explorers had shared the deserted freeway with them on the way into town. But by rush hour, Cleveland's main arteries would be choked with reluctant travelers slip-sliding away to work.

And so, Plato and Jimmy had dug the car out of the snow while Cal made breakfast: an enormous pile of sausages and ham and eggs and frozen toaster waffles with butter and syrup. In a single sitting, Jimmy Dubrowski had consumed most of the food in their refrigerator and freezer—which was another reason to get him to the hospital as quickly as possible.

"Police," Jimmy muttered. "You said no police, I'm not going back to prison, no way, nope, nuh-uh, I'm getting out now, *hasta la vista*, Baby, good-bye."

"Jimmy, *no!*" Cal whirled around in her seat. "We didn't ask the police to come; I don't know *why* they're here."

Plato peered out the window. Sure enough, a pair of patrol cars were huddled just outside the hospital's main parking deck, along with the coroner's van. And as Plato turned into the physicians' parking lot, they saw a stretcher being wheeled out one of the doors from the deck.

"*That's* why they're here," Jimmy muttered unnecessarily. "Somebody else got killed, but I didn't do it, nope, no way."

"I know, I know. It's okay," Cal soothed. She had a hypnotic effect on Jimmy Dubrowski; he trusted her completely. Cal had managed to talk him to sleep last night, and had woken him this morning with a promise that they would go to the hospital, that Jimmy would get the medicine that made the voices go away, but that there wouldn't be any police to take him back to Mansfield.

Before they left the house this morning, she had finally managed to get through to Jeremy on the telephone, to tell him all about what had happened. He had been pretty dubious about the whole thing, insisting that they still had no proof that Jimmy hadn't committed the murders, worrying that Plato and Cal were somehow being coerced, and even toying with the idea of meeting them at the hospital door with tear gas and a S.W.A.T. team. But Cal had persisted and won him over: Jeremy agreed to let them bring Jimmy in for treatment—provided his office could station a pair of plainclothes guards on watch outside his room.

"We know you didn't do it, Jimmy," she continued. "How could you have? You were at our house last night."

"Our house last night, last night, last night," he echoed.

"That's right." She leaned forward toward the windshield studying the gurney as though she might somehow be able to identify the person beneath. She shook her head and glanced at Plato; he could read her thoughts.

Who was it this *time?*

Riverside General was becoming a very dangerous place to work.

But as it turned out, the victim wasn't a Riverside employee at all. Walking through the hospital lobby with their charge, Plato and Cal bumped into Jeremy Ames. The detective's relief at seeing them safe changed to awed astonishment as he beheld Jimmy Dubrowski.

"This is our detective friend, Jimmy." Cal smiled. "The one I told you about. Detective Ames."

Jimmy Dubrowski held out a trembling hand. "Nice to meet you, sir. Meet, greet, really neat. Yup."

Jeremy squinted at the hand as though he was expecting some kind of a trick, then shrugged and shook it. He glanced at Plato. "Everything's ready up on the floor. The, umm, *doctors* are all ready and waiting."

"Good." Plato lowered his voice and gestured back to the parking lot. "I take it you're not here on a social call."

"You didn't *hear*?" He smacked his head. "Christ, of course not, how could you? Otto wasn't discovered until after you called."

"Otto?" Cal echoed.

"Otto, Otto, Otto," Jimmy added, taking up the refrain.

"Otto Browning," Jeremy replied, after giving Jimmy an odd look. "The newspaper guy."

Cal put a hand up to her mouth and shook her head. "How?"

"Strangling. Just like Ji—" He broke off and stared up at Jimmy again. "Just like the other cases."

"Otto *Browning*?" Jimmy's jaw dropped. "Otto is *dead*? No, nope, no *way!*" His face clouded up, and he looked like he was ready to cry. "Otto is my friend, he can't be dead, no way, nope, can't be . . . writes me letters at Mansfield, nobody else does, but Otto did, all the time all the time all the time."

"Otto *wrote* to you?" Cal asked gently.

"Wrote to me, wrote to me, wrote . . ." Jimmy squeezed his eyes shut.

"He wrote to you?" Cal repeated.

"You betcher. All the time, asking me what I remembered, who I saw, where I went, what I did when all those people got killed." He clutched his head in his hands, as though it were about to split in two. "Otto believed I didn't kill those people—that's why I broke out. Otto said he'd prove it for me, show I didn't do it, show Jimmy's not a killer, no way. But now Otto's dead." A tear trickled down his face; he clasped his hands in front of him and rocked back and forth on his heels, keening softly. "Dead, dead, dead, dead, dead."

"I don't think you killed them either, Jimmy." She touched his arm, then glanced at Jeremy. "*Nobody* does, any more. Do we, Jeremy?"

The detective frowned at Cal, then took a deep breath and sighed. "No. We don't."

But Jimmy wasn't listening; he was lost in his grief. "Gone, gone, poor Otto is gone, gone, gone. *Hasta la vista*, Otto." He shook his head. "Otto wrote me letters, he did."

"I know, Jimmy." Cal patted his arm gently. "I know."

"*Otto* knew I didn't do it, knew I was framed, picture-frame window-frame, tame tame window-frame . . . the FBI did it."

"The FBI?" Jeremy asked blankly.

Cal gave a quick shake of her head.

"*Oh*—the FBI. I see." Jeremy nodded. "We'll look into that, Jimmy—we certainly will."

"Wrote to me all the time . . . we were going to *meet*, but we never did." He glanced out the door at the coroner's van as it pulled away from the curb. "And now we never will."

"Then I guess that explains *this*." Jeremy pulled a plastic-wrapped sheet of paper from his briefcase. "Take a look."

Cal did, with Jimmy and Plato looking over her shoulder. It was a note, printed on plain computer paper—part of an entry from a journal or a calendar:

12/10, 8 P.M.: Jimmy Dubrowski called: frantic about manhunt, wants to meet early tomorrow a.m. He suggested Riverside General's parking garage, as deserted around that time. Be near the A-2 stairwell at 5 A.M.

"We found it in Otto's notebook computer case." Jeremy frowned at the document and shook his head. "It's just about the *only* thing we found; his computer was smashed to a total hash. Whoever killed him was trying to cover their tracks."

"And trying to make Jimmy take the fall," Cal agreed. "Again."

"Of course, we know it wasn't him now—" Jeremy broke off suddenly, looking over their shoulders and glancing around the deserted lobby.

Plato turned around and gasped. "Oh, shit."

While they had been studying the document—the slip of paper implicating Jimmy in yet another murder—their charge had disappeared. Once again, Jimmy Dubrowski was on the run.

"He's a pretty smart guy," Cal told the detective.

They were waiting to take the elevator up to the psychiatry ward. Jeremy wanted to contact his plain clothes guards and send them hunting for Jimmy.

"He was getting a degree in computer science," she continued. "At Cleveland State."

"I know." Jeremy's thin mouth puckered in a sour frown. "That's how he escaped from Mansfield—they finally figured it out. He was working on some college courses—got computer privileges and somehow hacked his way into the prison's E-mail system."

After that, Jimmy had simply added his name to a list of inmates scheduled to be transferred to the minimum-security area of the prison. He had slipped away during the transfer. His absence wasn't noticed at first because the other area didn't have him listed as a transferred inmate. Several hours elapsed before the authorities realized their error; by then, Jimmy had overpowered a guard and escaped.

"That's why he came *here*, to Riverside," Cal continued. "He broke into Tyler's offices one night last week, trying to find some evidence in their computers."

"What kind of evidence?" Jeremy asked quickly.

She shook her head. "I don't know—he doesn't exactly talk very clearly."

"So I noticed." He rolled his eyes. "I can't *imagine* that guy getting a college degree—or hacking his way out of a prison hospital."

"He's probably a lot better when he's taking his medicine," Plato noted.

Jeremy nodded. "Speaking of evidence, we found another motive for Joan Randall."

He described the partnership agreement between Joan and Tyler—a contract drawn up back when they were still married. The agreement stipulated that the surviving partner would receive the practice—and its assets—upon the death of the other.

"The partnership had some extensive investments—mutual funds, pension accounts, and so on. Almost two million dollars." Jeremy nodded. "And the practice was due to break up this spring."

The elevator doors opened and they all stepped aboard. Cal was only half-listening; she was still trying to remember what Jimmy had told her last night.

"He was looking for some program on the computers," she said. "Something about 'time studies' or 'time management.'"

"TIMETRACKER?" Plato asked.

Cal snapped her fingers. "That's it!"

The detective frowned at Plato. "What's a 'time-tracker'?"

"It's a computer program—one of my patients owns the company. And Jimmy used to work for her."

Plato told the detective about Francine Pryce and her computer consulting business. Their headline product was a program called TIMETRACKER, which recorded employee activities according to which program they were using, how long they worked on a particular document, whether the computer was inactive for more than a few minutes, and so forth.

"So they can tell if somebody's just loafing, or playing Solitaire, or surfing the Internet instead of working?" Cal asked.

Plato nodded.

"Pretty tricky." She shook her head. "Sort of like having Big Brother inside your computer."

"Too bad they didn't have TIMETRACKER installed at Mansfield," Jeremy mused. He sighed. "But what was Jimmy looking for?"

They stepped off the elevator on the eighth floor. Plato led them down to the locked ward, pressed a button, and had them buzzed in. Once inside, Cal replied.

"Jimmy figured if he hadn't done the murders, somebody *else* in Tyler's office did." She lowered her voice. "He thought it was Joan Randall."

"Not a bad guess," Jeremy agreed. "But how could he prove it?"

"By checking the TIMETRACKER record," Plato answered. "Seeing if Joan worked late that night, around the time of the first murder."

"Wow." Jeremy nodded. "That *is* pretty sharp—the killing took place after office hours, when just about everyone had left. Deirdre Swanson was supposed to close up the office that night, and Jimmy was the last patient—she was supposed to see him out the door. *Sup-*

posedly everyone else was gone, and the outer door was locked. But if we could prove that Joan really was working late that night . . ." He paused expectantly. "Did Jimmy get his evidence?"

"Nope." Cal shook her head. "The office got a whole new set of computers last year."

Jeremy's face fell. "So the data is gone."

"Right."

"Not exactly," Plato interrupted. They glanced up at him, and he continued. "We don't have data for the night of that first murder, but we may have information for *Saturday's* killing. Joan told us she was typing up her research paper all morning—remember?"

Cal nodded. "But if Joan *hadn't* used her computer that morning, she'd be on pretty shaky ground."

"Plus, she might have actually typed that fake note on her PC." Plato pointed to the plastic bag, still in Jeremy's hand.

"Right." Cal nodded. Then she frowned. "Too bad we don't have the slightest clue how to work the program."

"We may not *need* to," Plato countered. He smiled. "I've got an idea."

Just half an hour later, Francine Pryce was seated at Joan Randall's desk. The psychiatrist hadn't made it to the hospital yet, but the hospital president himself had granted permission to check Joan's computer. While the patient records were the property of Joan and her patients, the rooms and equipment were hospital property. Jeremy had promised to limit his search to the time-tracking software on the office PCs.

"Joan probably wasn't even aware that this software was installed," Francine explained as she booted the computer. "She was a psychiatrist, not a secretary—this data would be pretty meaningless for her. But we sold an umbrella contract to the hospital's Systems division, and I believe they installed it on every unit."

Francine pressed the F-12 key as the system came to life, the standard procedure for opening the TIME-TRACKER program. Sure enough, a WELCOME! screen responded:

ACCESSING TIMETRACKER™ PROGRAM. PLEASE ENTER PASSWORD.

Francine typed a reply and smiled up at them. "We always put a back-door key in; you wouldn't *believe* how many people forget their passwords."

WELCOME TO TIMETRACKER™! the program replied, apparently satisfied.

Francine typed a few commands, and the computer answered with a screenful of data: a column of dates and times, another column of program names, and more columns filled with arcane gibberish about CPU utilization, keyboard activity, hard disk seeks, and so on.

Even before Francine interpreted, Plato understood the results. He and Cal and Jeremy shared a disappointed sigh: Joan Randall had indeed put in some hefty computer time Saturday morning. From nine a.m. until noon, her word processor had been open and apparently in constant use.

"Let's see," Francine muttered. She peered at the screen like a psychic staring into her crystal ball. "You were most curious about the hour between eleven and noon, right?"

Plato nodded.

"No dice," she replied. "Joan was working straight through that time period—the keyboard shows almost constant activity, she opened a dozen files, and she modified three documents." Francine shook her head. "That wouldn't have left her time to go get a cup of coffee, let alone go murder somebody."

Cal sighed, then shook her head in confusion. "But how did Joan know that Tyler had been killed at the old bridge?"

"Easy," Jeremy replied. "Take a look."

He gestured to the window. From up here, on Riverside's eighth floor, they could easily see the black thread of the river, the breakwall and river walk, and the concrete pylon supporting the rusting hulk of the old railroad bridge. With all the coroner's workers and detectives clustered around Saturday afternoon, it would have been simple to guess where Tyler had been killed.

"Does that answer your question?"

Cal nodded. "Then I guess it wasn't Joan."

"I guess not."

Francine switched off the computer and sighed. "Anything else you want me to check?"

Jeremy shrugged. "I suppose we ought to look at—"

He paused, frowning. From the hallway outside, they could hear a gleeful cackling, along with a familiar voice.

"Jackpot, jackpot, jackpot," the voice said. "I found it, found it, yup, you betcher."

They rushed out into the hall. Jimmy Dubrowski was sitting at the receptionist's desk, a broad smile plastered on his face. He wasn't looking at another TIMETRACKER report; he had obviously thought up a much better idea.

Marianne's computer screen displayed a very familiar document. A copy of it was in Jeremy's briefcase:

12/10, 8 P.M.: Jimmy Dubrowski called: frantic about manhunt, wants to meet early tomorrow a.m. He suggested Riverside General's parking garage, as deserted around that time. Be near the A-2 stairwell at 5 A.M.

CHAPTER 23

"Hi, Jimmy," Francine said brightly. "Nice to see you again."

He stared up at the computer executive, blinked, and rubbed his eyes. "Ms. *Pryce*, pryce, Price is Right?"

"That's me." She patted his shoulder. "Where did you find that, Jimmy?"

"*Temp* file, uh-huh, yup, you betcher. Temp." He nodded solemnly and pointed at the screen. "Windows, temp directory, temporary—temperature—temper, temper, yup. Temp."

"What's he talking about?" Jeremy whispered to Cal, as though she could interpret.

Francine overheard him and replied. "Marianne probably didn't save a copy of the file. But the computer did."

She typed in a few keystrokes and nodded. "The computer automatically generated a working copy of the file."

Later, she explained, the temporary file would be erased and overwritten with the next temporary file. But Marianne hadn't used her computer since she wrote the note—last night.

"Jimmy searched Marianne's directory for a key phrase: A-2 stairwell." Francine turned around and leaned against the desk. "He came up with this file—officially, it had already been marked 'erased.' But since it hadn't been written over by something else, Jimmy was able to 'un-erase' it."

Beside her, Jimmy Dubrowski stood up from the desk chair and nodded.

"Lots of people don't realize you can do that," Francine continued. "But these days, there's a lot of redundancy in computers. Most of the time you think you've lost a file, you can find it again—if you just look hard enough."

Jimmy Dubrowski had apparently looked hard enough. While the rest of them were searching through Joan's computer, he had snuck through the open office door and checked Marianne's.

"I don't believe it," Jeremy said, shaking his head. His eyes had a dull, glazed look, like a boxer just before the knockout punch. "She and Nina are such good friends."

He reached over to pick up the telephone.

"Of course, this doesn't really prove anything." Francine shrugged. "*Anyone* could have written this note on her computer. As a matter of fact—"

Cal yelped. "Oh, my God!"

"What is it?" Plato cried.

Cal looked like she had seen a ghost—like she was still seeing one. She was squinting down at Marianne's desk chair—at the cloth seat and the back of the chair. She reached out and tweezed an invisible object between her fingers, holding it up to the light.

It was a blond hair. A short, straight Barbie-doll hair.

Plato gasped. He ducked down to the floor and hunted around. Sure enough, half a dozen more Barbie hairs were scattered on the carpet underneath her desk. There were even a few on the desk itself, as well as inside the drawers. Meanwhile, Cal reminded Francine about the

Barbie-doll prank—a crazy threat designed to terrify Cal into an even greater fear of Jimmy Dubrowski. A threat which had worked.

"I guess that proves it," Plato said. "Marianne must have gotten some on her coat or her clothes—maybe even inside her car—and carried them up here. They've probably been here all along."

Jeremy was still waiting for the telephone to ring. He was shaking his head, now looking like a boxer just *after* the knockout punch.

But Plato didn't get a chance to ask why. He was interrupted by a sudden commotion in the waiting room, a strident and familiar voice.

"*Marianne!*" it shouted, like a schoolteacher barking at a disobedient third grader. "Marianne Cosgrove! You're in *deep shit*, lady."

Joan Randall stormed through the door, staring around at the office's occupants without a glimmer of surprise. Her mind was focused only on her prey. "Marianne— where the hell *is* she?"

Jeremy had just hung up the phone. "That's what *I'd* like to know."

"Never mind *you*—I've got to find her. Now." She tossed her coat over a chair and shook her head. "That girl must have left the procedure room unlocked—*again*. I've got a nine o'clock treatment to give, and no machine."

"No machine?" Jerry asked blankly.

"The ECT machine," she snapped. "Somebody must have carted it off, God knows why. It's worth ten thousand dollars, but where would you sell it?"

"Oh, my God."

Cal rushed over to the detective. "What is it, Jeremy?"

"Nina is there," he replied dully. "At Marianne's apartment. Remember—I said in my message that I was sending her someplace safe? That's where."

"Maybe Marianne hasn't left yet," Plato suggested optimistically. "Maybe—"

"I saw her." Francine's voice was a horrified whisper. "Earlier this morning. When I was counting cars."

"What time?" Jeremy asked breathlessly.

"Just before you showed up, Plato." She stared down at the floor. "Marianne headed out to the employee's lot—she's got a purple car, and I recognized it."

"Was she *carrying* anything?"

Francine nodded. "A box. A big black box."

"That's it, then." Joan Randall's lip curled in a disgusted sneer. "She's got it, the little thief."

"She's not a thief," Jeremy snapped. "She's a murderer."

"I should have known," Jeremy said later. "As soon as we learned it wasn't Jimmy, I should have guessed."

"Jeremy, " Cal said. "There's no way you could have—"

"I could have," he replied bitterly. "I *should* have."

They were roaring out of town on Interstate 90. The road was reasonably clear; even better, most of the traffic was headed *into* Cleveland for the beginning of the workday. Jeremy had mounted his portable flasher on top of the roof; it was urging the few cars in the westbound lanes to the side.

Marianne Cosgrove lived in Westlake, on the near west side of the city—just up the road from Nina and Jeremy. The detective had phoned the Westlake police and they were on their way, too. He couldn't be sure that they would get there in time, that *anyone* could. But he was determined to try.

"Couldn't know, shouldn't know, nope, no way." Jimmy Dubrowski was sitting in the back seat, nodding. "You thought it was me."

Jeremy's mouth hardened into a thin line, but he finally relented. "Thanks."

"But you don't anymore, nuh-uh."

Like a stray puppy, Jimmy Dubrowski had followed them down to the front door of the hospital. When Cal tried to send him back upstairs, he had firmly shaken his head.

"Want to be there," he said. "I've got to help, got to try. Got to."

"We might have to break the door down," Plato reminded Jeremy.

That had decided it. And so the four of them were racing down the highway toward Marianne's apartment, hoping to catch her in time.

"Marianne was *always* attached to Tyler Cummings," Jeremy told them. "But he was never too sure about her—it was an on-again, off-again relationship going back for years. Nina told me all about it last Saturday; I really don't know Marianne very well. But Nina said she was deeply in love with Tyler, and awfully possessive."

Cal nodded; only now did she remember Nina's words at the shopping mall. Talking about jealousy, Nina had mentioned Marianne: *Women can be even worse. My old roommate—*

"I guess that explains Deirdre's murder," Plato noted. He frowned. "But what about the *other* folks—Luella and Jerry?"

"Jerry lived in Jimmy's apartment building—in *Marianne's* apartment building, and Luella lived next door." Jeremy sighed. "They must have seen something that incriminated Marianne. Maybe one or both of them could have given Jimmy an alibi."

"Luella was a good friend, good friend," Jimmy muttered from the back seat. "Good cook, too—Friday night fish night fish fry Fridays . . . Luella made great fish—flounder, mackerel, perch, salmon, shrimp. Great fish."

"Deirdre was murdered on a Friday," Cal noted.

They all glanced back at Jimmy Dubrowski. He was sitting shaking his head, mourning another lost friend.

"That probably explains Luella's murder," Jeremy said. "And Jerry may have seen it—seen Marianne going into Luella's house."

"We'll never know," Plato said.

"There's a lot we'll never know," Cal added.

"Like how the hell she faked those DNA tests." Jeremy glanced at Cal. "Have you ever heard anything like that before? I thought those things were supposed to be *accurate*, like one in a million chances of being wrong."

"They weren't wrong," Cal replied. "That *was* Jimmy's blood at the scenes."

Jeremy jumped. "Then—"

"Jimmy wasn't there," she continued. "But his *blood* was."

She explained her theory; it was the only way to fit the facts together. Jimmy's blood had been drawn for routine Haldol levels at Tyler's office that afternoon. Presumably, the vials were still waiting to be taken away by the lab courier when Deirdre was killed. All Marianne had to do was draw a sample of her own blood and label it as Jimmy's, then sprinkle his vial of blood at the scenes of the crimes.

"The only problem was, Jimmy's Haldol level was *too* low. Nonexistent—because it was *Marianne's* blood sample." Cal explained how Jimmy's blood had been tested for Haldol just a couple of weeks earlier, during a pre-employment physical exam. "I called Tyler about it—even *he* had trouble explaining the level dropping all the way down to zero." She took a deep breath. "I think he realized something then—maybe even guessed who had done the murders."

"And that's what got him killed," Jeremy guessed.

She nodded. Cal had to admire Marianne's sheer audacity and cunning. Thanks to a public and police force—and *deputy coroner*—all too willing to accept a schizophrenic's guilt, Marianne had easily pinned the murders on Jimmy Dubrowski. The receptionist had been a key witness in one of the killings, placing Jimmy near Jerry Tammerly's apartment at the time of the murder.

And when the alleged West Side Strangler escaped, Marianne had resumed a campaign of terror targeted at Nina and Cal—a campaign designed to throw even more suspicion on Jimmy.

Except Tyler Cummings had never taken the bait. He had never really believed in Jimmy's guilt. And when Cal's call had finally piqued his suspicions, he must have tipped his hand to Marianne.

And so, he and Otto Browning had joined with the other three victims in the string, putative casualties of a paranoid schizophrenic—but in reality, victims of a sane woman's rage. Five victims, Cal mused. *Six*, for you had to include Jimmy Dubrowski as well.

Hopefully, there wouldn't be a seventh.

"But why *Nina*?" Cal asked suddenly.

"I don't know." Jeremy shook his head. "She was due to testify against Jimmy—she had seen him near Luella's house on the night of the second murder. But they didn't need her testimony after all—they had a pile of evidence stacked up."

"All circumstantial."

"Right." The detective frowned. "She must have known something *else*, about Marianne. After all, they were roommates."

Cal nodded.

"Hopefully," Jeremy murmured, "we'll find out what she knew."

"We will," she assured him. "We will."

CHAPTER 24

"You've always been so good to me," Nina told her friend. "I really do appreciate this."

"What are friends for?" Marianne shrugged and flashed that bright smile.

It was so typical of Nina's old roommate to be so cheerfully giving. Always, when they had shared an apartment, Marianne had been ready to help with a favor, or a loan, or a ride in her car. When Nina had first come to the States, she had felt so lost and alone. Her father's brother—who ran the jewelry shop—was kind and generous, but very busy. He had a wife and six children of his own, and could hardly be bothered translating odd English words and phrases or teaching her how to drive according to American rules.

But Marianne had done all that. They had met in the shop, where Marianne was working part-time while she took some secretary's courses at the university. Nina was grateful when her friend asked her to share the apartment.

They had grown very close, more like sisters than friends. Sharing most of their dinners together, going on elaborate and regretfully expensive shopping trips, even flying to Cancun on vacation that first winter.

Of course, they had their differences, the occasional *argomento*; but who didn't? If Marianne had a weak spot, it was her jealousy. Whenever Nina had made new friends, Marianne tried to drive them apart—"forgetting" to pass on their telephone messages, or speaking rudely to them, or sulking for days after being left at home alone. What was Jeremy's term? Passive aggressive, that was it. Marianne could be very passive aggressive.

But all that changed when Marianne took her job at Tyler's office. She didn't *need* Nina so much, and her jealousy seemed to fade away. Even when the trouble began—the shock of that awful murder right at the office, and the horror of another two deaths in their own neighborhood—Marianne had leaned on Tyler for support. Still, it was a relief for both of them when Jimmy Dubrowski was finally arrested.

"You have *taught* me what friends are for," Nina said soberly. She nodded. "Always, Marianne, you have been the very best of friends."

It was true. For once again, Marianne had saved the day. Just a few minutes after Jeremy got that awful telephone call last night, Marianne had rung up. She was up late, worrying about Nina, wondering if her old roommate would want to spend a few nights in her apartment until it all blew over.

Jeremy was doubtful, but he understood. And when he saw the building early this morning, he was relieved. Marianne's new apartment in Westlake was quite a step up from the old building on the west side of Cleveland: twenty-four-hour security, an alarm system, and keyed elevators. The building was a fortress: the West Side Strangler couldn't reach her here.

"Some more coffee?" Marianne suggested.

Nina nodded. For some reason, she was awfully sleepy this morning. Maybe it was the apartment—so cozy and comfortable. This, too, was a huge step up from their old place: spacious and airy, with lots of windows and a beautiful balcony view of the lake. Framed prints on the walls and polished wood floors, a kitchen finished in marble and cherry, and two beautifully furnished bedrooms. Truly, it was nicer than anything she and Jeremy could afford.

Nina knew why, and she understood. Marianne and Tyler had been very close; the room was filled with photos of the happy couple, gifts from Tyler, and even some of his office files. She got the impression the two of them had spent as much time here as they did at his house in Pepper Pike. They had been planning a summer wedding; Marianne had already asked Nina to be matron of honor.

It would have been an honor indeed, but now it was all over. And that was another reason why Nina had come here. She had understood that Marianne's call was as much from concern for Nina as from sheer loneliness, a need to share the burden of her grief.

Marianne needed a friend, and Nina was glad to help.

"You're looking awfully tired, Nina." Marianne studied her face with concern. "Go ahead and take a nap if you want—I'm not going to work until later."

Nina nodded. Marianne had already explained—she had tried to make it to Riverside early this morning but she had stopped halfway. The roads were just too dangerous.

"I *am* awfully sleepy," Nina admitted, then smiled. "It's the baby, I think. The doctor said I'll need a lot more sleep these first few weeks."

"Then you just go right back to bed," Marianne said sternly, then giggled. "Doctor's orders."

"Okay, doc." She stood and yawned hugely, then gave her friend a hug. "And thank you, again."

"Any time," Marianne replied. "Any time at all."

*   *   *

Watching Nina padding off to her bedroom, Marianne knew she would have to work fast. The heavy dose of Valium she had put in Nina's decaffeinated coffee would send her off to sleep very soon. With luck, she could hook the device to her friend's scalp in just a few minutes, let it do its lethal work, then take it back to work again. Joan Randall hated snow—she usually canceled her entire mornings on bad-weather days. She would never realize that the ECT device had been missing.

Marianne would discover Nina's body after work tonight. The poor woman would be the obvious victim of a fatal seizure—not surprising, since she had been having reasonably serious seizures ever since a car accident when she was six years old. Marianne had even witnessed one of them herself, back in their old apartment. In the middle of lunch, Nina's eyes had suddenly rolled back in her head, she had fallen to the floor and started trembling. It was a horrible thing; Marianne had worried that Nina was going to die.

She hadn't, of course—thanks to Marianne's quick intervention. She had taken the hospital's lifesaving course, had recognized that Nina was choking on something. So, swallowing her fear, she jabbed a towel into her friend's mouth and plunged her fingers inside, pulling a bite of celery from the back of her throat. Nina had started breathing again, and the horrible convulsions had gradually faded away. An ambulance finally came and rushed her off to the hospital, and her neurologist had increased her anti-epileptic medication.

This time, she wouldn't be so lucky. With the help of the device Marianne had borrowed, her friend's seizure would never stop. Not in this world, anyway.

Marianne opened the black case with a genuine sense

of grief. Nina had been a very good friend, a very *close* friend, almost like the sister she had never had. Back when they were roommates, they had shared everything together, pooling their money to buy a decent stereo, sharing job listings and makeup secrets, joys and frustrations. Tyler had changed a little of that, even before Nina left.

But Nina herself had changed it even more. Making so many new friends that she almost forgot Marianne—forgot all that she had done for Nina when she first came to America. Still, Marianne found she could forgive the betrayal, especially once Tyler came along. She and Nina were still friends, even now.

Which explained why Marianne hadn't killed her long ago, like she should have. For on the night of Jerry Tammerly's murder, Marianne had left for the evening—and left her apartment keys on the counter. Nina had rushed downstairs to catch her before she drove away.

She had caught her, all right. Red-handed, just as Marianne was coming out of Jerry's apartment.

Jerry had seen Marianne walking into Luella Huckleby's house on the night of *that* killing. Marianne and Jerry had dated a few times, and he was still infatuated—often "watching over Marianne" to make sure she got home safely. After all, their little apartment wasn't in the best part of town, and they had that crazy guy living upstairs. Once Jerry realized what he had seen, the fool had telephoned Marianne herself, pleading for her to explain, to tell him it wasn't so.

Marianne didn't bother explaining; she just strung a lamp cord around his neck and let him figure it out for himself. She tried to rig it up to look like a suicide, not that it really mattered. If the cops didn't buy it, Jerry Tammerly would be chalked up as another victim of the

West Side Strangler. Just like Luella Huckleby and Deirdre Swanson had been—slipping that engagement ring under Dubrowski's door had been a stroke of pure genius. So were the drops of blood sprinkled at two of the crime scenes.

But as she rushed out of Jerry's apartment, Marianne saw her roommate coming back inside from the parking lot after searching for her. Marianne had never been sure if Nina spotted her or not. But she couldn't take a chance, even with a friend.

Especially not now, when the police were getting so close. Tyler had figured it out, and so had that dirtbag reporter, Otto Browning.

Marianne was really sorry about Nina. Just like she had been sorry about Tyler.

But what else could she do? Besides, who knew whether Nina might not have had another fatal seizure someday soon anyway? Marianne had saved her life four years ago; she was just calling in the debt.

She picked up her black box and crept down the hallway. Nina was sprawled on the spare bed, fast asleep. *Snoring*, in fact—something Nina never did. Apparently, she was deeply asleep.

Just to be sure, Marianne stepped into the room and clapped her hands, hard, right beside her friend's head. Nina didn't even stir.

Satisfied, Marianne opened her black box, plugged the machine into a wall outlet, and set to work.

CHAPTER 25

"Goddamned worthless security guard," Jeremy snapped as he slammed down the cellular phone. He hammered the steering wheel for good measure. "Stupid shit won't answer his phone."

Both Jeremy and the Westlake police dispatcher had been trying to reach the apartment's security guard for the past ten minutes without any luck.

But it didn't really matter now. They were just a block away from Marianne's apartment; Plato could see the intricate peaks of brick and granite rising above the smaller buildings nearby. The architecture was reminiscent of Ralph Jensson's Monastery. Pretty upscale for a receptionist at Riverside General, Plato thought—until he remembered that she had also been Tyler Cummings's fiancee. Presumably, after all these years, he had at least chipped in with some rent money.

They skidded into the parking lot and plowed to a halt in front of the tallest building in the center. Jeremy staggered out of the car and stumbled up the sidewalk with Plato and Cal trailing close behind. They rushed into the vestibule and pulled the inner door handle; it was locked. Behind them, Jimmy Dubrowski lumbered up the sidewalk like a hungry polar bear eyeing the breakfast seal.

"Can I help you?" a voice murmured smoothly from a pair of stereo speakers mounted above the door.

Jeremy whirled and spotted the security guard through the glass doors, seated at a table across the lobby.

"Let us in," he snapped. "Police business."

The guard rose and sauntered to the door. "Can I see your badge, sir?"

Plato's head whirled with a sudden rush of déjà vu: the scene at Siegel Medical College was being played all over again—except this time, the murderer had Nina instead of Cal. And once again, a brainless security guard was foiling their rescue attempt.

Even the security guard looked similar: another actor at play, with perfect hair and a perfectly polite smile.

"Here—sheriff's deputy." Jeremy whipped his wallet open and pressed the badge to the glass. He pointed a thumb over his shoulder at Cal and Plato. "This is a county coroner, and a doctor."

The guard reached for the lock, then frowned dubiously at Jimmy Dubrowski.

"Who's that?"

Jeremy glanced over at Jimmy. The stress was finally getting to him. Eyes closed, he was banging his head against the glass and making strange grunting sounds, like a moose with a hangover. He was still wearing Plato's sweats, but they hadn't held up to the strain very well. The pants barely reached his calves, and the seams were starting to split.

"That's my *partner*," Jeremy explained. "Undercover."

"Undercover?"

"He really gets into his roles." The detective hammered the door with a fist. "Now, let us *in*, damn it!"

"Number 342," the guard said, reading Jeremy's badge. "If you'll just hold on while I—"

"God-*damn* you!" The homicide detective reached into his belt and pulled out . . . *nothing*. He smacked his forehead. "Shit—I left it in the car."

Jimmy was grunting louder now, rhythmically banging his head against the door; the doorframes quivered like the wooden gate of a fortress. The security guard stared up at him like an Oklahoma farmer spotting a twister on the west forty and coming in fast. But he held his ground, unbuckling his holster and drawing his gun.

"Jimmy—*don't*," Cal pleaded, but it was no use.

Jimmy raised one enormous hand and battered the reinforced glass. Once, twice, three times and it finally shattered into a million icy shards. The security guard raised his gun . . . then lowered it again.

Behind them, Plato heard the wail of sirens and the thunder of feet pounding up the sidewalk. A pair of uniformed cops rushed into the vestibule. Jeremy whirled and flashed his badge, nearly weeping with relief when he spotted a familiar face.

"*Phil!*" He jerked his thumb over his shoulder. "Tell this idiot who I am."

"Deputy sheriff," Phil, the Westlake cop, barked. "Put that goddamned gun away and let us in."

"Yes, sir." The security guard meekly complied, opening the shattered door and standing back as they rushed to the elevators. He followed, slipping a key into the locked panel.

"Twelfth floor," Jeremy panted as they stepped into the car. He stabbed the button and glanced around at the other cops. "Thank God you guys showed up."

"We'd have been here sooner," Phil told him, "except Randy got stuck at a stop light."

"We hit a snow drift," Randy said sullenly. "Damn

thing nearly swallowed the car. Need a *tank* to get around this town today."

A bell rang, the elevator doors slowly sighed open again, and Jeremy squirted through the crack and into the hall. Rounding a corner, he shouted over his shoulder, "Room 1236!"

He was still there when the others caught up.

"No answer," he explained breathlessly. He lowered his shoulder and charged the door. It didn't even tremble; the door was heavy-grade steel and deadbolted for good measure. "Damn!"

"Here, lemme try." Randy, still wincing from his encounter with the snowdrift, lowered his shoulder.

But Jimmy Dubrowski was already there. After backing up a few steps, he rumbled across the hall and slammed into the door with the irresistible force of a wrecking ball. The steel puckered and bent and literally tore away from its hinges, slamming flat onto the floor. Jimmy knelt on top of it, mewling and slamming his bloody fist on the steel again and again, beating the door into submission.

Cal knelt beside Jimmy, crooning and calming him as the others rushed past. The apartment seemed empty, except for one closed door at the far end of the hall. Jeremy tried the lock and pounded.

Plato's heart sank as he heard a frightened wail from the other side of the door.

"Help!" The voice was Marianne's. "She's having a *seizure!*"

This time, Jeremy didn't need Jimmy Dubrowski's help. He lowered his shoulder and slammed into the door; the thin plywood shattered into shards and dust as he rocketed through.

Marianne was sitting on the bed, staring up at Jeremy

with a mixture of fear and false concern. She forced a relieved smile. "Thank *goodness* you're here. Nina—"

Jeremy pushed her away and rushed to his wife's side. Nina Ames was obviously in the throes of a full-blown epileptic seizure: her arms and legs trembled and thrashed, her eyes stared sightlessly at the ceiling, and a horrible cawing sound came from her throat. Her lips were gashed and bloody; Jeremy stuffed a handkerchief into her mouth to keep her from biting her tongue off.

From the other side of the bed, Plato checked her pulse and pulled the pillow out from under her head, in order to keep the airway clear. He glanced up at Jeremy as the convulsions slowly died away. "I think she's going to be all right."

"No thanks to *you!*" Jeremy growled at Marianne.

"What do you mean?" The woman's face was a mask of shocked innocence. "I was trying to *help* her!"

Standing in the doorway, Randy spotted something: his opportunity to redeem himself from getting stuck in the snowdrift. He darted over to the bed and reached underneath, emerging with a heavy black case.

"Is this what you phoned us about, Jeremy?"

Behind them, Marianne sprang for the door, only to encounter an immovable object in her path. Jimmy Dubrowski was standing there, glaring down at the receptionist with a very angry frown.

"Get out of my *way*, you big oaf!" She tried to shove him aside and dart past, but he was too quick for her. With one bleeding hand, he grabbed Marianne by the front of her stylish silk shirt and lifted her up in the air. She kicked her feet helplessly, like a frantic bunny caught by the scruff of its neck.

"Put me *down!*" she screamed. Desperate, she turned to the others for help. "Help me—this guy is *nuts!*"

"And you're a murderer," Jeremy said softly.

The full impact of her situation suddenly seemed to sink in. She squirmed and kicked, kneeing Jimmy Dubrowski in the chest and stomach, but he didn't even wince. She might have been dangling beside a gallows post—or a concrete bridge support.

She glared at Jeremy, eyes flashing fire. "He's *crazy*— he's the West Side Strangler! You're going to believe *him* instead of *me*?"

Jeremy glanced over at Jimmy and smiled grimly.

"Actually, yes."

He gestured, and Randy pulled out his handcuffs. But Jeremy wasn't really paying attention anymore. He turned away to watch as Nina's eyes fluttered open, then leaned over and kissed her forehead, very gently. "Welcome back, dear."

CHAPTER 26

Two weeks later, Plato and Cal were sitting beside the Christmas tree, opening the last of their presents. It was their *own* Christmas tree, and their own house. Marianne Cosgrove was safely behind bars pending a jury trial after the holidays, and Jimmy Dubrowski was free.

Bing Crosby was crooning carols on the CD player, and the air was filled with the sweet aroma of pine and scented candles and the pumpkin pies Plato had baked early that morning. The house was blanketed with a fresh fall of light snow, and the Christmas tree sparkled gloriously in the morning sunlight. Beneath its boughs, Plato's *American Flyer* cranked dismally around its circular track, like an arthritic centenarian running in the Boston Marathon. It clattered and clanked and wheezed and sparked, but it hadn't set anything on fire. Not yet.

Each time Cal spotted it, she winced.

But the ritual was almost over; Plato would turn it off once they finished opening the presents. He had already ravaged most of his pile—the usual clothes and books and the latest James Taylor CD. Cal had gone through most of her gifts as well—clothes and books and a Natalie Merchant tape. She was unwrapping her last present: an impossibly small box that Plato had sent around to her on a rusty yellow hopper car.

Cal opened the jewelry box and stared openmouthed at the contents. A sapphire necklace with a heart-shaped stone. Deep blue color and a long gold chain.

"To go with your engagement ring," Plato told her, slightly embarrassed. He still wasn't quite sure if she'd like it.

"Oh, *Plato!*" She crawled through the wrapping paper and scrambled into his arms; apparently she did.

"Open *yours*," she urged.

Plato reached for the last present of the pile: a big and heavy oblong box wrapped in bright silver paper with a gleaming red bow. He tore it open to find a simple cardboard box inside—unlabeled and unmarked. Puzzled, he lifted the lid and gasped.

It was a mint-condition American Flyer set—transformer and all. The tracks gleamed like quicksilver and the heavy black steam engine oozed raw power. Five brightly painted cars and a caboose were packed in neat compartments like so many precious eggs.

"Where did you *get* this?" Plato asked.

"From a restoration company. Jimmy Dubrowski told me all about them." She gestured at the transformer. "The power pack and the tracks are new—a couple of companies still make S-gauge—but the engine and cars are original. Circa 1948—postwar period."

"Gosh." He stared at her with awe. "You sound like you've been doing your homework."

She nodded, then cocked her head in a gesture reminiscent of Jimmy Dubrowski. "Do you like it?"

"I *love* it!" He shook his head. "This is one of the best Christmases I've ever had, Cal."

"It may get better," she replied cryptically.

But Plato didn't hear. In seconds, he had the train free of its box; in minutes, it was set up and running around the Christmas tree. The engine purred around the track, pulling its cars and puffing smoke with barely a clatter or clank. Plato lovingly packed his old engine and track into the new box; someday, he'd pay to have them restored. But for now . . .

Half an hour later, Cal dragged him away. "Come on, Casey Jones. We've got a turkey to make."

Reluctantly, he followed her into the kitchen.

As usual, Cal did the cleaning while Plato prepared the stuffing. She slit the plastic wrapper open and sat Tom in the sink. He was a huge bird, almost thirty pounds. But they were expecting a lot of guests for Christmas dinner—including one very big eater.

She frowned at the turkey. "I think we've got a homicide on our hands."

"Really?" Plato looked up from his growing pile of crusty stuffing bread.

"I'm almost sure of it." Cal studied the bird and peered inside both ends, finally extracting a curved, pink hose-like structure. She waggled it at Plato. "Cause of death: a massive blow severing the head from the neck—and the neck from the body."

"Cally—"

She frowned at the neck, then pointed inside the abdominal cavity. "Postmortem mutilation, too. Notice how all the organs are gone."

"You're disgusting."

Cal just shrugged. "I'm a pathologist. What do you expect?"

But she got to work, cleaning the bird with professional skill and dexterity. In just a few minutes, it was ready for Plato's famous stuffing: parsley and sage and onions and mushrooms and lots and lots of eggs. He packed and buttered the huge bird and tucked it in the oven under a cozy aluminum foil tent.

Plato started back toward the train set, but Cal headed him off, gently urging him upstairs. "We've only got half an hour before the guests arrive."

To save time, they showered together—something that never really worked the way it should. In a sort of sexual gestalt effect, double showers always took longer than two single showers would have. But they were dressed and ready when the front doorbell rang.

Cal rushed downstairs with Plato close behind. It was Jeremy and Nina, carrying a casserole of Nina's cheddar cheese broccoli and another pie. After a round of Merry Christmas wishes, Cal leaned close to Nina and whispered something strange; Plato wasn't sure if he'd heard it right.

"Did you bring it?"

Nina nodded, and they rushed upstairs together.

Homer arrived next, with a date: Janice Hathaway from the psych ward. Homer had met her while preparing the prosecutor's case against Marianne; she seemed to fascinate him even more than the arc-fountain at Tower City. Homer followed her around the room like a puppy dog—like Jeremy followed Nina, in fact. The prospects were good.

Plato had just served them drinks when the doorbell rang again, announcing their last guests. Jimmy Dubrowski was standing on the front porch, dressed in a three-piece suit that actually fit. Flanked by Ralph and Althea Jensson, he was holding a gaily wrapped Christmas present covered with pink bunnies and blue teddy bears.

"Merry Christmas!" he told Plato. "Here."

"Aww, Jimmy—I told you not to bring any presents."

"It's not for *you*," he explained with a shy smile. "It's for the *baby*."

Beside him, Ralph shrugged helplessly. Plato didn't have the heart to correct him; Jimmy's memories of his breakout were still rather muddled. So Plato simply thanked him and led the trio inside. Together with Francine Pryce, the Jenssons had taken Jimmy under their wing. He was doing a lot better, now that he was back on his medication. Jimmy would go back to school in the spring, and work part-time at Francine's company.

Holding a tall glass of Guinness, Jeremy frowned at Plato. "What's Cal up to, anyway?"

"I don't know." Plato shrugged. "I'll go upstairs and check."

"I'll come, too." Jeremy shook his head. "Something's going on—Nina kept giggling the whole way here."

"Is she all right?" Plato asked carefully. Nina had spent a few days in the hospital for observation.

"Sure." Jeremy beamed. "And the doctors said our baby's doing just fine."

Upstairs, they found the bathroom door closed. Plato rapped on the door. "Cally? Are you all right?"

"We're just fine." From behind the door came faint scrabbling noises, whispers, and *giggling*.

"Cal's been acting a little goofy lately too," Plato admitted.

"Speaking of goofy—did you hear Marianne is trying to cop a temporary insanity plea?"

"Temporary insanity?" Plato asked. "For five different murders?"

"She doesn't have a prayer," the detective agreed. "But it was the best her lawyers could do." His schnauzer nose twitched disdainfully. "My guess is she'll get five consecutive life sentences—which would make her eligible for parole sometime in the twenty-second century."

Plato nodded. The irony was that Marianne's insane jealousy might have worked as a defense for the *first* murder—of Deirdre Swanson. But the other four killings were obviously cool and calculated attempts to cover her tracks, and to throw suspicion on Jimmy Dubrowski. The huge prints in the courtyard had been matched with a pair of Tyler Cummings's boots found in Marianne's apartment, and several of the threatening phone calls had been traced to her office telephone.

No judge or jury would accept an insanity plea—especially since a battery of psychiatric tests had proven her to be perfectly sane.

"Are you guys almost done?" Plato asked. "We've got guests downstairs."

"Okay, okay." Cal finally opened the door, a faint smile lighting the corners of her mouth. "I was just getting my last Christmas present ready."

"*What* present?" Plato asked.

"This."

She thrust a white plastic object into Plato's hand. It was shaped like a very tiny egg cup. Inside, halfway down the top compartment, a piece of round white paper showed two blue dots of equal intensity: one at the center and one near the edge.

As a physician, Plato recognized it immediately. But he couldn't speak, couldn't *think*. So many of his hopes, of his dreams, had suddenly crystallized in this one moment. All he could do was to look into Cal's eyes in wonder and awe, sputtering like a motorboat with a bad plug. "Puh-puh-puh-puh . . ."

"What the hell *is* it?" Jeremy asked impatiently.

"Puh-puh-puh-puh . . ."

"What's going on?" Homer had climbed the stairs to frown at his cousin. "What's wrong with him?"

"Just wait," Cal told them. She grinned impishly at Plato. "He'll get it out."

He wet his lips and tried once more. "Cal is . . . I am . . . *we* are puh-puh-puh-puh—"

"Jesus Christ," Jeremy muttered. "Lemme see this thing." He snatched the object from Plato and read the tiny letters on the side. "Oh, my God! Cally is—"

"Pregnant!" Plato finally shouted. "She's going to have a *baby*!"

Jeremy slapped him on the back and squeezed Cal's shoulder. "That's fantastic! Congratulations!"

"I'm gonna be an *uncle!*" Homer cried ecstatically.

Behind her, Nina smiled at Jeremy. "Our baby will have a *cousin* to play with."

Cal moved in close and gave Plato a hug. "Merry Christmas, Dad."

"Merry Christmas . . . Mom." Plato was still numb from the shock, the surprise, the delight. "This is the perfect gift. Really. Better than *anything*."

"No kidding," Jeremy sighed, holding Nina in his arms.

Plato smiled and leaned down to pat Cal's tummy. Already, he imagined that it seemed a little bigger, a little rounder. "And Merry Christmas to *you*, little guy."

"Little *girl*," she corrected.

"Maybe both," Homer suggested. "Twins."

Cal shook her head. "No way, nope, nuh-uh." She stared down at her belly and frowned. "Don't even *think* about it—Jelly Bean."

SIGNET

Edgar Award Nominee
Bill Pomidor

"A delight! Bill Pomidor just keeps getting better!"
—*New York Times* bestselling author Tess Gerritsen

"Enjoyable...combines wit with wisdom, and the
result is both entertaining and charming."
                                              —*Romantic Times*

☐**MIND OVER MURDER**
                    0-451-19216-8/$5.99
☐**SKELETONS IN THE CLOSET**
                    0-451-18418-1/$5.50
☐**THE ANATOMY OF MURDER**
                    0-451-18417-3/$5.50
☐**MURDER BY PRESCRIPTION**
                    0-451-18416-5/$4.99
☐**TEN LITTLE MEDICINE MEN**
                    0-451-19214-1/$5.99

Prices slightly higher in Canada

Payable in U.S. funds only. No cash/COD accepted. Postage & handling: U.S./CAN. $2.75 for one book, $1.00 for each additional, not to exceed $6.75; Int'l $5.00 for one book, $1.00 each additional. We accept Visa, Amex, MC ($10.00 min.), checks ($15.00 fee for returned checks) and money orders. Call 800-788-6262 or 201-933-9292, fax 201-896-8569; refer to ad # 002

Penguin Putnam Inc.   Bill my: ☐Visa ☐MasterCard ☐Amex_____(expires)
P.O. Box 12289, Dept. B   Card#_____
Newark, NJ 07101-5289
Please allow 4-6 weeks for delivery.   Signature_____
Foreign and Canadian delivery 6-8 weeks.

Bill to:
Name_____
Address_____City_____
State/ZIP_____
Daytime Phone #_____

Ship to:
Name_____   Book Total $_____
Address_____   Applicable Sales Tax $_____
City_____   Postage & Handling $_____
State/ZIP_____   Total Amount Due $_____

This offer subject to change without notice.

SIGNET BOOKS

LAWRENCE BLOCK

THE BURGLAR IN THE LIBRARY

__0-451-40783-0/$6.99

After his girlfriend dumps him to marry another, Bernie follows the couple to a New England inn with his sights set on an autographed first edition of Raymond Chandler's *The Big Sleep*, located in the inn's library. But when a dead body appears and all the guests remain snowbound, it's up to Bernie to solve the case.

Also available:

__THE BURGLAR WHO THOUGHT HE WAS BOGART

0-451-18634-6/$6.99

__THE BURGLAR WHO TRADED TED WILLIAMS

0-451-18426-2/$5.99

__THE BURGLAR WHO LIKED TO QUOTE KIPLING

0-451-18075-5/$6.99

__THE BURGLAR IN THE CLOSET

0-451-18074-7/$6.50

__BURGLARS CAN'T BE CHOOSERS

0-451-18073-9/$5.99

Prices slightly higher in Canada

Payable in U.S. funds only. No cash/COD accepted. Postage & handling: U.S./CAN. $2.75 for one book, $1.00 for each additional, not to exceed $6.75; Int'l $5.00 for one book, $1.00 each additional. We accept Visa, Amex, MC ($10.00 min.), checks ($15.00 fee for returned checks) and money orders. Call 800-788-6262 or 201-933-9292, fax 201-896-8569; refer to ad #SMYS1

Penguin Putnam Inc.   Bill my: ☐Visa ☐MasterCard ☐Amex_____(expires)
P.O. Box 12289, Dept. B   Card#_____
Newark, NJ 07101-5289   Signature_____
Please allow 4-6 weeks for delivery.
Foreign and Canadian delivery 6-8 weeks.

Bill to:

Name_____
Address_____City_____
State/ZIP_____
Daytime Phone#_____

Ship to:

Name_____   Book Total $_____
Address_____   Applicable Sales Tax $_____
City_____   Postage & Handling $_____
State/ZIP_____   Total Amount Due $_____

This offer subject to change without notice.

MAYHEM, MURDER, MAGGODY.

THE AMERICAN MYSTERY AWARD-WINNING SERIES BY JOAN HESS

☐ *THE MAGGODY MILITIA*

Chief of Police Arly Hanks is the law in Maggody, Arkansas (pop. 755), a peaceful little Ozarks town snuggled in the heartland of America. Until a group of camouflage-clad patriots march in with maneuvers—and murder.
(407261—$5.99)

☐ *MALICE IN MAGGODY*

Arly Hanks soured on the Big Apple, which is why she took the sherrif's job in Maggody. She needed R & R. What she got was M & M—murder and malice. Because the quiet of the Ozarks is about to be shattered.
(402367—$5.99)

☐ *MAGGODY IN MANHATTAN*

The last place Arly Hanks wants to return to is New York. But when a friend is the prime suspect in a Manhattan murder mystery, Arly is there.
(403762—$5.50)

☐ *MIRACLES IN MAGGODY*

A televangelist has rolled into Maggody, set up a tent, and before you know it, the town is blessed by miracles—and cursed with unholy murder.
(406567—$5.99)

Prices slightly higher in Canada

Payable in U.S. funds only. No cash/COD accepted. Postage & handling: U.S./CAN. $2.75 for one book, $1.00 for each additional, not to exceed $6.75; Int'l $5.00 for one book, $1.00 each additional. We accept Visa, Amex, MC ($10.00 min.), checks ($15.00 fee for returned checks) and money orders. Call 800-788-6262 or 201-933-9292, fax 201-896-8569; refer to ad #HESS

Penguin Putnam Inc.	**Bill my:** ☐Visa ☐MasterCard ☐Amex_____(expires)
P.O. Box 12289, Dept. B	Card#_____
Newark, NJ 07101-5289	Signature_____
Please allow 4-6 weeks for delivery.	
Foreign and Canadian delivery 6-8 weeks.	

Bill to:

Name_____

Address_____City_____

State/ZIP_____

Daytime Phone #_____

Ship to:

Name_____	Book Total	$_____
Address_____	Applicable Sales Tax	$_____
City_____	Postage & Handling	$_____
State/ZIP_____	Total Amount Due	$_____

This offer subject to change without notice.